A HARD LIGHT

"A [heroine] who is intelligent, feminine but tough, clever without resorting to cuteness, and as resourceful as a Navy SEAL with a Swiss army knife. Long may she survive."
—*Los Angeles Times*

"Hornsby's fluent style carries this story to its satisfying conclusion."
—*Publishers Weekly*

"A winning series."
—*Library Journal*

"An action-packed adventure. Smart, tough, and idealistic, Maggie MacGowen is an appealingly unorthodox heroine in a fine series. This one belongs in every collection."
—*Booklist*

"Wendy Hornsby gets better and better. *A Hard Light* is an exciting whodunit."
—*Midwest Book Review*

A HARD LIGHT

A Maggie MacGowen Mystery

Wendy Hornsby

SIGNET
Published by the Penguin Group
Penguin Putnam Inc., 375 Hudson Street,
New York, New York 10014, U.S.A.
Penguin Books Ltd, 27 Wrights Lane,
London W8 5TZ, England
Penguin Books Australia Ltd, Ringwood,
Victoria, Australia
Penguin Books Canada Ltd, 10 Alcorn Avenue,
Toronto, Ontario, Canada M4V 3B2
Penguin Books (N.Z.) Ltd, 182–190 Wairau Road,
Auckland 10, New Zealand

Penguin Books Ltd, Registered Offices:
Harmondsworth, Middlesex, England

Published by Signet, an imprint of Dutton NAL,
a member of Penguin Putnam Inc.
Previously published in a Dutton edition.

First Signet Printing, July, 1998
10 9 8 7 6 5 4 3 2 1

Printed in the United States of America

PUBLISHER'S NOTE
This is a work of fiction. Names, characters, places, and incidents either are the product of the author's imagination or are used fictitiously, and any resemblance to actual persons, living or dead, events, or locales is entirely coincidental.

For my dear old dad,
Robert Westfield Nelson,
My rock, my best friend.

Chapter 1

"Maggie, you sure you got the right address?" Guido shifted his Steadicam from one shoulder to the other.

"First hovel past the sewer outflow," I said. "There, that one with the Budweiser poster for a door."

Minh Tam's alleged abode was an untidy, dun-colored assemblage of rags and cardboard propped up and strung up between two undernourished castor bean trees. Very little vegetation managed to sprout out of the stone-paved banks of the Los Angeles River where it dumped into the Long Beach Harbor. The trees, spindly though they were, must have been made of hardy stuff to survive at all.

There were several shelters along that barren bank, the last stretch of river before the stinking urban stew of back-yard runoff and industrial waste finally poured into the Pacific. The end, in many ways.

Guido, with one small camera, seemed burdened as Atlas might have been with his somewhat larger load. Usually a joy to work with, all day Tuesday Guido was crabbier than our task, the smoggy air, and too much of my company warranted. When I asked what nettled him, I got "Nothing" for an answer, twice. I quit asking, he kept grousing.

"This is nuts." Guido shifted the camera again. "We shouldn't be messing around down here. People live in shit holes like this because they're problem children in a major way. I don't feel like getting into a knock-down with some guy who hasn't had a bath since Christmas."

"Two of my film school interns spent three days walking Minh Tam's picture through every breadline in town just so that I could get to this point. Now it's time for the payoff. Be proud for me, boyo." I punched his hard shoulder. "Finding this shit hole may well be the crowning moment of my inglorious career nosing around in other people's business. So, if you don't mind, shut up and start the camera running. We need to document the moment."

Guido would not be bullied. "Doesn't look like anyone's home."

"Won't know if we don't go down there and find out."

"This Minh Tam guy could be armed."

"He could be. Just make sure you have the tape running if I get hit."

"The riverbank's too steep, Maggie. I don't want to fall with the camera." This from Guido, who had filmed incoming SCUD missiles in Iraq.

"Then stay up here." I handed him the heavy Nagra recorder I carried. "I'll go down and see if Mr. Tam is home. If he is, I'll deliver him to you up here."

"I think the camera's battery charge is low."

I reached across him and pressed the charge meter on his camera. We had ninety minutes on the battery, and a fully charged spare in the bag. I said, "Think of something else."

"I can think of only one thing," he said, his chiseled jaw clenched. "How bad was Khanh Nguyen hurt?"

"Khanh is more scared than hurt," I said. "She was tied up and threatened, she has some bruises. But she's physically intact."

"She's scared," Guido said pointedly, "because she's smart, Maggie. A home invasion robbery, something like that takes real mean motherfuckers to pull off. You get yourself too involved, you think those creeps won't come pay a visit to your house?"

"After what Khanh went through, the least I can do is help her find her friend Minh Tam. Give her some peace of mind to know he's okay. It's no big deal."

"It's none of your business."

I turned my back on him.

I make documentaries for a living, I don't locate people. And I certainly don't put myself in any situation that could conceivably involve contact with my former husband. Khanh was a longtime legal client of my ex; that's how we met. But Khanh's problem was real, the progress on my film project was stalled, and I was desperate for an excuse to skip a damned network-exec goon meeting that was scheduled for that Tuesday morning. Mr. Minh Tam needed finding at exactly the time I needed an out.

Guido and I took cameras along from habit and to avoid questions when we slipped out of the studio. Minh Tam had nothing to do with my film in progress, a sad tale about rudderless youth, a detail we kept from my executive producer.

Guido and I had parked the network's van at the downtown Long Beach marina and walked for maybe a quarter mile along a paved bike path to reach this garden spot. Down the slope behind us was the city's tow yard and street department storage, ranks of sagging barbed wire atop half a mile of cyclone fence. On the far side of the river in front of us, the city's westside ghetto.

"I just don't want you to get hurt." Guido was still arguing with me when I took a tentative step off the pavement down onto the rocky bank. Fist-sized stones shifted underfoot.

"Oh, for cryin' out . . ." Guido passed me back the Nagra and led the way, as I knew he would: Guido Patrini of the Sicilian Patrinis.

We were both off-balance to begin with—me with the strap of the recorder over one shoulder and Guido with the video camera cradled against his chest the way he would hold a baby. But Guido was the first to fall.

As he lost his footing, his free hand snagged the thick stock of a milkweed. He managed to stay upright, until I landed on my butt and slid into him, sending a cascade of stones bouncing all the way down to the sluggish gray water below.

We made a lot of noise and dust, but we only actually

moved a yard or two, sledding on our bottoms. After we came to rest, tangled together but sitting upright, there was a moment of icy silence between us that lasted until the splash of the final stone.

I took a sort of personal inventory and found all of my parts and the recorder intact. Guido was swearing, so I knew he was all right. I asked, "The camera okay?"

If looks could kill: "Yes, the camera is just peachy. My precious little ass feels like mincemeat, in case you're interested. But, yes, Maggie, the camera is perfectly fine."

"Good." I stood, found solid footing atop a concrete outlet pipe, and gave him a hand up. And then I gave him a hug. My uptight friend, a sack of bone and sinew inside a Mickey Mouse T-shirt, held me in a tight embrace.

"You're not hurt, are you?" he asked, a little quaver in his voice that showed more emotion than the mishap warranted.

"I'm fine."

Then he held me at arm's length and looked me over. "Tell me the truth. Are you okay?"

"Would I lie to you?" I patted his cheek and broke from his hold.

Guido and I had worked together, off and on, ever since my first TV job reading the farm report at a little independent station in central Kansas. He was an intern cameraman back then, both of us fresh out of college. I made a down payment on a nose job with my first paycheck, and Guido drove me to the appointment.

After Kansas, we did the news correspondents' tango, moving from city to city, now and then reconnecting, both of us rising with each move until eventually I was a big-city evening news anchor in full makeup and big hair and Guido was a network correspondent dodging bullets during Desert Storm. Then we both quit. I now make documentaries, he teaches film at UCLA.

For a lot of those middle years, other than Christmas cards and occasional late-night phone calls when something at the bottom of a scotch bottle reminded one of the other's face, we lost touch. Then, about a year ago, I accepted a contract with one of the big three networks, and moved from San Francisco to Los Angeles with my teenage daughter, Casey.

For one more go-around, I accepted all the hassle that goes with a network gig—endless oversight and accounting—because I needed, first, a steady paycheck, and second, some time in Los Angeles to work out my destiny with Mike Flint, detective, Robbery-Homicide Division, LAPD.

That hazy Tuesday morning, I was at a crossroads. Mike was three months and five days away from eligibility for a full city pension. Casey, my daughter, had only four more months of her junior year in high school, and an offer to attend a dance academy in Boston in the fall. My film in progress was the last project on the network contract. The lease on our rented house in South Pasadena would expire in June.

The question du jour was, once the project was finished, and Mike Flint was retired, and Casey was ready to move on, then what? The riverbank was not the only rocky slope I had to contend with.

One edge of the Budweiser banner that served as the hovel's door moved an inch or so. I called out, "Minh Tam? Mr. Tam?"

First one dark eye appeared, then a brown, leathery face. According to Khanh, Minh Tam was fifty-three, but he looked much older, beaten down by more than overexposure to the elements.

I repeated, "Mr. Tam?"

"You Sanitation? I don't bother anybody. This is my place. Go away."

"We aren't from the Sanitation Department, Mr. Tam. Or any other department. My name is Maggie MacGowen, this is Guido Patrini. We want to talk to you. I'm a friend of Khanh Nguyen."

"Khanh Nguyen?" He came out a little farther to look around, expecting, I supposed, to find Khanh.

"Khanh told me to show you this picture when I found you." I offered him a photograph of me and Casey picnicking with Khanh, her husband, Sam, and their four adult offspring. Mr. Tam studied the snapshot with the skepticism a passport inspector might have if he were on the lookout for a fleeing terrorist, comparing me to my smiling image.

After a long moment, he decided to come all the way outside, struggling upright from a squat, a skinny man in too-big khaki pants and a clean button-down shirt. There were gaps among his yellowed teeth, but he seemed more-or-less healthy. At least, his eyes were clear and his mind was sharp.

"Where is Khanh Nguyen?" He slipped the snapshot into his breast pocket without asking if he could keep it. "Does she come with you?"

"She's at home," I said. "In San Marino. She asked us to bring you some news about a family member, a Mr. Bao Ngo."

Mr. Tam's first reaction was a panicky retreat back toward his ragged pile of a house.

"Do you know Bao Ngo?" I asked.

He waved me off, his back to me. "Never heard of him."

"I have another photograph I'd like you to look at, Mr. Tam."

I held out a copy of an old black-and-white shot of two young men holding hands in the Vietnamese manner. One of them was Minh Tam before he had gray hair at his temples. This was the picture my interns had spread all over town, hoping someone would recognize Tam. A dozen or more people knew who he was, but the only person who knew where Minh Tam lived was a security guard working a harbor-front RV park.

I extended the picture to Tam. "Khanh says the man standing with you is Bao Ngo."

Tam turned and studied me again before he reached for the second snap. When he looked at it, the expression that crossed his face I can only describe as the joy you might feel taking the first sip of water after a long desert trek. He only said, "Ah," a short, sharp, happy bark. There were tears in his eyes.

"This picture is very old," he said.

"Khanh brought it with her from Vietnam."

As Tam angled the picture away from the sun's glare, Guido raised the camera to his shoulder and turned it on.

Khanh should have prepared me better. She should have told me more about the relationship between the two men.

I asked again, "Is that Bao Ngo?"

"You are not FBI?"

"No." I handed him my card with the Technicolor network logo embossed on one corner, and saw him scrutinize me with new appreciation; bless the power of TV. "I'm a filmmaker."

"You want to talk with me about my cousin?" His velvet brown eyes widened. "Are we exemplary in some way?"

"You're interesting."

"Interesting?" For the first time, he smiled directly at me, a sarcasm there that hinted at a wicked sense of humor. "I have been sought out for many reasons, but never for being interesting. What is interesting about my cousin Bao and me?"

"I located you as a favor to Khanh Nguyen," I said, stalling. I had a feeling that if I told Tam too much, too soon, he would be afraid to talk to me. "She was worried about you. She wants to talk with you about Bao Ngo."

"Ah. I see. My cousin Bao, he is dead?" Tam bowed his head, contemplative, sad. A breeze feathered his short hair at the crown as a father's hand might, gently, as his own hand brushed across the photograph he held. "I thought that must be true. Otherwise, if Bao is not dead, why have I not heard from him?"

I let his erroneous conclusion stand for the moment. "When was the last time you spoke with your cousin Bao Ngo, Mr. Tam?"

"Long time," he said. "In Saigon. April 29, 1975. I flew out on the last helicopter that was able to evacuate from the American embassy before the Communists reached Saigon. Bao did not make it in time. The last I saw Bao, he waved to me from the helipad as I flew away from him." Tam's face clouded over as he remembered. With his head bowed he asked, "Does my cousin Khanh know how Bao died? Did she learn when it happened?"

"Bao is not dead, as far as I know," I said. "Khanh saw him last week, at her home in San Marino."

"Last week?" Tam was startled, looked around as if there might be better information from somewhere else because what I said was impossible. "How could it be? Bao did not contact me all this time. I know he must be dead, or maybe it is too dangerous for him to write to me."

"Dangerous why?"

"The Communists." The word seemed to leave a bad taste in his mouth. "When he stayed in Vietnam, I knew that the Communists would take him to jail or they would execute him."

"Bao got out of Vietnam the same day you did," I said. "He missed the evacuation airlift, but he found space on a Canadian freighter. Bao Ngo entered the United States through the Port of Los Angeles in September of 1975."

Tam all but called me a liar, shaking his head, waving his hands to fend off my words. "Not possible."

"Last week, Bao invaded the home of Khanh Nguyen and held her hostage while he ransacked the house."

"Last week?" Tam seemed more stunned by the timing than by the deed.

"Yes. I'm sorry to be the one to tell you. What would make him do such a horrible thing to a family member?"

He brushed off the question to get back on the topic that bothered him. "But where has Bao been all the time?"

"I wish I knew, Mr. Tam," I said. "After he entered the country in 1975, there are no records of Bao on any known computer database. Other than some old photographs and the alien identification number that was issued by Immigration when he entered the country, there is nothing. He bypassed the refugee camps. Under his own name, he was never issued a Social Security number. Never had a driver's license or paid taxes. There is nothing known about him until Khanh opened her front door and found him standing there with a gun in his hand."

"The computer?" Tam's sly smile returned. "I think perhaps my cousin Bao did not want to be found."

I waited for three boats, the sound of spilling water and distant traffic exaggerating the silence between us.

I said, "Can we buy you lunch, Mr. Tam? We'd like to talk with you."

He was nodding assent to the lunch idea before I got to the talk part. He walked along with me and Guido back to the tourist village in the downtown yacht harbor, an upscale strip of ocean-front gift shops and restaurants. There was an arrogance about the man, the way he walked a little to the side to show that, while we were together, we were still strangers.

Tam chose tacos from the available options. We bought food from a take-out stand and carried it to the patio seating. I moved a bench to place him with his back to the rows of boats moored on the far side of a redwood railing. Downtown Long Beach, its new skyline of high-rises glowing pink and bronze, rich in the early afternoon sun, made a dramatic backdrop.

Light reflecting off random windows could be a problem for the lens, but not nearly so big a problem as the wandering tourists who are wont to duck into the field of vision and wave hi to Mom. Positioned as we were, unless someone rose up out of the water, we had the wavers blocked visually. To block them aurally, along with general background city noise, we set up the Nagra and clipped a mike on Tam's shirt, out of the camera's eye.

Guido, still crabby, rested his narrow haunches on a table about six feet away, wolfed down a greasy chicken taco, wiped his hands on a wad of paper napkins, then raised the camera to his shoulder, made a test, made some adjustments, then gave me a thumbs-up.

Tam's attention had wandered off to a pair of men who loitered nearby, watching us, I supposed, as the source of some variety in their day, something to go back to the office and talk about later. They looked like civil service types or mid-level corporate office workers. Short-sleeved, no-wrinkle dress shirts, generic neckties, dark slacks with the seats sprung from sitting all day; cheap, serviceable, low-maintenance clothes. They looked fit enough, putting me in mind of the detectives who worked with Mike Flint.

"Mr. Tam," I began, drawing his eyes back to me. "Tell me about Bao Ngo."

He considered for a moment, sipping Coke through a straw. When he spoke, he seemed to be detached, unemotional. Again, I read in his aloofness a certain arrogance: How could I not know these details of his life? As if the story had been told so many times before.

"I knew Bao Ngo from childhood," he said. "We grew up in the same village. Our fathers grew up together, and their fathers. Our families sent us away to school together. When my cousin married his sister, then we were family."

I said, "Khanh Nguyen told me you and she worked with Bao Ngo at the Musée de Tourane, the old colonial French museum in Da Nang, during the Vietnam War."

"Oh, yes." He bowed slightly, a formal recognition. "Madame Thieu, who was wife of the president of South Vietnam—the last president—asked Bao to be curator of the museum. Bao asked for my help, and for the help of Khanh Nguyen."

"The museum sounds like a family business," I said. "Was Mr. Ngo related to Madame Thieu?"

Again he bowed. "That is the way in Vietnam."

It occurred to me that for a man who lived in a hut on the banks of a river of sludge, Mr. Tam looked fairly well scrubbed. His accented English was perfect, his manner genteel. All the parts of the picture did not hold together.

"When the Communists invaded the north," he said, "we had one day, Bao, Khanh, and I, to crate the most important museum treasures and to load them onto military transport." He looked out across the harbor, remembering. "One day and four trucks were all we had to save eighteen hundred years' worth of a people's history and culture from certain destruction by the invading forces. That was not sufficient time, was it?"

"Wouldn't seem so." And probably wasn't necessary, though I refrained from the suggestion. The old French museum has been restored by the current Hanoi regime and renamed the Cham Museum after the people who traditionally inhabited the area around Da Nang. I doubted that the treasures inside were ever in danger of anything except slipping from the clutches of the fleeing Saigon leadership.

I asked, "Where did you send the collection?"

"To Saigon. We set out in four trucks with military escort. But I saw only two trucks arrive, mine and Bao's. The road was very crowded with people fleeing from the invading troops. A few miles south of Da Nang, deserting soldiers commandeered Khanh's truck. And the fourth transport, I don't know." He raised his hands, the delicate hands of a scholar. "After the first day on the road, we lost sight of it. It was impossible to go back and search for it. Maybe it arrived in Saigon later, I can't say."

"You fled with Bao Ngo and Khanh Nguyen and who else? Who drove the fourth truck?"

He studied me, a wariness in his gaze. And then his hand came up to shield his face from Guido's lens, halting the interview. "What did you say is your name?"

"Maggie MacGowen," I said.

Tam reached into his shirt pocket and drew out the business card I had given him earlier, checking on me. He studied the card and then he studied me. "MacGowen? Is that your family name?"

"It was my married name. It's still my professional name. The IRS knows me as Margot Duchamps."

"Is it a common name, MacGowen?"

"Fairly."

He nodded and put the card away, still cautious, I thought. But he didn't get up and leave, as I was beginning to fear he might.

"The fourth truck?" I prodded.

He waved away the question. "Long time ago. Who can remember?"

I moved on. "What happened to the museum collection after you delivered it to Saigon?"

He shrugged. "I did not stay to find out. We parked the trucks behind the gates of the president's palace, received diplomatic credentials for our efforts, and then we went directly to the American embassy to wait our turn for priority evacuation. That is all."

I prompted him. "You left Vietnam."

"Here I am." He spread his arms, suggesting that I should not ask him the obvious.

"You seem to have fallen on hard times. Tell me about your life in this country."

"I opened a small gift shop, but it was not a success. Then I found work as a cook." He smiled, his lips stretched taut over his discolored teeth. "Cooking in a restaurant is not the job my family had in mind when they sent me to university, but I managed."

He rattled the ice in his cup, gazing off toward the boats. "You are partially correct, Miss MacGowen. Art was indeed the family business. My father, and his father, were exporters, however. Not collectors. They assisted in the looting of Vietnam."

"Do you have a job now?"

"I am not currently employed." His expression showed more anger than chagrin. "I had an argument with my last boss. The issue is of no consequence. But he tells everyone who will listen that I am an informer for Hanoi. Now my old friends don't want to be seen with me, and no one will hire me."

"Informer for Hanoi? The war is over, Mr. Tam."

He leaned back, crossed his arms. "Is it?"

I didn't want to debate the sorry state of the Communist menace with him. I waited a beat, and then asked him, "When you fell on hard times, why didn't you go to your family for help?"

"Pride," he said. "Pride is one of the seven deadly sins in your culture, is it not?" He tapped his chest. "Behold a sinner."

"If you wanted to find out where Bao Ngo has been since 1975, where would you start?"

"How did you find me?"

"The IRS has an address for you. We went to the address and the landlady told us you had moved out but that she still sees you in the neighborhood now and then. It was just a matter of showing your picture around until someone recognized you and could tell us where you lived," I said. "But we have nothing to help us find Bao Ngo's trail after he walked off the boat. I would like to know—the police would like to know—where he has been since 1975. Khanh says no one in the family has heard from him."

"No one." Tam thought about it before he shrugged. "If he did not contact the family, then that is your answer. Bao did not wish to be found. Who can say why? I think it is wise to stay off the database, like my friend Bao Ngo."

"Do you have any ideas where to begin looking?"

"I would expect Bao to do as I did when I left the refugee camp: to seek work at auction houses, galleries, and museums that have Asian collections. Maybe a fine arts importer. There are not many. Maybe someone remembers him. Put his picture on the television. You can do that?"

"Not easily," I said.

"Ah." Tam gazed away, apparently deep in thought. "I cannot help you."

"Do you know any reason why Bao would want to hide?"

"Not one."

I thought his answer came too quickly. The next few questions earned only one- or two-word answers. Clearly, Minh Tam, his lunch finished, paper wrappers folded into a neat stack beside his folded hands, had nothing more to say.

Reluctantly, he agreed to speak with us later if we had more questions, and asked us to give his regards to Khanh Nguyen when we spoke with her. But for the moment he was finished. We said our good-byes and left him basking in the sun.

Guido picked up both the recorder and the camera and headed at double-time off toward our van. He still seemed miffed, oddly silent for the loquacious Guido.

"How about a beer?" I called to his back. "On the expense account."

He stopped, thought, redistributed the weight of his load, said, "All right."

We locked up the gear in the van, and then walked along the waterfront to the very end of the marina village to a fish house with an outdoor deck.

It was a typical February day, clear and breezy, mid-seventies. The truth is, except for some hot days in August and September, a week or ten days of rain after the first of the year, and some fog in June, the weather was typical of nearly every day around coastal L.A. The only atypical aspect of the day was Guido's moodiness.

A waitress wearing short-shorts set two cold beers in front of us. Guido didn't even glance at her young backside. He leaned his elbows on the table, ignoring the frosted glass in front of him.

"What was the point of all that?" he asked.

"You know the case Mike is working on?"

"Yeah." Guido frowned. "Kids torture an old perv. We're using them in the new project."

"Pedro wasn't old—only twenty-two," I said. "His killers remind me of Bao. Maybe we can fold him into the project."

"Fold him in?" Guido scowled. "Pedro's dead and Bao's a thug. Where's the connection?"

"Can't you see it?" The heat in my voice surprised me, shocked Guido.

He tucked in his chin the way boxers do before they go inside. "What's going on with you?"

"I don't want to finish this film as it's planned. I don't want to talk to any more pubescent sickos or their ineffectual mothers. 'My baby ain't bad.' " I fell into the mournful whine I'd heard from every mother of every single delinquent we had filmed. At least, every mother we could locate. " 'The system failed my baby.' "

"You need a break," Guido said. "You've done three films back-to-back."

"The problem isn't the workload, it's the rut. Three films in a row I've done about the evil spawn of the urban nightmare. Guido, I just can't gut this one out."

"I hear you." He relaxed a little. "You're a victim of your own success, kid. The first film you did for the network did really well, so the network wants you to go with the winning formula and keep making the same film over and over. That's how they operate, and you're stuck with it as long as you're in their pocket."

"I want out of the pocket."

"But I don't see how Bao Ngo is going to give you your segue. What are you proposing to do, find out where Bao Ngo has been for the last twenty-some years? Like a video Where's Waldo?"

"Maybe. I like the myth Bao has become. Man, missing over twenty years, shows up to assault family. You can't deny the mystery here."

"Myth," Guido muttered. "Mystery."

A fuss at the far end of the patio distracted us. The same two men we had seen earlier, the men in short-sleeved shirts who had watched us tape Tam, argued with the hostess about the table she offered them. They wanted something closer to the water, up where Guido and I sat. But the hostess didn't want to give them the only table available, a table for six, because she had a large party waiting. The men were pushy and ugly with her, intimidating: Civil service, I thought, low functionaries or inspectors of some kind. Petty tyrants who need to throw their weight around.

I was glad the hostess didn't give in. I didn't want loud-mouth neighbors, perhaps nosy neighbors. The pair left in a huff, the taller of them punctuating their exit by pushing over a wrought-iron chair.

I moved my chair out of their path as they swept past. Watching them, Guido said, "Pissants."

I put my hand on his arm and he turned back to me. I

said, "What would happen if we scrap the dysfunctional *Brady Bunch* shit we've taped so far and head off in a new direction?"

"If I say 'budget' or 'deadline' or mention your esteemed executive producer's blood pressure, will it matter?"

"What can she do?" Saying that, I felt as if a blockage had just blown away to reveal something I should have seen all along. "I'm at the end of the contract. Let them fire me. Most of what we've done so far on this project, Guido, has been done before. Directionless youth grow up to become neighborhood bullies, convenience store thieves, precocious rapists. So what?"

"So what? I'll tell you so what. The footage we have so far is really dramatic, great, insightful, magical stuff, Maggie."

"We can do better. Think about this: Pedro's killers and Bao Ngo spent hours tormenting their victims, and earned damn little for their efforts. So, I ask you, what actually was their reward?"

Guido began to chew on his lower lip as he thought about it.

"Try this," I said. "Pedro's crime is, he underestimated his prey. He thought he was going to get something for nothing, and had to be taught a lesson."

"What was the lesson?"

"I'm not sure, but I have a feeling he needed to be shown who was in charge," I said. "Pedro is young and randy, he has a week's pay in his pocket. He wants sex, but he doesn't want to go out on the boulevard and pay a pro. So he goes to the park where he knows a group of teenage girls hang out; he's seen them there many times before. He knows they're poor. He thinks that because they have babies they're gullible, easy. For pocket change and a six pack, he thinks, they'll give it up to him. Maybe he can just talk a little booty out of them. In his own mind, Pedro is one charming guy. He thinks that's why the girls invite him home with them."

I looked sideways at Guido. "I wonder at what point

during the nine hours of torture, Pedro realized he had made a fatal miscalculation about who was in charge."

"Hmmm." Guido thinks in pictures, and I knew a whole new reel of images was running through his head.

"Those girls didn't have babies because they were push-overs. The babies are their meal ticket, the boys who fathered them are their pawns. For those girls, sex is power."

"Yeah, okay, I see that. I even like it. But where does Khanh fit in?"

"She had something Bao Ngo thought he was entitled to."

He wasn't a buyer. "You want to scrap a whole month's work?"

"Not all of it." I sipped my beer as I ran through the contents of the tapes filed in my office at the studio.

"San Marino is a million light-years away from the ghetto," Guido said. "You give any thought to the shift you're making? Jeez, Maggie, you'll need the frigging Golden Gate to bridge the gap."

"For crying out loud, Guido." I rubbed my eyes and then I looked at him, at his scowl. "Try this: It's Tet. Time to celebrate the family. We talk to Khanh with Tet as subtext. We go down to Little Saigon and film the parade on Saturday. Better yet, we fly up to San Francisco for the dragon parade down Grant Avenue. Can't you see footage from the celebration bursting open the cinder-block and barbed-wire backdrop we have so far?"

"No point arguing, is there?" Guido ground his back teeth and watched seagulls without apparent interest.

"Argue what?"

Slowly, he focused his big brown eyes on me again. "Bao Ngo has nothing to do with Mike Flint, does he?"

"Not one thing."

"And Pedro has everything."

I nodded. "Pedro is Mike's case."

"I get it, Maggie." I didn't care for the know-it-all smugness that came over him. "I see the segue you're going for, and it doesn't have a goddamn thing to do with this film or any other film or Bao Ngo, either. It's Mike's pocket you really want to get out of, and you think you've found your rocket. But I don't think your personal problems can fly on the back of this film."

"You don't know what you're talking about." But there was some truth in what he said. Damn him.

The air was heavy with something else left unsaid. I leaned back and stared at the side of Guido's face. "What?" A challenge in my voice.

As if startled, he echoed, "What?"

"Spill it, Guido." I set down my glass. "Something has been on your mind all day. If I have done anything to upset or offend you, I want to hear about it."

"There's nothing." Another answer that came too quickly.

"And?"

He watched seagulls some more. Drank some of his beer.

"Guido?"

Finally, he met my gaze. His big eyes were moist. "How long have we been friends?"

"A long time."

"Good friends?"

"You're as close as a brother to me."

"We're family?" he said.

"Damn near."

"Family tells family what's going on, Maggie."

"If something is going on, I missed it."

"Are you all right? Physically, I mean."

"I spend every day with you, Guido. If I wasn't all right, wouldn't you know?"

He folded his arms across his chest, pugnacious, angry. Like an accusation, he said, "Your mother flew down Sunday morning. She's still at your house."

"Mother visits happen to the best of us. Your mother has been known to fly into town to stay with you, too. So?"

Guido's posture went rigid, defensive. I had hurt him, an offense by omission, because I hadn't brought him inside.

He said, "Liam Farrington from Channel Four News

was at Cedars Sinai Hospital Saturday night following up on a hit-and-run. He saw Mike carry you into the emergency room."

"So Liam went straight to the phone and called you for the scoop?"

"He was worried about you. He said there was a lot of blood. He said you were crying."

"He wanted to know if there was a story," I said.

"Is there a story, Maggie?"

I sipped my beer, holding the bubbles at the back of my throat because I could not swallow. When Guido reached across the table for my hand, I pulled back because if my composure slipped at that point, it would set off a floodtide.

Early Saturday night the world divided for me into two categories: the people who knew and the people who didn't. The people who needed to know, knew: Mike, our children, my parents. And the people who didn't? What happened between me and Mike was none of their business.

I managed a breath. I finally swallowed. Looking over Guido's shoulder at the *Queen Mary* anchored across the channel, I said, "We forgot to get Tam's signature on a release. We have to go back down there."

"Maggie?"

"And we need more footage of his hut, for background." I scooted back my chair. "You ready?"

"If you are." He wouldn't look at me; I thought he was trying not to cry. He dropped money on the table and rose, held the back of my chair as if I needed help. As if I were suddenly delicate.

Minh Tam had moved from the patio seat where we left him. I was relieved that he was gone, because at that moment I really didn't want to talk with him. Later, maybe, but not right then.

All the way back down the bike path, Guido and I talked about the quality of digitized film, and how easy that process made mixing 35mm footage with VHS footage when it came time to edit. The subtext of the conversation was how far the two of us had come together. As close as the two of us were, though, Guido could never get inside that indefinable thing that exists between me and Mike Flint. No one could.

We were nearly abreast of the sewer outflow when I saw the Budweiser poster that had been Minh Tam's door, floating down the river. Tied to it still was the collection of rags and cardboard and the broad green leaves of the two castor bean trees that had been his walls and foundation. All of it tumbling toward the open sea.

Chapter 2

Minh Tam pulled off a good disappearing act. The only trace that he had ever called the riverbank his home was a small ring of blackened rocks where he, or someone, had once built a fire. I kicked around the area for a while looking for something he might have left behind in lieu of a forwarding address. But there was nothing to see other than the general weather-beaten detritus that was strewn all along the river.

"Good-bye, Mr. Myth; hello, plan A." Guido had a cocky sort of attitude, as if he had won a round. "*Killer Babies,* a film by Maggie MacGowen."

I threw up my hands to signal that I was conceding the round, though I was not, and made my way back up to the top of the bank where Guido waited. As far as I was concerned, Bao Ngo had become plan A. With Minh Tam or without him.

There were a few missing parts to the story Minh Tam told us, essential parts, that I already knew. Parts I had neglected to share with Guido and would withhold from my executive producer, Lana Howard, until the time was right.

No filmmaker pretends to be objective about the material in a project. There is, however, a line that should not be crossed between a personal story and blatant self-interest. By searching for Bao Ngo, I already had one toe over the forbidden line, and was casting about for some way to go all the way over without losing face or professional credibility. *I* needed to find out what Bao Ngo was up to.

I brushed my hands on my jeans. "We have a meeting with Lana. Better head back to the studio."

Guido drove, pushing early rush hour traffic all the way up the 405—the dreaded San Diego Freeway—and over the Sepulveda Pass into the Valley. Endless snaky lines of cars in both directions, everyone getting just about nowhere, trapped into the same commuter ordeal morning and night. A terrible price to pay just to live with good weather, I thought.

After twenty-five years with LAPD, Mike Flint was desperate to leave the city, any city. I was merely desperate to leave L.A. and its freeways.

When we arrived at the studio in Burbank, we were late for the meeting I had set up to introduce Lana to Arlo Delgado, a licensed private detective who specializes in finding lost people and ferreting out protected information.

On our way upstairs, we stopped by my office cubicle to pick up a tape the film library had put together for us, a collection of clips culled from prime-time news broadcasts over the last year. I had ordered the clips as background for several of the segments we were developing and wanted Guido and Lana to see it as soon as possible.

"You'll hate this stuff," I told Guido, passing the tape to him. He only grunted.

I also collected a handful of messages from Fergie, my red-haired assistant. Most of the calls were work related and nonurgent. I left them to deal with later. Five memos, however, I held on to: My daughter needed money for new dance shoes; Mike Flint was working late; my mother, the human dynamo, had gone to the county arboretum with an old school friend and the two of them were going out to dinner; my ex-husband, Scotty, left a pager number. The last of the calls was from my father.

Dad never phoned me at work just to say hello, and, anyway, he had called during breakfast only that morning, saving me from the bowl of iron-rich hot oatmeal Mom had set in front of me. I dialed his number in northern California to find out what could be, using his phrase, so all-fired important.

In May we would celebrate Dad's seventy-fifth birthday. Mother was a few years younger, both of them still living in the big old house in Berkeley where I grew up. They were healthy and strong, all things considered. Just the same, calls out of the blue made my palms sweat. Besides, I missed them. I missed living in San Francisco where I was only a quick subway ride away in case of emergency.

Dad's answering machine kicked on after the third ring. Still feeling uneasy, not knowing why he had called, I left a message and hung up. If there were an emergency, Dad would have called my mother first. If he couldn't find her, he would have his baby brother, my Uncle Max, track me down. Knowing all of that was small comfort.

On my way out, I asked Fergie to keep trying my dad and, if she reached him, to forward the call to Lana's office.

By the time Guido and I made it upstairs for Lana's meeting, Arlo Delgado already had his laptop set up on her massive granite conference table, his modem connected to a phone jack, and Lana completely enthralled. We wanted his help finding the missing parents and other family members of some of the kids we were interviewing. We also wanted a peek at their sealed juvenile histories. Abandonment, a family history of drugs, and alcohol were the common links among the baby criminals. The scoop on their histories was essential, but the system froze us out. The need to know was only half of the reason Arlo was there.

Arlo, paunchy, balding, on the downside of fifty, has charisma. Lana was working her way through divorce number three and feeling unlovable. They were a good pairing. I knew from our producer's girly-girl posture as she draped around Arlo that I had sent in the right takeover salesman for the deal I wanted to pitch.

I learned long ago that in the fickle world of network

television, the execs need to be constantly sold on projects even after they have signed off on them. The execs are less likely to capriciously cancel a project or interfere in obnoxious ways if they believe they have made creative contributions. The meeting with Arlo was totally fluff, a hand job for Lana to keep her attention from straying.

I knew that Arlo hoped to charm his way inside as a centerpiece in our film, when Guido and I wanted him for only one purpose, and that was information access. If Arlo appeared in the final cut, he would be seen sitting at his computer for a very few moments, nothing but video wallpaper to front narration about information gathering. No talk from Arlo, just an image. That was the deal we made. He would be paid, and his name would be in the credits. Period.

The usual one-day pass onto the studio parking lot and lunch in the employee dining room among network stars great and small were not going to satisfy Arlo's celebrity urge. He told me this fantasy he had about everyone recognizing him, about walking down the street and people saying, "Weren't you on TV, Mr.?" Wanting a talking part too much left Arlo vulnerable. I was not above taking advantage.

"We tried to call you from the van," I said, accepting Arlo's big hand. "You'd already left your office."

"One thing I learned working street patrol with Philly PD." He smooched the back of my hand. "Never be the last one to a party. Anything special you wanted to tell me?"

"Just wanted to tell you not to hurry. We were stuck in traffic. I know your time is valuable. Sorry you had to wait."

He winked at Lana. "Don't be sorry on my account."

Guido didn't bother with greetings. He headed straight for the TV system built into the far wall and slipped the tape we had picked up into a VCR. He turned the volume low and ran the tape. Background sound: "Girls, eleven and fourteen, arrested in slaying of elderly neighbor, their long-time friend." "Six-year-old held in savage beating of infant in crib." "Family defends accused rapist, age eleven, as outcry grows." The clips showed, in sequence, a snapshot of two smiling girls with similarly bad teeth, a sheriff's deputy carrying a tiny wrapped figure out of a worn-out-looking apartment building, and a skanky woman with uncombed hair, an unfiltered cigarette burning between her fingers as she cursed the system that let her boy down and the neighbors who wanted him locked up.

At the conference table, Arlo scooted back his chair to make room so Guido and I could watch over his shoulder as he demonstrated his stuff. He smelled of coffee and day-old whiskey, and fresh manly sweat. Lana stood close enough to just breathe him in.

"Got the social security number? You type it in and, bam." Arlo smacked the table next to his computer as screen after screen of files scrolled past. "The Life and Times of Mr. Ronald Coffey. It's so easy, Maggie honey, I can do it anywhere. All I need is an electric outlet and a phone jack. I don't need an office anymore.

"See here?" Arlo's thick thumb tapped the screen. "Mr. Ronald Coffey holds a mortgage on a house at three-zero-uno Spruce Street, Beaverton, Oregon, where his subscriptions to *Car and Driver* and *Playboy* are delivered. Same address is listed on the lease for a two-year-old Jeep Cherokee registered with the Oregon Department of Motor Vehicles."

"This is so fascinating." Lana's slender hand crept from the back of Arlo's chair onto his shoulder.

"Fascinating?" Guido said. "It's scary as hell."

Ronald Coffey's personal life, including his spotty credit history, poured through the modem connection. As he read, Guido clutched the neck of his shirt as if someone might come along and snatch him naked. I had a similar impulse.

You've had that dream where you're walking down the street nude, or you find yourself standing in front of all the people at work and you're wearing nothing but flimsy night-clothes? It seemed to me, watching Mr. Coffey's life displayed on the computer terminal, that maybe that particular nightmare had come true. We all just might as well walk around naked because none of us has any secrets anymore.

Right then, I promised to say six Hail Marys for every microphone and camera I had thrust into the face of some poor soul who didn't want to share his private tragedy or felonious gaffe with a national TV audience. How many times had I held up the press shield, claiming the public's right to know, when the truth was my story was nothing more than good and juicy dish?

I said I would ask for atonement. I didn't say I would stop doing it.

I crossed my arms protectively across my chest as Coffey's military history followed his list of unpaid parking fines, a wage garnishment for child support, and the results from a pathology lab: His enlarged prostate showed negative for malignancy. If I were to do a film about privacy in the computer age, the title would be *Snatched Naked*.

Moving the cursor to the beginning of the medical records, I said, "This can't be legal."

"Legal, schmegal. That's for the boys on the city payroll to worry about, not me. I'm private." Arlo sneered. He never would talk about the circumstances under which he left the Philadelphia Police Department, but I had a feeling they had something to do with not following other people's rules.

He said, "To me, whether it's legit or not hinges on how I use the stuff. It's not like I'm going to blackmail some guy. Most of the time, all I want to do is find the address of someone who doesn't want to be found, for someone with a good reason and enough money to buy my services. How I do the job is my business. And I sure as hell don't give my client more than he needs to know. I don't want some hothead coming back on me with a lawsuit or a loaded revolver."

"A credit report is one thing, but medical records?" Spicy taco grease rose in my throat. "You must need credentials of some sort to get access to this sort of information. It's protected."

"Oh, I got credentials up the butt. I'm licensed here and registered there. You'd be surprised how easy it is. Medical I get because I do collection work; I get the original, itemized bill. But most of the time, I don't even need a service. See this?" Arlo held up a CD ROM disk. "Contains the numbers from every phone book in the country. You can buy one of these in any computer store."

Arlo slipped the CD into the drive, and came up with Ronald Coffey's Beaverton phone number and address. "I'd say that's dead bang. You want him, Maggie, go get him. You can even call him and tell him you're coming."

"The daughter he walked out on needs some help. She's being tried for murdering her mother," I said. "I doubt Coffey meant to hide from her. But suppose he did. How easy would it be for him to disappear?"

"Depends." Arlo absently moved Lana's hand from his shoulder and pressed it against the side of his neck. "If Coffey lived under an assumed name, never made contact with friends or family, used only cash, didn't own anything, pay rent, work, have a phone, get sick, use the mails, or file a tax return, then it would be a little tougher. But if that's what he's doing, then the law is probably after him, too. In that case, it's best to give the authorities any data you have and let them do the work."

"Cooperation with the law, that's refreshing advice." Guido nudged his way past Arlo's wide shoulders so that he could type in *Bao Ngo* and several variations, city unknown, and got a screen full of possible phone numbers and addresses. He said, "I don't have any problem accessing the phone book because that's already public information. But the rest of it, I don't know. The police can't even use the DMV files without authorization. This other stuff, like financial records, they'd need a subpoena. Medical they couldn't have at all."

"That's why folks hire me." Arlo stretched. "I got no one to beef me but deadbeat dads and skip artists."

I said, "What if all you have to go on is a fairly

common name and a twenty-year-old alien identification number?"

"No social security?"

"Nope."

"That's a tough one, honey."

Guido tapped the print icon, and a hard copy page of Bao Ngo addresses and phone numbers emerged from Arlo's printer.

Arlo took the page from him. "You want this guy?"

I said, "Yes."

"Let's give him a try."

There were plenty of Bao Ngos living in America. But none of them had the right age or date of entry.

I asked, "Can you access alien ID numbers?"

Arlo shook his head. "Only if there's a cross-reference with Social Security or IRS files. And we aren't finding one here. The Immigration people aren't real helpful, and I can't get into their database. Best thing, go into the community and ask around. Put an ad in the Vietnamese language papers. You need more than a name to get a good hit."

"What's in a name?" Lana spoke up for the first time. "A rose by any other name . . ."

"Yeah, I know, it's still a rose," Arlo chuckled. "Your only hope may be if someone recognizes this Bao Ngo's smell. A whole lot of people change their names when they cross the border. He could be calling himself Becky Thatcher by now."

"The hunt is the thing," I said.

Guido glanced at the video playing on the far side of the room. A young honor student was denied admission to Harvard when it was revealed that she had been convicted of murdering her abusive alcoholic mother. The story was sadder than hell—she did her time, she got no break—but it was a story already worn out by daytime talk shows. All of the clips on the tape were well-worn territory. Child crime gets a lot of attention.

When Guido turned to me, I asked, "Was I right?"

"Yes. I hate it." He folded the Bao Ngo list and stuffed it into his back pocket.

"Maggie." Lana reached for me, oblivious to what Guido had said. Oblivious to everything except her immediate program, namely, Arlo. "How will Arlo's demonstration scan?"

"On film? It won't," I said. "All we can do is show him sitting at the computer. We can't hit the information on his screen. There are privacy issues the legal department is worried about."

It was time right then to say that I did not intend to film Arlo at all. Clearly, Lana's interest was in Arlo live, and not in the film's form or structure. The need to keep Lana's interest piqued, however, overrode good judgment and any sense of fair play on my part.

Lana was all mushy over Arlo. She took a few steps back, framed him with her hands, the way a director might, and made a show of imagining Arlo on screen. Behind her back, Guido rolled his eyes when she said, "I see Arlo shot full-face. We'll pan in over the top of the computer and come in close on that wonderful face."

"Get the logo on the back of the computer while you're going in, Lana," Guido said, nudging me. "We'll snag us some product-placement money."

"I don't know." Arlo suddenly had qualms. "Maybe you should put one of those blue dots over my face like the gal that Kennedy kid raped."

"Allegedly raped," Guido corrected.

"Whatever." Arlo winked at me. "I don't want some allegedly irate deadbeat recognizing my handsome mug and coming after me."

"Don't worry, Arlo," Lana cooed. "I'm sure you know how to take care of yourself."

"You bet I do." He knew he was being handled. I think he wanted to be handled.

Lana threw an arm around his shoulders. "Then we have a deal?"

"A deal."

We already had a deal, and Lana knew it. Pointedly, she turned to me. "Where does Mr. Delgado fit into your shooting schedule?"

"We'll work something out," I said. "Arlo, my people will call your people."

I make the decisions about who and what I shoot and when I do it. Until Lana decided she liked the scent of Arlo, I had never known her to interfere as long as I was on deadline and close to budget. She certainly never stooped to schedule interviews. I thought her input was a cheap move to make a thirty-second TV star out of some poor guy just so she could ease him out of his trousers. I had a sick feeling, as if I were procuring for her.

I added, "Arlo, when Guido and I get back from Montreal, we'll call you."

Guido jumped as if I had goosed him, but didn't challenge me.

"Montreal?" Lana parroted. "What's in Montreal?"

"An auction house. A couple of items stolen during a recent home invasion robbery showed up in their inventory. The rightful owner and I sure would like to know how they got there," I said. "What sort of arrangements can we make with a Canadian affiliate for auxiliary crew and equipment on short notice?" I nudged Guido. "You know how tough it is, taking a crew out of town. Save us having to lug everything with us if we can get what we need near location."

"None. No arrangements." She seemed nonplussed. "That's Canada. Canadian broadcast law won't let us have affiliates. I don't know anybody up there."

"Then we'll have to schlep everything. Guido, who do we need? What do we need?"

"Union minimum." He ground his teeth again. "We have to do this?"

"Depends," I said, turning to Arlo. "Can you access ships' manifests?"

"I've never tried it before. What do you want?"

"I want the name of the ship Bao Ngo arrived on in September of 1975, names of the crew and other passengers, the ship's cargo manifest. The captain's log would be nice. What do you think?"

His chest swelled. He was cocky, boastful, in the way

he said, "When do you need it?" as if no problem was too big.

"I need it now. I don't want to go to Montreal."

"Let me work on it, make a few calls." He began closing computer files. The meeting was over. "I'll get back to you, honey."

Lana's face flushed. Anger, frustration, both—I don't know. Arlo, clearly, was preparing to leave, all business now that he had an assignment.

Arlo is a big flirt, but I never knew him to be easy. I thought that it was entirely possible, considering Lana's obvious behavior, that Arlo was relieved to have a graceful out. Now that poor Lana wasn't going to get what she wanted that afternoon, I had a feeling that she would somehow extract payment from me.

While Arlo packed up his equipment, I used the phone on the conference table to call Fergie. I told her to check out airline schedules and the availability of a bare-bones film crew. She groaned, but promised to get right on it.

When I hung up, I caught Lana watching me. Her tone was cold when she asked, "Is there a budget line for this trip?"

"I'll work it out with the location auditor. We'll find a way to shuffle funds from one pocket to another."

She said, "Uh-huh," without much expression, and then gave her attention back to Arlo, giving him one more shot before releasing him. Lana and Arlo were still together in the conference room when Guido and I excused ourselves.

Guido punched the elevator button. "Montreal? You serious?"

"Let's see what Arlo turns up, first. If we go with the Bao Ngo angle, I want to interview the owner of a Montreal gallery. He accepted several pieces of lovely Asian sculpture, subject to appraisal and verification of provenance. I want to know whom he talked to; the pieces all came out of Khanh's house. He spotted them on an Interpol list, and Interpol traced provenance to Khanh."

"It's February." Guido held the elevator door for me. "You have any idea what the weather is like in Montreal in February?"

"Cold, Guido," I said. "It's cold in Montreal."

It was almost five o'clock when I sat down at my desk to return calls.

The kids—my daughter, Casey, and Mike's twenty-year-old son, Michael—informed me that they were going out for pizza and then Michael was taking Casey to his college library to help her with a research project. They said they would be home by ten. Neither of them had heard from Mike.

When I called Parker Center downtown, the Police Administration Building where Robbery-Homicide Division is quartered, I was told that Mike was in the field. That could mean a lot of things: He had forgotten to sign out, the guy who answered the phone had no clue, Mike was investigating his current case, or he was up at the police academy bar having a few with the boys and his colleague didn't want to snitch him off.

I paged Mike, punched in four-four, our code for Hi. If he could call me, he would. In the meantime, there were a few chores I wanted to get through before I went home for the night. I was about halfway through the list, maybe half an hour later, when Mike called.

He asked, "How are you?" Not the usual formula greeting, but a question fraught with concern: How *are* you?

"I'm ready for this day to be over," I said. "But I'm okay."

"Want me to come and get you?"

"No need. I'm a little tired, but I'm fine. The kids are going out, Mom has been out with a friend all day. So, if no one's at home, I'll wait around here a while longer and let traffic clear before I get back on the freeway."

"Your mom is out? What happened to chicken soup and pillows under your feet?"

"Mom isn't much of a fusser, Mike, and I'm not very good about being fussed over. She gave me two full days' worth of chicken soup. The oatmeal this morning was her grand finale. Now she's at the arboretum with a friend, checking out drought-resistant plants."

"If you're feeling up to it, I may have a break in the Pedro case for you. I'm waiting on the mother of one of the witnesses to come in: Can't question the kid until the mother shows up." I heard him shuffle papers. "The mom is going to try to get off work a little early."

"Going to try?" I said. "Her kid is in Parker Center because she was involved with a murder and Mom is going to *try* to get there?"

"I caught a bad one this time, Maggie." His tone was heavy, dragged down by too much reality; Mike was in all ways ready to retire. "My last case, and it sure as hell isn't the way I want to go out. I keep asking myself, what's it all been about? Twenty-five years I spend trying to get bad guys off the streets so the kids can grow up safe. And what does it come down to? We aren't safe from the kids."

"You really are down, aren't you? Why don't you have the mother come in early tomorrow and you and I go home and have a quiet evening?"

"I wish I could." He cleared his throat. "I shouldn't have let you talk me out of putting in for vacation time this week. If I had, one of the other guys would have caught this one and I'd still be working the cemetery scam. You know, the cemetery owner who dug up old graves and resold them? It's a weird case, but there's no homicide involved. All that our guys have to do is watch the forensic anthropologists dig through the bone pile and give updates to the press."

"You don't have to ask my permission to take vacation time," I said.

"What's the point of me staying home if you go in to work?"

I said, "There was a time, not so long ago, when you'd sing Hank Williams songs to me when I called you."

"I don't feel like singing. If the mother shows up, I'm going to spend half the night questioning a fourteen-year-old girl about her part in the torture of a little guy who was only looking for a piece of teenage ass."

"Mike?"

"Don't go PC on me. We're not talking about deflowering a virgin. This kid already has two assault charges in her file, and a baby to take care of."

"She's a child, Mike."

"She's a whore who got an early career start. I don't have any soft spot for her because she's only fourteen. She's been gang-banging half her life. Pedro sure as hell isn't her first victim. I only hope the judge gets some message from her record and lets us try her as an adult."

I had nothing to say.

"You don't know how it is out there, Maggie."

"Sure I do."

It was his turn to fall silent.

I said, "I called because no one will be home all evening."

"I'm sorry, there's no way I can get off. If you don't want to be alone, maybe Guido . . ."

"You miss the point. No one's home, Mike. It's a rare opportunity. If you ever wanted to walk around the house in your boxers and scratch, now's the time."

"Scratch, huh?"

"As in, relax?"

I heard him tapping the end of his pencil on his desk, tapping out a thinking rhythm. I gave him time to work through whatever was on his mind. He said, "If you feel up to driving downtown, we can go have dinner as long as it's somewhere close. I'm on the pager."

"I'm leaving now."

Fergie put her head in the door. "Your dad's on line two."

I promised Mike I would see him within the hour and said good-bye. Then I switched to the second call.

"Dad?" I said. "You okay?"

"I'm fine." He sounded okay.

"What's up?" I asked.

"It's the damnedest thing, sweetheart," he said. "I had a call this afternoon from your San Francisco neighbor, Jerry, the real estate guy."

"Is he okay?"

"He's fine. He thinks he's hot on a commission." Dad drew it out to build suspense.

"And?"

"Maggie, someone wants to make an offer to buy your San Francisco house."

Chapter 3

At the end of every work day, when the commuters have vacated downtown L.A. office buildings, a second shift—winos and junkies and the ambulatory insane—slips out from the shadows with their bottles in brown paper bags and their bedrolls on their backs to claim Civic Center lawns and sidewalks as their rightful domain.

I arrived downtown during the transition, when dark-suited city workers and the homeless shared the side-walks in nearly equal numbers. In another hour, most of the suits would be gone and the neighborhood would begin its nightly, underworld carnival.

I left the car in a lot in Little Tokyo and walked across First Street to Parker Center, the LAPD's big blue administration building. The Glass House, inmates call it. There is no fondness attached to the sobriquet, and no special respect or fear.

Parker Center is falling down. Twenty years of deferred maintenance, a trio of fair-sized earthquakes and no budget for cosmetic repairs, as well as general overuse, have rendered the onetime showplace an embarrassment to civic pride. Maybe it's a good symbol for the city's general state of affairs; no effort is spent anymore to keep up appearances in the face of too much reality.

A recent commission decided that the facility was beyond fixing and should be demolished. In the meantime, cops make do, dodging falling ceiling tiles and broken flooring, ignoring gaping holes in the plaster, trying to patch into the information age with an antique electrical system and insufficient telephone lines.

I walked toward the main entrance past families waiting for loved ones to get processed out of jail. They lounged on the scruffy grass out front or sat on the memorial to fallen officers, some of them picnicking on fast food brought over from the mall underneath the Civic Center across the street. The air all around held the heavy perfume of burning marijuana.

The reception officer signed me in on my press credential and let me go upstairs without an escort. I wasn't stopped again until I reached the door of the third-floor Robbery-Homicide Division bull pen where Mike worked.

At the door, a dozen or so onlookers were kept out, as I was, by a working four-person news crew: cameraman, soundman, gaffer, and an on-camera face with a battery pack spoiling the line of his custom-tailored jacket. A lavaliere mike served as his tie clip.

I knew the face, a veteran city reporter named Henry Jacobs who worked for the same network that signed my paychecks. That made us colleagues, I suppose.

Inside the bull pen, Mike Flint was seated at his desk with eight or ten veteran detectives perched around him, all of them in shirtsleeves and all of them grinning. From my vantage point in the doorway, the focus of attention seemed to be Mike Flint's polished black shoes.

Henry Jacobs faced the camera and read his notes in a deep, *Dragnet*-imitation voice. "The thief struck by night, brazenly breaking into the very heart of police headquarters looking for loot. Night after night, his nocturnal crime wave taunted our fair city's elite Robbery-Homicide detective division. In the end, it was the perpetrator's greed that foiled him.

"Hoping to catch the criminal at his game, veteran Detective Mike Flint set a trap, and the wrongdoer fell for the bait. Caught in the very act of pilfering a piece of fine, aged cheddar, the suspect put up a brief struggle before he met his violent end. Had he survived, his legal defense might have been, 'Entrapment.' "

I could see in the cameraman's monitor a very dead

mouse with his neck pinned under an old-fashioned spring trap that Mike had set in his bottom desk drawer.

"A motto for would-be thieves to keep in mind," Henry intoned. "Live by the cheese. Die by the cheese."

Everyone in the room laughed. When the gaffer lowered his lights and the cameraman stopped his tape, there were handshakes all around. Henry passed his batter pack and lavaliere mike to the soundman, and the crew decamped. As I backed out of the way to let them through the door, I caught Henry's eye. He gave a little jump as if startled to see me.

"Maggie MacGowen," he said.

"Henry." I offered my hand. "Slow news day?"

"That's an understatement." He leaned in closer, as if he hoped to buy something illicit from me. "You working on a story?"

"No," I said. "I don't do the news anymore. I'm only here to have dinner with the executioner over there."

Henry glanced in at Mike, who was still surrounded by detectives and staffers trying to get a look at the mouse.

"Flint, huh? Guess I heard about you two." Henry suddenly had a gleam in his eye, an old reporter's is-there-a-story-here gleam.

"Police press office call you with the dead mouse tip?" I asked.

He shook his head. "We've been hanging around here all afternoon, hoping to get some new developments on this cemetery scandal in time for the five o'clock. But it's a no go. I think Flint took pity on me. When I asked the team for an update, Flint said the only story breaking was the mouse, but I could have an exclusive. If we get nothing on the cemetery by six, I think we're going to run the mouse tape."

"Can you get me a copy?" I asked. I had a growing archive of Mike Flint clips culled from prime-time news. I planned to run all of it at his retirement party in May.

"No problem," Henry said, giving my hand a squeeze.

"I wouldn't mind if you passed any little insider tidbits my way. You know, home team advantage."

"Count on it, Henry. You know Mike isn't on the cemetery case anymore?"

"He told me. He has some juvenile thing going down." Henry scowled. "I hate juvenile cases. Can't use names, can't use photos, all the charges will be sealed, and no one will give me a quote. Does me no good."

Something, maybe the tone of Henry's voice, made Mike look our way just then. When Mike met my eyes, he blushed, seemed embarrassed; so unlike Mike. He dropped his gaze from mine. Ordinarily, I would have walked straight to him, but the look on his face chilled me. The night before, when I rolled up against him in bed and put my arm around him, as I had hundreds of nights before, instead of turning toward me, he had turned away and pretended to be asleep.

What happened Saturday night left him either afraid to touch me or loathe to touch me. I couldn't read him, and he wouldn't talk about it. This I knew, as I stood there, feeling alone only a few feet away from him: If he didn't start talking about what was on his mind pretty soon, then we wouldn't have anything left to talk about.

Mike slipped the mouse, trap and all, into a manila evidence envelope. He sealed the top with red tape and carried the package over to us.

"Souvenir, Jacobs." Mike handed the envelope to Henry, acknowledging me with a wink.

"Thanks, Flint." Henry took it. Seemed quite happy to have it, in fact. Henry is a notorious prankster. I was certain he would pass on this little gift to some unsuspecting soul.

Mike gripped my shoulder; real detectives don't smooch in front of the boys, but I expected a more familiar greeting. He said, "Hello."

I was tempted to put my hand on his ass while everyone was still watching him. Just to do it. Instead I said, "Hello."

"I'll get my coat," he said, sounding formal, the way one talks to strangers. "Be right with you."

I watched him cross the big room to the coatrack, knew the contours of the shoulders inside the starched shirt when he raised his arms, knew the flex of the gabardine-covered thighs when he walked. Knew his body almost as well as I knew my own. Knew his body, but could not get inside the mind.

Tall, white-haired at forty-eight, Mike still has the hard, sinewy body of a marathon runner. He's handsome the way Bogart was, with the map of a full life etched on his face. You look at him and you know he'll be either a good time or a very, very bad time. Depending.

Mike has a bit of a swagger that is part of his charm. The swagger comes from pride, and the pride, until recent notorious events in the City of Angels, came largely from his job with LAPD's elite Robbery-Homicide Detective Division.

"The best job in the world," he would say when I first met him. But during his last couple of years on the job, when anyone asked where he worked, Mike clammed up to avoid the inevitable browbeating. Not a healthy state of being for a prideful man.

Mike signed out with his partner, an old-timer named Cecil Renfrew, and I said good-bye to Henry.

On the way to the elevator, Mike slipped into his suit coat and then patted himself to make sure all the essentials were in place: police photo ID on his lapel; money clip in his front pocket with a handful of keys; on his belt his polished shield, pager, cuffs, extra ammo clip, and 9mm automatic. Maybe I got into the habit of patting him on the ass because the rest of him is usually so cluttered.

"Beef dips at Philippe's sound okay?" he asked, pushing the down button. "Not fine cuisine"—pronounced coo-zeen—"but the service is quick and it's just a few blocks over."

I said, "Anything is fine, as long as you're with me."

Alone in the elevator with Mike, I put my arm around his back, brushed my lips across his sleeve. He pulled me into a strong embrace and buried his face in my hair.

It was a nice moment that lasted only long enough for the elevator to descend one floor.

Six women officers in maternity uniforms got in at the second floor and rode with us all the way down to the garage. From their conversation I got the impression that they had come from a medical benefits meeting. Mike was unusually quiet and tense around them, not a single comment about the perils of working in the fertility zone or the smell of dill pickles in the air. I put my hand through his, but he wouldn't look at me.

In the underground garage, we got into his ancient city-issue car and pulled out onto San Pedro Street, headed north through the dusk. Mike still seemed deep in thought, shrouded behind this wall he sometimes drops when something is on his mind.

At the first red light, he pulled himself back to the surface. He turned to me. "Tell me what your dad said."

"My San Francisco neighbor called him. Remember Jerry, the real estate guy? Someone contacted him and wants to buy my house."

"No lie?" The light changed and Mike drove ahead across the freeway overpass, the last of rush hour flowing like a river of light below us. "How much are they offering?"

"We didn't get into that yet. Dad told Jerry that if he had a serious buyer he should go see my Uncle Max and draw up a formal offer."

"Could be bullshit," Mike said.

"Could be. I called Lyle and he told me that he had seen some people taking pictures last week. Two men in dark suits. Corporate types."

The corner of Mike's mouth drew up in a smirk. "Lyle forget to tell you about them?"

"What's to tell?"

Lyle was my former housemate. Casey and I acquired him the evening the Loma Prieta earthquake turned his home behind ours in the Marina District of San Francisco into a rubble-filled lot. Our offer of shelter until Lyle rebuilt evolved into something more permanent, something more like family. Lyle, Casey, and I got used to looking out for each other.

When Casey and I moved south to be with Mike, I had to rent out the house to make ends meet. I never had time to worry about where Lyle would go. We found tenants for the house, oceanography graduate students who sprouted a new variety of kelp in the master bathroom tub. And Lyle moved in with my mom and dad in Berkeley to help out with the heavier domestic chores. The arrangement worked well until the grad students' grant ran out. My house had been vacant since the end of the winter quarter, and the financial drain was ruinous.

Mike parked in a red zone in front of Philippe's, hung the transmitter of his police radio over the rearview mirror so that he wouldn't be ticketed. His city parking pass, he called it.

"Can you take Friday afternoon off?" I leaned in close to him as I got out of the car. "I'm thinking we could fly up to San Francisco, check out the house, and see if there's anything to this offer. Then we'll have the whole weekend. We could go to Chinatown to watch the big New Year parade. It's a good party. We'd have fun."

"That's a big trip for a weekend." He wrapped his arm around me. "Are you up to it?"

"Sure. Maybe the kids will come with us. We're due for a family outing."

"Might be too soon for you." He gave me a sidelong appraisal. "Can't Uncle Max fax the documents to you?"

"I feel like getting out of town."

He wasn't listening to me. "Why don't I fly up tomorrow morning, take a look at the offer with your dad and Max? I can be home by this time tomorrow."

"I'm fine," I said, hearing the edge in my voice. We hadn't moved away from the car. "I am certainly strong enough to read a legal document."

Mike shook his head all the time I talked. When I paused, he said, "It's not about reading the papers, it's about the wear and tear. Two days ago you passed out walking up the stairs."

"Three days ago I was in the emergency room. But today, I worked all day and I'm perfectly fine. I need to be busy."

"Give yourself some time. It's too soon for a big trip."

I pulled away from him. "There's a remote possibility I may go to Montreal tomorrow. If I do go, I can be home late Thursday, and we can fly up to San Francisco on Friday afternoon."

"Maggie," was as far as he got before he couldn't say anything more.

His look of deep anguish made me feel sad, and made me feel inadequate all over again. I wrapped my arms around him. "I'm sorry, Mike."

"Sorry for what?" He stood rigid.

"I'm sorry about the way things turned out." I pressed my face against his hard chest and smelled his skin through his crisp shirt. "And I'm okay now. But I don't know if you are. Sooner or later, you have to talk to me, Mike."

A panhandler rose from his squat in a nearby doorway, sidled toward us, changed his mind, moved on. Mike didn't seem to notice. He began to pat my back, as he does when he's upset, and stood there silent for a long moment. I waited until he figured out what he wanted to say. Or not say. After a while he took a deep breath.

"When Michael got serious with his girlfriend," Mike said, his voice thick, "I started getting used to the idea that I could be a grandfather in the not-too-distant future. It was a real nice notion, the thought of having a baby in the house again. Then suddenly, out of nowhere, it's me who's going to be the father. Me. Old Mike Flint. I'm ready to retire, and you and me are going to have a baby. The reality of it hardly sinks in, and then the baby is gone. Poof. Just gone."

"A little more than poof," I said.

"I can't get the picture of what might have been out of my mind." His voice wavered. "I liked the picture a whole lot, Maggie."

I started to pat his back. I was sad, too. But more for Mike than for myself.

"I tried to get the lieutenant to take me off the Pedro case today," he said. "I don't have the stomach for it. I listen to these little assholes, thirteen, fourteen, fifteen years old. They talk about how far they'll go to get a little money for drinking and toking and screwing around, and all the time their babies are crawling around on the police station floor.

"I look at them, and the babies are so damn cute. But no one watches after them the right way. They're nothing but raw material for the next generation of criminals. Another ten years, I'll be hooking them up and bringing them in, just like I brought in their moms and dads."

"You won't be around in ten years to hook up anybody."

"It's just, I get so pissed." What he didn't say was, why did they get to have babies when we didn't? "What a waste."

I said, "I love you."

"I know." He chuckled deep in his throat, a self-deprecating tone. "Can't for the life of me figure out why."

"Because you always take me to the nicest places. Are we going to eat, or what?"

"Yeah. We're going to eat." He squared his shoulders, adjusting himself as if he had just dropped a heavy load. "I'll put in for a vacation day Friday. We'll have a good time this weekend."

"Good." I reached up and kissed the underside of his jaw, felt the twelve-hour beard against my lips. "Lyle says he'll move back into the house until we figure out what to do with it. Just so it won't look abandoned."

"Best thing would be to sell," Mike said. And said it not for the first time. "Let's hope this offer is legit."

As we walked down the block toward the restaurant, I mumbled something about the bad real estate market and that we would be lucky if the offer was big enough to cover the mortgage, much less the sales fees. Mike didn't seem concerned.

The hills of San Francisco around my house are so steep that you can't always see what's down the other side until you're over the crest and headed into, well, whatever is down there. That's how I felt that Tuesday evening—rapidly approaching a blind descent.

The house was after all just a house. And an expensive liability. No question about my attachment to it: The house had sheltered Casey and me through the two Big Ones, the divorce and the earthquake, in that order. Still, it was just a damn house.

Okay, this is the truth: As much as I loved Mike, I always knew that if things didn't work out between us, I could always go home. Selling my home required a leap of faith in our shared future similar to heading downhill blind.

Philippe's is a city landmark, a turn-of-the-century sandwich shop about halfway between Olvera Street and Union Station just north of L.A.'s Civic Center. There's nothing elegant about the place—long tables and sawdust on the floor, an eighty-cent cup of coffee served with the original hot beef dip on a French roll—but it is a constant in the sea of urban change.

I found two window seats at the far end of the narrow dining room while Mike ordered from the counter. Experience taught him to have the food wrapped to go, just in case. He had no more than sat down and added milk to his coffee, when his pager buzzed.

"Wouldn't you know?" he muttered. He had to put on reading glasses to see the two-line readout. "It's the office. The mother is in. I gotta go."

I'm not a crier and I'm not clingy, but I felt like being both as soon as that damn pager beeped. I didn't know where the sudden flood of emotion came from, and that upset me even more than the surge of tears I had to fight down. While Mike gathered everything together, preparing to leave, I walked over to the counter to grab a handful of napkins we didn't need just to have a few seconds to myself, to get a grip.

Mike waited for me at the door. I tucked the napkins into the top of his sandwich bag. “No wonder you have mice in the office, always taking meals at your desk.”

“I’ll be home as soon as I can, Maggie.” He took my arm and we walked out.

Chapter 4

I called Khanh Nguyen from Parker Center before I said good-bye to Mike.

"I found Minh Tam," I said. "I have him on videotape."

"I am impressed," she said. "My faith in you was well placed. How did you manage to find him so quickly?"

"Knocking on doors," I said. "The pictures you gave me helped. Someone recognized him."

"You can assure me that Minh is all right?"

"He is as all right as a homeless man can be."

"Now that he is found, I hope he will call me." There was hardly a pause before she asked, "Did you tell Minh about our cousin Bao?"

"Yes, but I'm not sure he believed me."

"The situation is very difficult to understand," she said. Her voice thickened, took on a pleading tone. "May I see your tape, Maggie? May I see Minh for myself?"

After what she had been through, the home invasion and all, who could turn her down? Sam and Khanh's house in ritzy San Marino was only a ten-minute detour if I stopped by on my way home, so I told her I would come that evening.

I turned onto Khanh's street, looking for addresses. It had been a long time since I visited, and I had never paid much attention to landmarks before because, in the old days, Scotty had always been the driver.

San Marino is an enclave for old money, quiet wealth secreted behind wrought-iron gates and other barricades well camouflaged by landscaping. Security generally was tight, but only Khanh's house had uniformed guards standing sentinel.

I hesitated before pulling up to the gate and announcing myself. The circular drive inside was lined by half-a-dozen or so sleek Mercedes and Jaguars, enough for a party. Under the circumstances, I knew there was no celebration, I just didn't want to walk in on something.

Sam and Khanh belonged to a world from which I had been exiled by divorce, the hard-edged, globe-trotting sphere of my ex-husband. Here I was, after several years' absence, putting in an appearance—an appearance wearing the same blue jeans that had gone sliding down the foul bank of the Los Angeles River early that afternoon. There was some brown stuff I could not identify, a smear, down the back of my left leg.

The Nguyens and their friends were elegant, gracious people, the exiled power elite from a country that existed only in history. The women, always beautiful in designer dresses and real jewelry, would talk about their children at Harvard and Oxford. The men, in perfectly tailored dark suits, talked business and debated what went wrong during the Bay of Pigs.

I am not shy, but in their house I always felt like a clumsy outsider, like a snot-nosed kid peeking through palace gates for a glimpse of the queen.

A guard carrying a cell phone in one hand and a flashlight in the other walked out to meet me. He shone his flashlight into the back of the van, and then turned it on me. "Miss MacGowen?"

When I said, "Yes," he opened my door and held it for me. "I'll park your car. Go ahead. You're expected."

Security guards watched from behind hedges as I walked up the long drive to the front door. It was too late to turn back, but I hesitated before ringing the bell. Something didn't feel right. Maybe it was the specter of Scotty. If he was there, I would leave as quickly as I could.

I shuffled the tape I had brought from one hand to the other, knowing that this visit would elevate me to topic number one in a new round of gossip among Scotty's old clients and their shiny wives for a while. In my mind, I worked through the worst scenario—Maggie looked so . . . —and decided I didn't care what they had to say. I pushed the bell.

Khanh herself opened the door.

"Maggie." Khanh held a cell phone similar to the one the gate guard carried. She bowed slightly rather than reaching for my hand. "You are so good to come."

"If I'd known you had company, I would have come another time."

"It is not company." She touched my arm then, as if sharing a confidence. "Sam is having a meeting."

Khanh, wearing house sandals, waited while I took off my sneakers and lined them up at the end of the rank of polished black leather shoes next to the door. A quick count said maybe a dozen pairs, about two pairs for each car in the drive. And all of them men's shoes.

Khanh smiled while she waited for me to pull up my socks, graciousness personified.

Khanh was probably in her early fifties, though there wasn't a line on her face to give away her age. She was exquisite, her perfect features—dark almond eyes, high cheekbones, a surgically westernized little nose, a curtain of black, sculpted hair as smooth and shiny as polished obsidian—and her graceful carriage, conspired to give her the illusion of being delicate when, indeed, she was anything but.

I walked with Khanh across her wide marble foyer to a small, dark-paneled sitting room: teak desk, deep chairs, big-screen television. She closed the door behind us, shutting out the male voices coming from the another part of the house.

"May I get you a drink? Something to eat?"

"No, thank you. I need to get home." I handed her the copy I had made of Minh's interview. "You may keep the tape."

"Thank you." She set the tape on the arm of a green leather club chair. "I will watch this later, when Sam has finished his business."

I was puzzled: If she had been in such a hurry to have the tape, why was she waiting to see it? When she raised her hand to sweep back the silky curtain of hair that fell across her face, I saw bruises and abrasions like ugly bracelets around her wrists where, I guessed, Bao had bound her, and a yellow-green doughnut-shaped circle where he had apparently pressed the barrel of his gun into the center of her forehead.

I asked, "Do the police have any news of Bao?"

"Nothing." She picked up a television remote control and pushed a button. "The police took the tapes from our security cameras, but they gave me this to show our friends. Here is Bao."

The television came on, a flash of snow across the screen, and then a pale face below dark hair. The camera was placed too high so it shot downward on the person standing outside the front door, foreshortening the man and distorting his features, making it impossible to judge his height or see his clothing clearly, or to see his features at all unless he looked straight up, which he did not do.

The image on the screen rolled, bobbled, and then changed to another camera, a different angle, this one shooting outward from, I guessed, somewhere beside the front porch.

Against the dark of night, a white, ghostlike blob approached up Khanh's driveway. The figure triggered a motion-sensitive spotlight mounted on a tree, and bright light washed the man in color. It was still impossible to see his features: He had turned up the collar of his windbreaker and kept his chin low as he jogged toward the house.

There were two other figures, just shapes against the hedge, loitering near the front gate. A hand loomed large in the lens, and the screen went dark.

I said, "There were three men?"

"I saw only two." She held up two manicured fingers: long, perfect tapered nails. "Bao was alone when I opened the door. I cannot tell you how surprised and how happy I was to see an old friend I thought all these years was dead. Of course, I invited him inside. I did not see where the other man came from. He was suddenly upon me and my hands were being bound. It happened so fast."

"The other man tied you?" I said. "Who was he?"

"I never saw his face. All I can say is he was tall and his voice sounded like a white man."

"Is it possible that Bao was a hostage, too? Could he have been forced to go along with the raid?"

"Forced?" She shook her head. "Oh, no. Bao gave the orders. He told the other one what to take and where to look. It was Bao who held the gun to my head when I would not give him the combination to the safe."

"Were you in the house alone?"

"Yes. Bao seemed to know I would be alone. He knew that it was the housekeeper's night off and he knew that it was the night I stayed home from the restaurant. Bao kept telling the other man to stay calm because there was plenty of time. He would say, 'Sam is just closing the restaurant now,' and 'Sam is counting the register now,' and 'Sam will get into his car now. Time to go.' "

"He's been watching you," I said.

Khanh shuddered. "I want to move away from here. But Sam says, no. Any affliction will only follow us, he says."

"Not if Bao is caught."

"Even then."

I heard bitterness in the tone of her voice. I said, "What a nightmare."

"I'm all right." She pulled her long sleeves over her bruised wrists. "Some things are gone that can never be replaced." Her glance fell to a side table where I remembered seeing a jade carving on an earlier visit.

I asked, "How much did Bao take?"

She turned her back to the table. "I do not dwell on material possessions we lost, Maggie. I think instead of the peace and sanctity of my family's home that has been stolen."

"I'm sorry," I said.

"Thank you for all you are doing to help me." Again, she reached out and touched my arm. "To celebrate the new year, after what has happened, Sam and I are especially anxious to have our family and friends in our house again, to exorcise our great fear. Will you and Casey and your man friend be able to join us on Saturday evening? Everyone will be here."

"Does everyone include Scotty?"

"Scotty and Sam are very close." She grew prettily sad. "We have missed you and Casey at our Tet celebrations the last few years, Maggie. Every time Scotty walks through my front door, I think in my heart that I will see you, too. But beside him there is only empty space." She paused, coughed to clear her throat. To clear her gaffe. "Not empty exactly. Sometimes Linda is with him. But you know what I mean to say."

"It's very kind of you to ask," I said. "But if Scotty will be here, it's best for everyone if I don't come. Anyway, we're going to San Francisco this weekend to take care of some business."

"Business?" She tapped her porcelain-smooth chin, thinking over something. "We haven't spoken together for so long, and there is so much to say. But tonight is not a good time; Sam and his associates are waiting for coffee. Can we set a date, before you leave for San Francisco? Before Tet?"

"If you want." I ran through the week's schedule in my mind. "How is Friday morning for you?"

"Friday morning is fine. I have shopping to do before the children arrive, so I will be out early."

"How about nine o'clock at my house? We aren't leaving until after noon. If we go."

"I am writing our date on my calendar right now." She walked over to the desk. "I will be there. Nine o'clock Friday."

By the time I got down the front steps, the security people had my van waiting inside the gate, lights on, motor running. The gate didn't begin to slide open until I was in the driver's seat with the door closed and the gear knob in drive, ready to roll.

I drove away, feeling I had escaped a haunted place.

Chapter 5

Cops look out for each other. When Mike and I decided it was time to move our families in together, one of his old Academy classmates offered to lease us his grandmother's vacant house in South Pasadena, a small sanctuary of a town a few freeway miles northeast of downtown Los Angeles.

At one time, the old house had been a beautiful example of turn-of-the-century craftsman design. But Grandma had let the place fall to ruin long before she moved into a nursing home. Mike and I were given a huge break on the rent in exchange for making repairs.

We didn't mind the work. After six months, we had restored the house to something like its original state of grace. But after six months, even though I could see my handiwork everywhere, I still felt like a paying guest.

When I got home, the house was dark and quiet, uncomfortably so. I put Vivaldi on the CD player and curled up on the couch in my workroom to return calls. Our dog, old Bowser, sauntered in from the backyard to finish his nap at my feet. I was glad to have his company.

The location auditor and I were haggling over budget manipulations when Arlo Delgado called.

"Caught the scent of your boy," Arlo said, sounding less than triumphant. "But you're dead right that the trail gets cold in a hurry."

"Tell me what you have."

"This Bao Ngo guy arrived in Wilmington aboard a Canadian-registered freighter, the *Manatee*. Cargo was mostly Canadian embassy furnishings, personal possessions of embassy personnel—household furnishings—and one dozen passengers. Diplomatic stuff is exempt from search. All the crates were sealed and shipped over to LAX, on their way to Canada."

I said, "There's an invasion underway, refugees are desperately trying to get out of the country, and people take up space with their furniture?"

"Looks like it." Arlo guffawed. "But it gets interesting, Maggie. According to the manifest, the ship was at maximum load, and it towed a fully loaded barge behind. Barge cargo was more household goods that got sent up north." He paused for effect. "There was also a container of artworks and antiques, property of the Republic of Vietnam. I should say, property of the late Republic of Vietnam. And it was manifested to your guy, Bao Ngo."

"Bao Ngo got out with a load of booty?"

"That ain't the beauty part. You ready?"

"Lay it on me, Arlo."

"Your buddy Bao Ngo has to clear Customs, cuz he's stayin' in this country and he ain't no diplomat." Arlo paused again, milking all the drama he could from his tale. "He has this stack of documents saying all the shit is valuable art and antiques. Madame Nguyen Van Thieu, the president's wife, is supposed to be the official trustee, and this Bao guy is her agent. He has a fistful of papers with seals and ribbons all over them to prove he has the authority to be in possession. Bao also has a catalogue from some museum, and the stuff in the container is supposed to match up with it. He's supposed to be on his way to some museum here that's going to safeguard the stuff until someone figures out where it belongs." I heard ice cubes clinking on Arlo's end of the line. "The scam is, you don't have to pay duties on fine art. So, the inspectors open everything to have a peek, and you know what they found?"

"Jimmy Hoffa."

"No way." Arlo thought, belatedly, to laugh. "Maggie, it was mostly all fakes. Just crap."

"Can you document this, Arlo?"

"Yeah, sure. I can transmit you a copy of the report from Customs. Is a fax good enough?"

"For now," I said. "Did you get me any names?"

"I got a dozen names. I've tracked down a couple of them from Customs. Want me to try and locate the rest?"

"Please."

"I'll leave anything I find on your e-mail. That okay?"

I said it was, thanked him, and promised to call him in the morning.

I looked at my watch and decided that it wasn't too late to call Khanh.

Right off, she said, "Do you have a conflict with our date on Friday?"

"No," I said. "I found out something new about Bao." I repeated the information Arlo gave me about Bao and the cargo he brought out of Vietnam.

Khanh laughed—not the reaction I expected. She seemed neither surprised nor scandalized. "All fakes? Poor Bao. How can that be? Bao would know the difference."

"Would he?"

"Of course."

"Can you think of any reason he would knowingly bring in fakes?"

"I can think of only one possibility at the moment. Do you know the story of the boy who every day came to the border pushing a bicycle with a small bag of flour over the handlebars? And every day the suspicious border guards inspected the bag, and every day all they found was flour inside. The guard was afraid to be shown for a fool by a mere boy. Every day he grew more and more angry, because every day the boy came home across the border wearing something nice and new. Every day they repeated the ritual as the boy crossed the border, and every day the boy came home richer. But never did the guard find anything. Do you know what the boy was smuggling?"

"Bicycles," I said. "So what was Bao smuggling?"

Again she chuckled. "That is the question, isn't it? All that we can say is, he did not have valuable artifacts to sell."

After we said good-bye, I called Guido.

"Cool," he said when I had filled him in about Bao's phony cargo. "When are you going to tell me the rest?"

"That's all there is."

"I'm here, Maggie," he said. "When you need me, I'm here."

I said, "I love you, too, Guido," and hung up.

I rummaged through the videotapes stacked on my shelves until I found the one I had made of a conversation with Khanh a long time ago for a short film I had done about the immigrant experience. Something she had said during that conversation suddenly clicked.

On tape, Khanh told me how she left Vietnam in a panic. If she'd had time to think, she said, if it had occurred to her that she wouldn't be able to return for decades, then she might have stayed, as her cousin Honey Thi Nguyen had, and faced the consequences. When I mentioned that for Honey the consequences included ten years of forced labor, Khanh, sitting in her elegant living room overlooking her quarter acre of landscaped backyard, said that there are many forms of prison.

Khanh said she longed to go home, but she was afraid that her name was still on a blacklist.

"That's your friend, huh? The one who got roughed up." Mike's voice startled me. He slouched against the door frame watching the video, jacket slung over his shoulder, hands full of unsorted mail he had picked up from the front table. "Have I met her?"

"You met her." I moved over to make room for him beside me. "I didn't expect to see you so soon. Did your little murderer's mother stand you up?"

"No. She came in."

"Did you get me permission from her to interview the girl?"

"Got it." He handed me a signed waiver form. "You can call her and set it up."

"Any possibility I can go talk to the girl in juvenile

hall tonight? Might be good stuff; she has to be scared to death."

He looked at me askance, chagrined maybe. "The kid went home."

"To sleep the sweet slumber of the innocent?"

"Sho', you right." Mike dropped down beside me, jacket and mail on his lap. He let his head drop wearily against my shoulder.

I turned off the volume but let the video run. "So, the girl is innocent?"

"Says her. There were seven kids in that house working on Pedro. According to my girl, it was the other six who did it all: nine hours of torture. They beat him, they burned him, they carved their gang names on his chest and back, poured bleach down his throat. The whole time that was happening, she says, she was in the next room watching TV and taking care of her baby. She admitted she knew what was going on, but she didn't participate except once, when she burned him with a hot spatula from her mother's kitchen."

"Do you believe her?"

"Hell no. But she agreed to give up the other six, so we're letting her walk."

"If she didn't stop the others or call for help, isn't she just as responsible?"

"If she doesn't talk, then we don't have enough to file the case and they all walk. She wasn't the shooter, so I won't lose sleep letting her kick this time. She'll be back in the system on something else soon enough." He picked up the telephone bill and slit it open. "Anyway, if I book her, her baby goes to foster care."

"What did the girl's mother have to say?"

"The mother?" Mike had a sardonic grin. "Not much. She's pissed about this going down in her house. But pissed is a long way from taking responsibility. She told me that when she got home from work and saw Pedro bound hand and foot in one of her bedrooms, she told her daughter's friends she was going down the street to play dominoes for a couple of hours and she wanted the mess cleaned up before she got back or she would call the police. Pedro was still alive at that point. The kids didn't know what to do with him. So three of the boys stuffed him into a laundry bag, dumped him into a grocery cart, then pushed him down the street to a school yard and shot him three times."

"Jesus, Mike. Why?"

"So he wouldn't identify them."

"I get that. But *why*? Did Pedro do something to them?"

"Complete stranger they picked up in the park. His crime? He let these predators see his wad." He glanced at the phone bill. "What'd I tell you? The city has gone to shit. But what do I care? After May, I'll be a long way into somewhere else and I won't have to see it or smell it or try to fix it anymore."

Nodding toward Khanh's image on the screen, he said, "Where did I meet her?"

"You met her and her husband, Sam, around Christmas. We ate at their restaurant. Remember? Big holiday party."

"There were a lot of people around that night. She and Sam are legal clients of Scotty? Is that the connection?" A furrow appeared between Mike's white eyebrows as it often did when my ex-husband entered the conversation.

"Clients of Scotty. Friends of mine." I wasn't sure how far to explain things. When Scotty and I divorced we divided the china, the bank accounts, and most of our friends. Rightfully Khanh and Sam Nguyen belong to Scotty, but we stayed in touch. They weren't my best friends, but they were old friends, and that was worth something.

I said, "Guido and I helped her find a relative down in Long Beach this morning."

"Oh?" Mike narrowed his eyes, raised his chin so he could look up at me; a cop look, an expression of doubt. A challenge. "What did she want the guy for?"

"Mostly just to know that he's all right."

"Did you tell me this before?"

"Dunno. We've both been working so many hours that we've let a lot of details slide."

"Out of the blue, she wants you to find this relative?"

"Not out of the blue," I said. "After what happened to her, she wants to gather her family around her. I think that's natural."

"Mmmm."

"Could you do me a little favor?"

"Could be. What do you need?"

"Can you call the San Marino police and get a copy of Khanh's burglary report? There are some details I would like to know."

"Is there a reason you can't just ask her?"

I held up my hands in front of him and spread my fingers, looked at my short fingernails. "What would happen to a woman's fingernails if she was tied up for the better part of a day?"

"I know what handcuffs do to a whore's manicure. Why?"

"Khanh's nails are perfect. And they aren't fakes."

Mike frowned, thinking things over. He reached for the trashcan and set it in front of him and began sorting the mail. He tossed the junk—the greater part of the stack—into the can, and the rest of it he sorted into piles on the floor in front of him. Without looking up, casually, as if the answer to the question was of no consequence to him, he asked, "This gal still a client of Scotty?"

"Yes."

"I'll give San Marino PD a call tomorrow."

Casey and Michael were home, chattering as they came through the house from the back. The dog heard them, too, and went out to meet them. When Casey and Michael walked into the workroom, Bowser was beside them, dragging his leash.

"Hey, Pop. Hi, Maggie." Michael, a taller, handsomer version of his father, sidestepped Bowser, came and perched on the arm of the couch next to Mike, rested his arm across Mike's shoulders. "How's it going?"

"How was the library?" I asked.

"Awesome," Casey said, big gray eyes lit. "Michael's college is so hot, Mom. It's, like, really huge. The bookstore is this total mall."

"She asked about the library," Michael prodded.

"Library was good." Bowser burrowed his muzzle into her armload of books. "Better than the public library, unless I went downtown. And who has time for that?"

Michael tossed a small pillow at her. "If you didn't procrastinate."

Bowser, impatient, barked.

"I'm not going to walk you, old man," Casey scolded. "I have to type a paper. I'll be up all night."

Casey appealed to Michael with a saucy little moue. Michael raised his hands and backed away from her. "He isn't my dog."

Bowser looked from one to the other of them, expectant, the clip on his leash clanking on the hardwood floor as his head snapped back and forth.

I stooped over and snapped the leash onto Bowser's collar. "Let's go, old fella. Just you and me unless I hear from volunteers."

Mike groaned. "It's late, Maggie."

"Tell the dog."

"Guess a walk won't hurt." Mike got up, took off his tie, and came with me, stopping to trade his black oxfords for the old sneakers he always left beside the kitchen door.

Bowser was happy to be outside the fence. The cool evening air was a relief after a day that I remembered as essentially one freeway excursion after another.

Mike talked about going to the morgue to observe Pedro's autopsy. I told him about going to Minh Tam's hovel. He liked the part about the hovel floating out to sea the best.

Walking slowly, we were less than two long suburban blocks from home, Bowser trotting beside us holding the handle of his leash clamped in his mouth, when I heard Casey call.

"Mom!"

We turned and waited for her to catch up. My ballerina daughter was already six feet tall. I loved watching her run, long skinny legs fully extended, toes pointed, loose hair. The streetlights, shining through the massive old trees along the curb, covered her in a moving canopy of pale yellow lace.

"There's a sight," Mike said, hugging me. "The hell of it is, you make good babies."

"You do, too."

Casey was moving so fast that she almost overran us.

"Glad you decided to join us," I said as she caught me in her forward momentum and spun me.

"I don't have time. Mom, have you talked to Dad?"

"He left a pager number with Fergie, but we haven't spoken since last week. What's up?"

"The Sequel called." As in, the second Mrs. Ian Scott MacGowen. The Sequel was the latest of Casey's titles for her stepmother, replacing The Immaculate Linda. Casey took a breath. "She wanted to know if I'd heard from Dad. She doesn't know where he is."

"Honey," I said, stopping myself from commenting on history repeating itself, or mentioning that Linda should be familiar with Scotty's M.O.: Linda was the reason I didn't always know where to find Scotty during the last year of our marriage. I said only, "Your dad's a big boy and he can take care of himself. Probably, he got busy today and he forgot to check in. You know how he is. Sooner or later, he'll remember and he'll call home."

Casey wasn't mollified. "She hasn't heard from him for almost a week."

"Is he out of town?"

"It doesn't matter if he's out of town or not, Mom. He has a cell phone, a pager, a secretary, and a message service after hours. I can always find him. Except, I just tried him and the call went to an answering machine. That never happened before."

Mike said, "There are plenty of possibilities, Casey. He could have lost the pager, or broken the damn thing. Maybe he's out of cell range and the message service is out for coffee. Is it possible he just doesn't feel like talking to anyone right now?"

She thought over the possibilities, pacing back and forth in front of us with her hands jammed into the back pockets of her jeans. She stopped, cocked her head, and looked at me, as if unsure of what she had to say. Or what was safe to say. After she had studied me for a while, she said, "Dad and Linda have been fighting a lot. Maybe they had a fight and he's still punishing her. You know how Dad is."

"Indeed," I said. "I'm sure it's nothing more than that. He's all right, or he would have said something to Fergie when he called me this afternoon."

"Right." She was still thinking it through. "What was the longest he ever left you for after a fight?"

"Forever," I said. "And after the last fight we had, he wouldn't talk to me for six months. If he had anything he needed to say, he left me a note. Tell Linda to watch the mail."

"Oh God. Dad and his stupid notes." She made a complete pirouette. "I hate his stupid notes. Jeez, if he has something to say, why can't he just say it to your face?"

"What, and give someone an opportunity to answer back?" I caught her hand and drew her nearer to me. "Why don't you call Linda? Tell her we heard from your dad today and there's nothing to worry about."

"Don't have time." Casey shrugged, a big theatrical shrug finished with a full sweep of her arms. "I have a paper to type. I'll be up all night."

"Better get to it, then. But call Linda first."

"Bye." She jetéd away down the street with Bowser loping beside her, trailing his leash.

Mike said, "Now it's just you and me, kid. You want to walk some more?"

"A little." I slipped my arm through his and we walked on toward the park at the end of the street.

"Mike," I said, "what do you really think?"

"About what Scott's up to? He's like the Unabomber. Now and then he has to remind everyone he's still around." Mike rubbed his cheek. "Does Scott know what happened to us?"

"Not from me. But why should he care?"

"I don't know, but I think he does. I think he cares a lot."

We reached the end of the street and started back toward home. Mike walked slowly, in no hurry. He said, "I'm not the one to bring this up, because what does it say about me? But, I don't get it, Maggie."

"Get what?"

"How did you hook up with that asshole to begin with?"

"Forgive me, Jesus, I couldn't help myself. I was sixteen and he drove a Porsche."

"That's it?"

"Close enough." I snuggled in against Mike and looked up into his face. "He was also handsome, older, worldly. Dangerous."

Mike nudged me. "Not exactly the answer I was hoping for."

I nudged him back. "And he's a big bully. The truth is, I've been through so much crap with Scotty that I cannot for the life of me remember what the appeal was."

"You like bad boys."

"I like you."

Mike kissed the top of my head. "You never told me how you met Scotty."

I didn't want to talk about Scotty. I let go of Mike and said, with exasperation, "Who cares?"

"Not a big deal. You just never told me how you met him." He gave me that narrow-eyed cop look again. This wasn't idle conversation. It was a grilling. "How'd you meet Scott?"

"He knew my big brother in Vietnam. He came to Berkeley to pay his respects to my parents the spring after Marc died."

"Driving a Porsche."

"Yep. First time he took me for a ride, I decided that I was going to marry him. And six years later, I did."

"Six years, huh? How much longer are you making me wait?"

"Dunno." There was nothing safe to say on that dangerous topic.

This marriage idea was a sore subject between us. For Mike it was all pretty easy. When you fell in love, you got married. If you fell out of love, you got divorced. He had gone through the process twice before I met him and bore few visible scars.

After my one and only failed attempt at marriage, I still felt as though I had gaping wounds. Even when, too briefly, I was pregnant with Mike's baby, I wasn't sure I was ready to try marriage again. How could I take the big risk a second time until I understood where I went wrong the first time? I loved Mike. But I didn't have a very good history with men.

My mother's rented Ford rounded the far corner. I reached for Mike's arm and stopped him. "I want to tell you something before we go back inside."

"Sounds ominous."

"It's not, but I want you to know up front, before Guido and I get any further along with Bao Ngo. Before we go up to San Francisco."

When Mom turned into the driveway, her headlights hit us square on for an instant, washing us in white. I saw Mike's face in that quick moment, saw something that looked like terror. Maybe it was a trick of light, I couldn't be sure. I knew only that I had to be very careful or I might hurt him. Mike acts tough, but he is not.

With no embellishment, I told him about the evacuation of the Cham Museum in Da Nang, about Bao Ngo and Minh Tam and Khanh Nguyen each accompanying an army truck loaded with art objects. And about how Bao Ngo dropped from view as soon as he entered this country. Mike was keenly attentive, but he seemed impatient, kept waiting for me to get to the punch line. What I told him was clearly not the sort of bombshell he expected. I just hadn't gotten to that part yet.

"There was a fourth truck," I said. "Right after they all left Da Nang, the fourth truck disappeared."

"In the evacuation," he said, a sort of counterpoint to the story, urging me forward. "A lot of stuff probably got lost."

"A lot of it did. Some of the museum collection left behind. Some of it had turned up in the international marketplace."

"And . . ."

"And it's the museum that connects Khanh and Bao and Minh Tam. I have a feeling that what Bao did to Khanh is related somehow to the booty that got out of the country."

"I thought it was all fakes."

"Bao had fakes when he went through U.S. Customs," I said. "But the U.S. wasn't the first stop that Canadian ship made."

"You say he's a scam artist?"

"He's a survivor."

"What does all this have to do with us going north this weekend?"

I looked around at the neighborhood at night, dark in the last phase of the moon except for streetlights that were shrouded among the huge old sycamore trees. All was quiet, sweetly peaceful. Every house holding its own set of secrets.

I looked up at Mike, his white mustache defining the curve of his frown. I said, "Scotty and I both earned decent money. His law practice was successful—is successful—I was a prime-time TV anchor. We shouldn't have had any problem covering the grocery bills. But sometimes we did."

"You've lost me."

"Scotty's a gambler. Not penny-ante Vegas crap, but big-time: stock market, real estate, ventures. Every time one of his deals blew up—and they regularly did—just at the point where I expected us to go under, Scotty always managed to come up with a windfall and save his ass."

"Living on the edge is what turns gamblers on."

"I hated it," I said. "I used to worry about where the

windfall money came from. I half-expected a goon squad to come kneecap Scotty during the night."

"Go back. What does Scotty's gambling have to do with this museum caper?"

"I told you Scotty knew my brother in Vietnam. He also knew Khanh Nguyen. He was attached to the United States Agency for International Development, supposedly as legal advisor to the American cultural attaché."

"Probably CIA. And?"

"And Scotty drove the fourth truck out of Da Nang."

Chapter 6

A storm blew in off the Pacific during the night Tuesday, bringing the first major rain in eleven months. The sound of rain pounding against the upstairs windows filled my dreams: Minh Tam floated away down the river at floodtide, his head a dark marble bobbing above the churning current. In the dream, I ran along the stony bank calling his name, trying to catch him. Casey was a new little baby I clutched against me as I ran in a panic, terrified that I would fall with her and she would be swept away, but too afraid that Minh Tam would be lost to stop running.

I woke up worried about where Minh Tam was spending the night. When I sat up to straighten the tangled sheets, I remembered something else from the dream: Like Minh Tam, my home had been washed out to sea.

After months of drought, rainwater poured off the hard-baked land as it would concrete. The storm drains in our neighborhood were clogged with rubbish—the skeletons of Christmas trees and other domestic refuse—so there was nowhere for the water to go. By the time we got up Wednesday morning, the gutters along our street were already flooded and, according to the traffic report on the kitchen radio, the freeways all across town were at a standstill.

"Good day to stay home," I said, looking out the kitchen window at the lake our backyard had become.

"Can't." Casey slathered cream cheese on two bagels. "Have to turn in my paper, and we have tryouts for *Cinderella* this afternoon. I have to be at school."

"Me, too." Michael stood beside Casey at the counter, making sandwiches. "I can't miss my bio lab."

Two days a week, Casey took a city bus to school. Michael drove her the other three days. He was a good driver and a conscientious youth. I never worried about him. But, like almost everyone in California, he had very little experience driving in bad weather. People forget from year to year what to do on those few days when the roads are wet.

As if that isn't bad enough, the first storm of the year always floats up accumulated road grime and motor oil and makes a slime that lies as slick as ice on the asphalt. Rush hour becomes a nightmare of bumper cars. I didn't want the kids to be out there.

I looked at Mike and some of the panic I was trying to hold down must have shown on my face; I had a flash of the kids floating away as Minh Tam had in my dream, sliding down a river of oily ooze in Michael's tiny Toyota.

"Michael," Mike said. "Heads up." When Michael turned, Mike tossed him the keys to his four-wheel-drive Blazer. "Take it slow, stick to the surface streets, and watch out for all the knuckleheads."

"I know how to drive, Dad." Michael fished his Toyota keys out of his pocket and gave them to his father in exchange.

"Give the guy ahead of you extra room and watch out for tailgaters."

"Dad?"

A look passed between them, and Mike threw up his hands, relenting, backing off. "Just be careful."

"You know it."

My mother walked into the kitchen from the living room, where she had been reading the morning paper in front of the fireplace. She set the folded paper on the table next to Mike's plate.

"Mike," she said as she refilled her coffee cup, her tone abrupt, almost accusing. "I looked through the entire paper and there is not even one mention of your case. There are several truly lurid accounts of the misdeeds of those cemetery folks, but nothing about your Pedro."

"Pedro's not the sort of victim anyone cares enough to write about. Press doesn't want him," Mike said. "Same goes for his killers."

"No one?" Mother thought that over. She sat on the chair next to Mike and folded her hands on top of the paper, focusing her gaze on Mike. When she is thinking things through, the intensity of her stare can be disconcerting. She doesn't mean to be rude, or to make people uncomfortable. It's just her way.

My mother is the perfect faculty wife, intellectual, sweet, independent. She even looks the part: tall, patrician, disdainful of makeup or artifice of any kind. She wore, on that dismal morning, a blue heather twin set she bought in an Irish wool shop probably twenty years ago, well-tailored gray wool trousers, and sneakers with a lug sole. I have known her to wear canvas shoes to the symphony because she forgot to change them, and to not much care when she discovered her lapse.

Every morning, as far back as I can remember, Mother twisted her gray-streaked hair into a loose bun and nailed it in place at the back of her neck with two small tortoise-shell combs. Amazingly, the bun stayed put all day long, defying the laws of gravity, as if Mom, the wife of a physics professor, had a special exemption from nature.

"Tell me, Mike," she said, her tone intense, one long-fingered hand touching his arm to rivet his attention on her. "Do *you* care?"

"Me?" Color rose on his face: My mother dwells in Berkeley, one of the great bastions of political correctitude. Her questions can be minefields. Mike, whose family consists of two sisters he never sees and an alcoholic father that he sees too much of, worries endlessly about saying or doing something that would diminish him in Mom's eyes. She is, to him, the embodiment of an idealized picture of all that a family should be that he has carried around, longed to join, for his entire life.

He did not want to lose my mother's love. The truth is, he could not. Mother just takes people as they come.

Mike said, "I care about the kids who killed Pedro the way a farmer cares about weeds in his cornfield. Pedro? I won't say he got what was coming to him, but he didn't go into that house to pray with those kids."

"Why did he go into the house?" Mother asked, her unplucked brows rising as her eyes widened.

Before he gave an answer, Mike looked from Casey to Michael and then back at Mom. Pedro had gone into the house hoping to trade beer and bus fare for sex with a couple of teenage girls, but Mike wasn't going to say so in front of Casey.

"Milk for your coffee, Mom?" I set the carton in front of her, a diversion.

"Thank you, dear." Mom's eyes slid toward the children. "Of course."

Mike reached back and tapped Michael's elbow. "You two should probably get going if you don't want to be late. Traffic's a bear."

"We're going." Michael packed the sandwiches he'd made into two brown bags, added an apple and a granola bar to each, and then dropped one into his backpack and one into Casey's. He handed Casey her backpack. "Ready?"

"Ready." Casey gave him a bagel wrapped in paper napkins and a plastic cup full of orange juice. Holding her own bagel and juice in one hand, with her backpack and dance bag slung over her shoulder, she still had a hand to open the back door so that Michael had hands to raise an umbrella.

Heedless, young, invincible, she tossed her head and offered a breezy, "Bye, Mom. Bye, Mike. Bye, Grandma. I love you."

"Be careful," Mike called after them as they went out, both of them huddled under the same umbrella.

Suddenly there was silence, nothing but the constant pounding of the rain. Mike and I stood for a moment watching Michael and Casey, a single dark mass moving through the gray deluge on their way toward the garage.

I turned to Mike when they were gone and he just shook his head, let out a big sigh, and then began gathering dishes off the table.

"Aren't they lovely?" Mother said. "Those two have become truly good friends, haven't they?"

"Yes," I said. "We're lucky."

She smiled at me as if I were a clever child. "It isn't luck, Margot, dear." She is the only person who uses my given name. "You and Mike have been very wise to make the youngsters dependent on each other. They have to break away from you and Mike, that's the job of teenagers. How fine for them to move toward sibling bonds."

"They aren't really siblings," I said.

Mother looked at me askance. "Aren't they? Are they aware of that?"

Mike chuckled. She was, after all, his chief ally in our domestic union argument. She adores Mike.

"What are your plans for the day, Mom?" I asked.

"I'm going home. Now that I see that my dear girl is indeed healthy, there's no reason for me to clutter up the place. Anyway, tonight is bridge night and you know how your father hates to miss his bridge. I leave from Burbank at noon, the weather permitting, and Daddy is meeting the flight in Oakland. All is arranged."

Mother rose and hugged me, a little gingerly, because that is her way, always careful of personal space. "Thank you for letting me hover, Margot. It is much easier for children to be independent than it is for parents to let go. If I tell *you* to be careful on the road today, both of you, you will indulge me, won't you?"

"Sure, Mom." I kissed her cheek, as soft and dry as fine silk against my lips. "I'm glad you were here. I needed you."

"My dear Margot," she said, her voice rich with affection. She stroked my face, a quick cool line drawn with a long finger. And then, abruptly, she was all business again. "I should pack."

Mike received a pat on the arm, then Mother took her

coffee and went up the back stairs. When we heard her bedroom door close, Mike said, "Quite a gal."

"One of a kind," I said. "What's on your agenda for the day?"

"Questioning another one of the kids in the Pedro case. Her mother is supposed to bring her in."

"Have any of the fathers shown up?" I asked.

"Nope. Don't expect any, either." He shrugged. "What are your plans?"

"Depends on you." I stacked cereal bowls. "The location shoot in Wilmington is obviously off."

He said, "Mm-hmm," as he wiped up a milk spill. "Maybe you can stay home, at least until the rain lets up. Stick around to see your mom off."

"I don't think so. Mike?" I caught his hand. "The rain woke me up last night and I couldn't go back to sleep."

"Uh-oh." He pulled me against him. "So, you lay there thinking, right?"

"Right."

"Inspiration happened."

"Sure did," I said.

"Why do I suddenly have a sense of impending doom?"

I bumped him with my hip.

"And?" he said.

"What's the possibility I can tape your initial interrogation sessions with this girl you have coming in?"

"We tape all the interviews. You can listen to the tapes. No problem. I told you that a long time ago."

"No," I said. "I want to be in there with you."

He frowned, his eyes narrowed to those dark, shiny slits, cop slits. "Run that by me again."

"I want to come into the interrogation room and videotape you questioning these little murderers for the first time."

"Too many legal implications in that and too many layers of permissions to get through. So far everyone has agreed to talk to you at some point. Isn't that enough?"

"No. I want them before they get their stories straight. I want them scared. And I want their mothers."

When he started to shake his head, I put my hand against his cheek before he could say anything I'd have to argue him out of. I said, "This fits too well for you to say no to me. Khanh gave us a family fragmented by one sort of war. Now I want what you have, families fragmented by war of another sort. See the thread?"

"No."

"No, you can't see it? Or, no, I can't do it?"

He studied me in his inquisitor's way. And then a slow smile crossed his face, an almost shy sort of expression. "You just can't stay away from me, can you?"

"Excuse me?"

"If you want to spend the day with me, I can think of a hundred better places than the interrogation room."

"I'm serious, Mike."

"Okay." He handed me the coffeepot so he could wipe the table under it. "I'll talk to the lieutenant and see what he says. But you only. No Guido. No crew. Just so you know, I'm only agreeing to this so I can keep track of you."

"Peter, Peter, Pumpkin Eater," I said.

"It's not like that and you know it. It's just, it seems to me this world has pretty much gotten out of hand, Maggie. When I look at all that rain outside, it makes me think, what if God has decided it's time for another forty-day flood to clear out all the sinners again? If I were him, I'd have cleaned house a long time ago. I'm getting a little nervous."

"I don't recall God giving us any instructions to build an ark, Noah. If this is the great flood, we must not have made the nonsinners cut."

"If nothing else, then, we'll go to the bottom together."

Mike had his back to me, putting the milk and margarine into the refrigerator. He turned and winked at me, a vague sadness in his expression. "You know it's a juvenile case. It can be rough, listening to what they have to say."

"I know."

On the radio, the weatherman was saying that the National Weather Service satellite had picked up three large storms backed up across the Pacific. "Expect intermittent heavy rainfall through the weekend," the reporter said.

Mike moved the salt and pepper shakers and the napkin holder back into the middle of the scrubbed oak table. "What did I tell you?" he said. "This little sprinkle is just the beginning."

The front doorbell chimed. I said, "I'll get it."

My mother called out to me from the upstairs landing as I crossed to the door. I couldn't understand what she said. I called back, "Are you expecting someone?"

I had my head cocked, trying to hear her answer, when I opened the door. When I turned, my focus was aimed straight ahead, expecting to look into the eyes of whoever was there. What I saw instead was the shiny, 24-carat gold tie tack of Ian Scott MacGowen, Esq.

Chapter 7

"Tell me it isn't true." Tanned and handsome, Scotty had his ain't-I-swell mask firmly in place. I didn't invite him inside where he might feel comfortable enough to let the mask slip. Rage *en croute,* his legal partner called him: rage contained only by a pastry shell. One hand in a trouser pocket, like a *GQ* version of success, he said, "Word is, you sold the house."

"Casey isn't here." Showing up unannounced, Scotty caught me off guard, made me feel vulnerable, so I put up a front of my own. The greatest boon of divorce from Scotty was that I never again had to stick around for one of his tantrums. I kept one hand on the edge of the door, ready to shut him out at the first word he uttered above a normal, conversational tone. "Casey has been worried about you and your wife has been calling."

"You should have given me right of first refusal." Still, he smiled. "As a courtesy."

"As a courtesy? Suddenly you want the San Francisco house? Why?"

"Why?" The tone said any idiot should know. I did not know.

Some men get better looking as they age, and Scotty was one of them. He was a tall man, six-six, and big boned. Extra middle-aged padding softened his angularity, made him seem less intimidating than I remembered. Crow's-feet, little wattles under his square jaw, a comfortable roundness under his belt, silver at the temples—Hollywood would easily cast him as a judge or a senator. Typecasting: Scotty was one of the most notorious litigators on the West Coast until he moved to

Denver with wife number two, where he became the terror of the Rocky Mountain State.

"Where are you staying?" I asked him, ready to close the door. "I'll have Casey call you."

"I'm at the Four Seasons," he said. "You haven't answered my question. Did you sell?"

"I haven't even seen the offer. But I'll probably accept it. Max says it's clean."

Scotty flinched and lost his smile, but wasn't yelling yet. "If I ever thought that you would just piss the place away, I would never have let you have it."

"You *let* me have what?"

"The house."

"You let me have the mortgage and the earthquake repair bills and the property taxes. Is there some part of that you want to lay claim to now?" I didn't raise my voice or even put a sarcastic twist on it. "You let me have the house because that made it easier for you to turn your back on Casey and start over again. Which reminds me. Linda is worried. You should call her."

I recognized the hard glaze that dropped over his eyes, the air he hauled in to fuel an impending explosion. He hissed, "Don't tell me what I did or did not do. Or what I need to do."

"I'll tell you this, Scotty. If the sale falls through, I'll have my attorney call you. Be warned: I'm only accepting cash offers."

The mask was gone. His breathing grew noisy, his face flushed, sweat shone on his brow—primal, like a man near the point of orgasm. But I knew from experience that the only ejaculation was going to be a stream of invective and threats. He took a step forward. "We have to talk. Now. Let me come inside, I'm getting wet."

I held my ground long enough to say, "Casey is the only subject you and I have to talk about, Scotty. Anything else, call my lawyer. Now, go call Linda." I closed the door, leaving him outside in the rain.

"I tried to warn you." Mom, carrying her toothbrush, had been eavesdropping from the living room. "I saw him drive up."

"Damn him." I snapped on the dead bolt.

"Think he'll do something, Margot?"

"Something like screw up the sale? He can't. I have legal title. There's nothing he can do."

"Nothing?" With the lift of one eyebrow, Mom expressed more sarcasm than anything I had said. "Scotty?"

"He doesn't want the house, he just wants someone to mess with. My bet is he's breaking up with Linda."

"They have small children." Sounded like disbelief; in my mother's world people with small children did not break up. "What about the children?"

I said, "What about the children, indeed."

"Was that who I think it was?" Mike walked over to the front window and drew back the drapes. The three of us stood shoulder to shoulder and watched Scotty climb into a chauffeur-driven Town Car and disappear into the deluge.

"So, Noah." I closed the drapes.

"Yeah?"

"Suppose Scotty thought he had an invitation for this boat ride you have planned?"

Mike chuckled. "If he did, he was wrong."

The night before, I had driven home in one of the studio's big Ram vans so that I could go straight down to Wilmington without driving all the way out to the Valley first. It was a good thing I had the van. Neither my car nor Michael's little compact would have made it downtown that morning without stalling and leaving us stranded We took the van.

A trip that normally takes twenty minutes during rush hour stretched over a harrowing hour. Mike drove and I kibitzed the entire way: "Fair Oaks looks flooded, try Orange Grove." "There's a tree down in the street ahead, turn right at this alley. Now." When he dropped me off at the downtown library on Hope Street, we were both short-tempered and happy to split up, even if only for a short time.

Mike's partner, Cecil, had volunteered to pick up the girl suspect and her mother in South Central. They weren't due at Parker Center for another hour, meaning they probably wouldn't arrive for two. Mike wanted that time to get approval from his lieutenant for me to shoot the interview, and he wanted me out of the way while he groveled. I had some library research to do, so the schedule worked out all right.

A few years ago, an arsonist set a fire in the stacks of the city's downtown library, destroying the original old art deco landmark. Out of the ashes rose a brand-new post-modern structure, part deco, part Dr. Seuss, part neo-mall, that is now the pride of the city center.

On that rainy morning, the library teemed with patrons, many of them obviously homeless folks looking for shelter. I rode the long central escalator up to the main floor and waited for a turn at one of the card catalogue computers.

An hour and a half later, with much help from several librarians and a lovely woman who attached herself to me because she thought I was an old friend of hers named Wilma—she also conversed with a mutual friend that only she could see or hear—I had several good volumes on Southeast Asian art and a list of galleries in the area that specialized in Asian works. I also had a printout of news stories culled from the Internet about home invasion robberies.

Mike paged me while I was in the main-floor bookstore, talking a clerk into giving me a plastic bag to wrap my books in. I found a public phone near the security desk and called him back.

"You're cleared," Mike said. "The lieutenant says you can sit in on the interview, and you can have a camera. But if at some point he decides you have to leave, you gotta go."

"I can live with that," I said.

"Then swim on over."

Chapter 8

The girl was young, big, hard-looking. Worldly. What impressed me most about her as she slouched in her chair in the hallway outside the interrogation room was that she seemed more annoyed than scared.

Her mother sat next to her, but with her chair turned purposely so that her back was to her daughter while she went over paperwork with Mike and his partner, Cecil Renfrew. Other detectives on the third floor walked around them, hardly bothering to notice the unfolding drama, the way water pours around boulders sticking up in the middle of a rushing stream.

I snapped a couple of Polaroids of the girl and her mother to check the light, and neither of them reacted. When the videocamera came up to my shoulder, though, the girl balked.

"Why you doing that?" she demanded.

"You signed off on the video," Cecil snapped at her.

"Not me," she snapped right back.

"You're a minor. Your mother signed for you." Cecil was awfully harsh with her. "Just keep still until we're ready for you."

Mike glanced at me, embarrassed, I thought, by his partner's tone. He said, "We'll be in that first room behind you, Ms. MacGowen, if you want to go on inside and get set up."

I wanted to tape the girl's parting with her mother because I thought it would be telling. But I went ahead as Mike suggested. The lieutenant had made it clear that he was uneasy about my being present at all until he had an official okay from the city attorney. This was a juvenile case, he reminded me. He was all for a Scared Straight approach, but juveniles have special protections. My toehold in the interrogation process, as he defined it, was so tenuous that I decided to be just real cooperative. For the time being.

I stopped at the open door of the secretary's office to watch a special news broadcast of the storm's ravages on her little TV. Out in the Valley the Tujunga Wash, normally a muddy trickle, had become a tumbling river powerful enough to carry along uprooted trees, an Edison repair crew's truck, a horse, and five small houses. An encampment of homeless men and their dogs had been washed out. At least one of the men had drowned, another clung to the underside of a fragment of washed-out bridge, waiting for the water to rise another foot and sweep him away. A rescue helicopter hovered over him, fighting both the rain and high winds as a fireman tried to persuade the frightened man to let go of the bridge and grasp the dangling lifeline.

The secretary looked up and saw me watching her TV. She turned up the volume a notch for me. "Can you believe this rain? They've started calling it the hundred-year storm. The heaviest rainfall on record for a single day. I want to go pick up my kids from school, but the lieutenant says to stay put. He says they're better off at school than in a car. He's probably right, but I'm getting nervous."

"Me, too," I said. "Mike's talking about building an ark."

She laughed. "Mike would do it, too."

The rescue squad got the homeless man tethered to the lifeline and flew him to high ground, like a bundle of rags swinging below the chopper.

I said so long and walked on down the hall, wondering if the rescue would have any influence on the man's life. He was safe for the moment, but where was he going to sleep at night?

The interrogation room Mike sent me to was about the size of a broom closet, barely big enough for its scarred Formica table and two old oak chairs. The acoustic tiles on the walls and ceiling didn't block very much outside noise, but they protected any conversation going on inside fairly well.

My microphone set off feedback squeal in the room's hidden sound recording system. From somewhere down the hall I heard an anguished, "Cut that out," probably from the poor guy who was setting up a new tape for the interrogation. I laid my mike on a parallel range and taped it down. Then I ran a quick visual check: The overhead fluorescent light gave the scene a harsh, industrial quality that I liked. A hard light that would show every line and flaw on the subjects' faces.

When the door opened, I started the camera running, backing into the far corner as Mike and the girl walked in.

"This is the setup I told you about," Mike said, pulling out her chair and pointing at the seat, meaning she should sit. "You know that everything you say is being recorded. Your mother signed the paper."

She looked at me and swallowed hard. After that, both of them seemed to forget I was there.

Sitting across from the girl, interview forms on the table in front of him, Mike began to talk. His tone was flat, not friendly, nor unfriendly. The girl was nervous, popped her gum, fussed with the fan of stiff hair that crested up from her forehead, couldn't decide what to do with her hands. Mike spent no time reassuring her or helping her to get comfortable.

"Okay." Mike took the cap off his pen. "What's your last name?"

"Woodson." The girl watched his hand as he wrote.

"First name?"

"Cantina."

"They just call you Tina, don't they?"

"Most people do."

"Middle name?"

The name sounded like, "Champagne."

Mike glanced up. "How do you spell it?"

"C-H-A-M-P-A-N-G-E."

"That's how your momma spells it?"

"Uh-huh."

Mike looked at what he had written, then he shrugged and went on. "What is your address, where your momma lives?"

"Four-one-oh-five. It's on Mayfair Drive." She rolled the street name over again as if unsure. "Yeah. Mayfair Drive. But that's not where I stay. I stay at my sister Daquie's house."

"Your momma's your legal guardian, so her place is your legal address." His hand moved down a line. "How tall are you?"

"Five-eight."

"How much do you weigh?"

"One-thirty-two."

"What's your birthday again?"

She gave him a date in May, and the year. He paused, did the math, and said, "That makes you thirteen."

Tina nodded.

"You need to say the answer for the tape. Was that yes?"

"Yes."

They went through the form, place of birth, mother's name and age—Shirley Johnson, forty-one—her mother's phone number. The answers came easily until Mike got to the father.

"Father's name?"

"Waquin Boudreau. Please don't ask me his age cuz I don't know it. And I don't know his phone number, if he even has one."

"Okay, Tina." Mike had not smiled at her even once. "Ever been to church?"

"When I was a little girl."

"How long ago?"

"Last year."

"Who took you? Your mother?"

"My mother? She don't go to church on account she got no way to get to church. I used to go with my sister and my aunt."

"Did they teach you the difference between right and wrong?"

"In church?"

"Anywhere," Mike said. "Do you know the difference between right and wrong?"

"Yeah."

"Who taught you the difference between right and wrong?"

"My sister and my older brother. My mom taught me a little."

"Give me an example of something you think is wrong." His head was bowed over the page.

"Shoplifting," Tina said.

"Give me another example."

"Lying."

"Give an example of something that's right."

"Going to school, getting my education."

"Something else."

There was a long pause. Tina stared at the camera lens as if waiting for the right answer to appear there, the closest thing to a TV in the room.

Mike kept his focus on the end of his pen as he prompted her. "Is doing what your mother tells you right or wrong?"

"Right. She always say, go to school, try to make something of myself."

"Is committing a crime right or wrong?"

"Wrong."

"What kind of crime do you think of as wrong?"

She thought before she answered. "Breaking into a store. Breaking and entering." Stealing seemed to lie heavily on her mind, though she skipped right over murder.

Mike turned a page. "Have you ever had your constitutional rights read to you before?"

"Not me," said with virtuous indignation.

"I'll read your constitutional rights to you. If there's anything you don't understand, you just say so."

He read the entire rights statement in the same flat

voice. Then he looked at her. "Do you know what having the right to remain silent means?"

She frowned. "A little bit."

"It means you don't have to talk to me. If you give up that right, I can use anything you tell me in a court of law. Know what that means?"

"Yeah."

"Know what court is?"

"Court is where the judge is at."

"Know what an attorney is?"

"Like a lawyer?"

"Yes. You have the right to have a lawyer here while we talk. Anything about this you don't understand?"

"I understand."

"All right. Do you give up the right to remain silent? Are you ready to talk to me without having a lawyer here?"

"I guess so."

"You guess isn't good enough. Want to talk to your mother about it first?"

"Guess I should."

Mike rose. "Let's go do it."

I followed them out into the hall.

The mother, Mrs. Johnson, had her eyes closed—napping maybe—and seemed annoyed about being disturbed from her repose by her daughter. She opened her eyes, but did not otherwise move, stayed slumped down with her skinny arms crossed over her protruding belly, and her head resting against a dark streak on the wall left by counterless others who had sat on that same chair, waiting outside the interrogation room. The cuffs of her long-sleeved blouse weren't long enough to hide the black tracks that her wrist veins had become. All around her, there was a strong smell of both wet clothes and alcohol.

Mrs. Johnson snapped at Tina. "What'd you do this time girl?"

"The man says I don't have to talk. He says I can have me an attorney."

"Well, you ain't getting one. You know what you done. You go back in that room and you tell the man. And don't you come out here again until you're finished."

Before Tina could mouth off, Mrs. Johnson turned to Mike. "I gotta be somewhere. Can I go now?"

"No, you can't. You need to stay right here. Tina and I will be inside for a while. If you want to get yourself a cup of coffee, that's okay. There's a machine downstairs. But the law is real clear about you being on hand during the interrogation. I can only release Tina into your custody."

"Release her?" Mrs. Johnson scowled. "Ain't you gonna process her into juvie?"

"We haven't even talked yet. Whatever way it goes, you need to be here when we finish."

"This girl is a trial, I tell you. Nothin' I can do to control her. No use me takin' her home. Only way to keep her out of trouble is book her in. You hear what I'm sayin'?"

"I hear you," Mike said. "Just wait out here, Mrs. Johnson."

Tina grew sullen. I closed in on her face as she turned away from her mother and mouthed, "Bitch."

Mike said to Tina, "Ready to go back?"

Head down, dejected, looking suddenly far younger than her thirteen years, Tina went with him. Loudly enough for her mother to hear, she said, "I ain't going home with her. You can release me over to my sister's house."

"I can't do that," Mike said, waiting for her to enter the room before him. "You're only thirteen. Once we take you into custody, we can't release you to anyone but your momma. If you want to leave your momma's after we take you there, if we take you there, and go back over to your sister's, that's up to you."

Mike sat down and picked up his pen again. "You feel better now? You ready to talk to me?"

"Uh-huh." Tina hadn't finished her snit, but she sat down. She gave it one last try. "I want to go back home with my sister."

"You know why you're here," Mike said. "Why don't you start telling me what happened that night."

"At night, I had already left."

"Then go back to when this all started."

"Okay." She settled into her chair, leaned her elbows on the table. "Me and my friend Angie and my sister Daquie had went to the park."

"Why did you go to the park?"

"We took the kids. We took Angie's baby and Daquie's little girl. You know. To play. This Mexican guy walks up and picks up Daquie's little girl. Angie went to get the little girl to come back over there where we were. The man came back with her and started playing with her baby—Angie has a five-month-old baby. Then after a while, he asked if we want something to drink. Angie says she doesn't have any money, but he says he'll pay. So I walked to the store with him."

Mike wrote notes, but he seemed to be only half-listening. He rarely looked at her, seemed to avoid eye contact. He said, "What was the man's name. Do you know?"

"Pedro," she said. "I walked over to the store with the man. He bought himself a twelve-pack. Angie drinks a forty-ounce, so he got Angie that. We went to go pay, and it looks like the man just got paid. He asked the clerk to cash his check, but the clerk says no. So the man, he takes a fifty out of his wallet."

"Pedro had a wallet?"

"Uh-huh. We walk back to the park and he's talking about why don't people get along?"

"Did he get you something to drink?"

"I drink a couple beers, but that stuff tastes nasty to me."

"He went back to the park with you."

"Uh-huh. We played dominoes and stuff."

"Who all was playing dominoes?"

"Me and Angie, my sister Daquie, and the man."

"You drink beer, he drinks beer."

"He put down two beers in a couple of seconds, and I

say, Dang, that's a lot of beer." She was laconic, emotionally flat. "I never saw no one drink beer like that."

"Was Daquie drinking?"

"She's eating on some chips. Then the kids were getting wet cuz the sprinklers came on. So we say we're going home to get them some dry clothes. Then he says he's going to leave then, too. We were all packing up the baby bottles and the kids' shoes, and he picks up Tyrone, Angie's baby, cuz he's asleep. We all walk to the house and the man carries Tyrone inside."

"Who invited Pedro to come inside?"

"No one did. He just walks right in because he has the baby. I say, You better leave. He's pretty drunk."

"You told him to leave?"

"Yes, I did." Now she feigns outrage, as if trespassed upon.

"Where in the house did he go?"

"First, he's sitting on the couch to feed the baby cuz Tyrone woke up. Then he goes to the kitchen to get some more beer. After a while we say, You gotta leave cuz we're leaving and we gotta lock up. Then my sister Daquie says, You think he'll give me bus fare cuz I have to go up to the county building. She don't want to ask him. So I asked him, Can you give me some money? And he gives me ten dollars. I give Daquie five and I keep five for myself."

"After he gave you the money, what happened?"

"This man gets pissy drunk and then Angie starts talking about boosting the man. He's got a couple hundred and stuff."

"Who started talking about boosting the man?"

"Angie. The reason why we did this is because we got no food in the house to feed the kids."

"So, you're going to boost him for food money?"

"And we got to pay rent."

"Where was the man when everyone was talking about boosting him?"

"Not everyone. My sister Daquie got nothing to do with this."

"Who all was in the house?"

"Me and Angie, my sister Daquie, Angie's sister Zeema, and her friend Too Short. And the kids."

"Where was Pedro?"

"He was sitting in Zeema's bedroom."

"Where were you?"

"I was in the tub. I had just came from my male friend's house before we went to the park. I came back to change my clothes cuz I hadn't planned to stay all night."

"So you were in the tub."

"Angie comes in and says there's this fool in the house who's pissy drunk, and about the kids need some food and all that. I say, You go do what you gotta do."

"What did you do?"

"I get out of the tub, go sit down in the living room, and watch the TV."

"You got dressed."

"Yes." She seemed scandalized. "I got dressed. What do you think?"

"Where was Pedro when you were in the living room?"

"They got him in Zeema's bedroom. They tell me to go back there. I go back there and this man ain't got no clothes on."

"Who took his clothes off him?"

Innocence this time. "I don't know."

"So then what happened?"

"Angie let him kiss on her to make him think she would do something, cuz the man wanted to have sex with somebody. By then they had called Shannon. I walked back to the living room and I see Shannon coming."

"When they told you to go into the bedroom, were you the one who was supposed to have sex with Pedro?"

"No. No." With heat rising, innocence offended: "They just want to make him think that."

"Did any of the girls have their clothes off?"

"No. The only one has clothes off is the man. All he have on is his underwear and his socks."

"When you went back there, who was he kissing on?"

"Angie."

"Were they on the bed?"

"No. He was laying flat on the floor. I ran back and told Angie that Shannon had come."

"Who called Shannon?"

"They all said it was Angie. He came walking up pretty fast."

"Who told you that Angie called Shannon?"

"Angie's sister Zeema and her friend Too Short. They was just talking. You know, like conversation. Angie was in the room with the man, and Zeema says, Keep me out of this. Even though they were in her bedroom, she's not going in there."

"You found money in his sock?"

"Uh-huh. I took his sock off him and this twenty falls out. I don't know who picked it up. Then Shannon comes in and Angie runs right out of there. So I go too cuz I don't know what's about to happen. Shannon just walks in and busts the man right in the face. Then he starts hitting him and hitting him. So I try pushing him away, cuz I say, Shannon, this don't make no sense. And then they blindfolded the man."

"Who did?"

"Shannon did."

"Who tied him up?"

"Shannon tied him up. He used a white extension cord he found in the bedroom."

"Okay." Mike drew a deep breath. His neutral expression had hardened, but he wasn't giving away any emotion. "Okay. What all did Shannon do to the man?"

"He beat the man. But I had left cuz Angie and Zeema's momma came home from work. She walks in and she's cussing me, call me a female dog. Her and me, we don't get along. I mean this is all day everyday."

Mike stopped her tirade before she got any further with it. "You don't live in her house?"

"No. I just go over there."

"What was Shannon doing to Pedro?"

"Beating him. Every time the man tries to get up,

Shannon hit him. The man was crying, No more, no more."

"Why was Shannon beating him?"

"I don't know. He told me that during the riots a Mexican shot at him and he don't like Mexicans ever since that." She raised her hands to show that the whole incident was beyond her understanding.

"Were you there when they dragged Pedro out of the house?"

"No. I had left on the bus to go back over to my male friend's house."

"What's your friend's name?"

"Turf."

"If I ask Turf, he's going to tell me you were there all night?"

"Uh-huh."

"What time did you leave Angie's house?"

"Not sure."

"Before midnight?"

"Way before. Night was falling."

"Night falls at six o'clock. When Shannon came over, was it still daylight?"

"Yes."

"Now, Tina." Mike leaned forward, all of a sudden paternal and firm. "Everyone I've talked to so far has told me you're the one who told Shannon the man had money."

"No. It wasn't me."

"Listen to me. Don't get yourself into trouble. I know everyone is telling stories and you want to look out for yourself. But I've talked to four people already who were there. I know what they did, and I know what you did. Now, I don't want any lying. What you've told me so far is not the truth."

Tina whines, "That is the truth."

"Part of it is. But not all of it. Yes or no, were you in that room when Pedro was getting beaten on?"

"Yes, I was."

"Did you hit him?"

"Only one time. Angie came in with a spatula from

the kitchen and I laid it on the man. His skin goes s-s-s-s cuz the spatula was hot."

"That's all you did to him?"

"That's all."

"Who else was in the room?"

"Me, Angie, Shannon, and Too Short. Zeema walked in a couple of times to get things for her baby, but she walked off. Except, one time she put the spatula on the man, too."

"Who else was there?"

"Pen and Snoop, my two male friends."

"How did Pen and Snoop get there?"

"Angie called them"

"What did Pen and Snoop do when they got there?"

"They saw all the blood and stuff and say, Dang. They was like, Hit the man with your best shot. Pen and Shannon held the man up so Snoop could hit him. They was trying to knock the man out. But they just couldn't do it."

"Did anyone try to talk Shannon out of beating Pedro?"

"We tried to push him off, but when we turn our back, he's back in there."

"Tell me what you told Shannon when he first came."

"I said, The man is in the bedroom."

"You told him the man had some money."

"I said, It looked like the man just got paid. I said, He has a couple hundreds and a couple fifties."

"When you went through his pockets what did you find?"

"I didn't take nothing. I had the wallet in my hand and Angie took it out of my hand. I don't know how much she took, but I didn't get none of it."

"What about the twenty that came out of his sock?"

"I picked it up, but Shannon took it off me. He said, I gave this man a hundred-dollar ass-kicking and didn't get me none of it. So I gave him the twenty. It ain't my money anyway."

"How much did you walk away with that night?"

"I already told you. The five dollars the man gave me."

"Did you see Shannon carve his initials in Pedro?"

"I wasn't in there. Daquie wouldn't let me go in there."

"You weren't in the bedroom?"

"No." Tina's voice rose. "I was in there when Angie and Zeema's momma came home. She was crying and stuff saying she didn't want her grandkids around this shit. She gave me money to get her cigarettes and a beer from the store. She called me a ho'."

"Everybody I've talked to said you were the one who promised Pedro sex, and that's why he came home with you."

"That's a lie."

"I'm saying you're the one who gave Pedro the impression he was going to get sex in that house."

She sat up primly. "He wanted me to, but I didn't tell that man nothing."

"Did you let him kiss you?"

"Nope."

"Did he touch you?"

"The only thing was, I was rubbing on his leg and up here." Tina spread her hands over her crotch. "I was rubbing on his leg, then I jacked him off."

"You jacked him off?"

"Yeah." The way she said it was so offhand, as in, so what?

"Before or after he had his pants off?"

"He was naked."

"Where were the others?"

"He was kissing on Angie. That's when I jacked him off."

"Did you do anything else except jack him off?"

"No, I didn't."

"When did you stop jacking him off?"

"Zeema came to get something for her baby and she said Shannon was outside."

"You went out to open the door for Shannon. You told him where Pedro was."

"Yeah."

"Who all decided to boost Pedro?"

"Angie brought it up to me."

"Whose idea was it to let him pretend to have sex?"

"Angie. He said he was going to leave. Then Angie started doing all that."

"Why did you want him to stay?"

"I don't know."

"Were you waiting for Shannon to get there?"

"I didn't know he was coming."

"If Pedro had all his clothes off, why didn't you just take his money and let him leave when he wanted to?"

"Huh?" She said this, a quick ejaculation, as if Mike had come at her out of left field.

"It never occurred to you to let Pedro leave?"

"No. That never occurred to me."

"How did you figure they were going to rob him?"

"I don't know."

"Yes, you do." Mike was suddenly argumentative. "Think about it. You're not a dumb girl. You're not going to just go in there and jack off some strange guy for the fun of it. What did you think was going to happen to Pedro?"

"That they were going to rob him."

"Who are they?"

"Angie and Shannon."

"How much money did Angie get?"

"I don't know."

"Where was Pedro when you finally left the house?"

"In the room. All tied up."

"Who cleaned up the mess?"

"We did. The man was lying there and Shannon said, Get this blood up."

"You're cleaning up the blood and Shannon is still hitting Pedro?"

"He's laying there."

"What did you do with all the bloody rags?"

"Left it on the counter in the kitchen with all the Ajax and bleach and stuff."

"Was Pedro conscious when you left?"

"Sort of. He was drunk. They bought him a Cisco and

some Thunderbird. They was trying to keep the man drunk."

"Who was?"

"Shannon was. He says, If the man is drunk, he won't say what happened to him. Angie had some bleach, cuz she was cleaning up, and she put it in the Cisco and the Cisco turned all white and Shannon made him drink it. He must have got tired drinking it cuz he started spitting it out. Angie made Shannon stop giving it to him because the man kept spitting it out all over the floor and she didn't want to clean it."

"What were you doing?"

"I went and laid down on the bed in the other room with Angie's baby for a while. Then I say, I can't take no more of this, and I left to go to my male friend's house."

"Pedro was still tied up when you left?"

"Uh-huh." She shrugged. "Next thing I knew about what happened, I'm playing dominoes with my friends and I hear that at the high school some man got killed. I say, that can't be true. So I call the house and ask Zeema, Did they kill the man? And she tell me she don't know nothing about it, you have to ask someone else. Then Shannon was over where I was and he says I ran off with some of the money and he wants it. I say, I didn't run off with nothing but the five-dollar bill the man gave me. I say, Shannon what did you do? He says, I had to shoot the man in the head. I say, Tell me you didn't drag him over to the school, and he says he did."

"Shannon told you he shot Pedro?"

"Uh-huh. They couldn't knock the man out, and Angie's momma wanted him out of the house. Shannon said they had to shoot the man."

Mike wrote, didn't look up, gave Tina plenty of time to get edgy. She looked at me, looked at the other three corners of the room, watched Mike write. I saw her crane her neck, trying to get a look at the form Mike was working on. Her face began to glow with sweat. After about five minutes of silent treatment, Mike tattooed the end of a line with a hard dot. Then he signed his name.

"Okay," he said, scraping his chair back as he rose. "Come with me."

"I want to go to my sister's house." She was persistent.

"Not today, you're not. We're going to get your mother, and she's going to go through the booking process with you."

"Booking?" Tina gripped the sides of her chair, nostrils flaring, eyes bugged out. "What do you mean, booking? I ain't going to jail. I didn't do nothing to nobody."

"Let's get your mother." Mike opened the door and waited for Tina to decide to get out of her chair.

"I told the truth. Thank you, Lord, I told the truth."

"Let's go." Mike stood beside the door with his hand on the light switch. Lumbering, stooped forward, arms hanging in front like a kid imitating an elephant walk, Tina followed. She was bright. She was half-formed.

When they were gone, I slipped a new battery and a fresh tape into the camera. All the time that Mike questioned Tina, she called Pedro by name only one. The rest of the time, he was "the man." He was no one, just the man.

When I listened to Tina casually talk about masturbating a stranger, I thought of my Casey when she was Tina's age, thirteen, the time she had to deliver a health report at school. Casey is no prude, but every time she said the word *condom* her color rose and the entire class giggled. Her world seemed a million miles away from the world Tina brought into that tiny interrogation room. How protected Casey was, and how vulnerable.

Mike looked weary as he explained to Mrs. Johnson what would happen to Tina. He was booking her into Central Juvenile, and she would stay there until the juvenile court judge and some social workers figured out what to do with her. She was too young for a jury trial, and that would save her, Mike said. The DA was considering trying eighteen-year-old Shannon for capital murder. But first Mike had to find the kid and arrest him.

Mike loosened his necktie. When he caught me filming him, he pulled up the end of the tie like a noose around his neck. "Sixty-seven more days I have to put this on," he said. "Sixty-seven more days."

Chapter 9

Manhole covers popped up all along downtown streets, lifted on geysers of water. The runoff pouring through the underground flood control had huge force and volume and nowhere to go. Muddy sprays four feet high spewed up from the storm drains at many intersections; streets were fast-moving rivers. The scene was dramatic and strange, like something dreamed up by a studio special effects team run amok. But the cost and the peril were real.

Across the street from Parker Center, the five-level parking structure under City Hall East was inundated by runoff because debris clogged the long-unused drains. An entire lot full of city employee cars was submerged, every car a total loss. No one could locate a maintenance man who had gone down to the lowest level to turn off a natural gas line just before the wall of water flowed in.

Cantina Champange Woodson was transported from the garage at Parker Center to the covered receiving bay of Central Juvenile Hall without being touched by a single drop of rain. A symbolic beginning, I thought, to her incarceration. Cocooned, isolated from the world outside.

I didn't have clearance to follow Tina inside. All I could do was film her back as she was escorted up a ramp and through a heavy door, a social worker holding one arm, Mike holding the other. She looked back at me once and I finally saw something I had been looking for all morning; Tina was scared.

While I waited for Mike to return to his city-issue car,

I made calls. The cellular signal was fuzzy, but at least the calls went through. According to the radio, many power and telephone lines were down.

I had spoken with my mother before she left for the airport, trying to persuade her to wait for the weather to clear before flying out. Mom has great faith in technology. As long as the tower okayed takeoff, she was leaving. Bridge night, remember?

It was just past noon. I called Burbank Airport for confirmation that Mom's plane had left the ground. Then I talked to my dad in Berkeley.

"How's the weather?" I asked him.

"Beautiful," he said. "Absolutely beautiful. Crystalline, in fact."

He also told me that my Uncle Max had a firm, written offer from the people who wanted to buy my house. The dollar amount was five percent above bank appraisal. "All cash," Dad said. "They want to take possession in thirty days."

I shivered, pulled my raincoat up around my neck.

"Max says it looks like a corporate offer. Big Asian company probably needs executive housing. They came in a little high because they don't want to haggle. He says accept it or say no. Don't bother with a counteroffer. The buyer wants a decision by close of business Monday."

"I have a lot to think about," I said.

"Don't think too long, sweetheart. Max says it's a good deal, considering the sorry state of the real estate market."

"What if I decide I don't want to sell?"

"Do what you want to. But Casey isn't going to be around much longer, and it's a big house for my little Maggot to rattle around in all alone." In my father's mind, Mike would not be part of my household until we were legally linked. "Max said to tell you to call him as soon as you get into town. He'll bring the papers right over."

I said, "Fine," and made a mental note to pick up a

bottle of bourbon on the way into the city. "See you tomorrow, Dad."

Fergie had a dozen messages for me, most of them junk. I wrote down the few numbers I wanted to return, and asked Fergie to call a few others and say that I would be on location all day, and would get back to them in the evening. The remaining five or six didn't require a response.

Minh Tam had called. I was both intrigued and enormously relieved, so I called the number he left first.

"Starbucks, Pine Square." The voice was young and perky. "How can I serve you?"

"This number was given to me by a man named Minh Tam. Does he work there?"

"Gee, I don't think so. Let me check."

I heard her ask if anyone knew "Minnie Something." There was some conversation, then she was back on the line. "I'm sorry, no one by that name works here."

And then, close beside her, more conversation, and Minh Tam was on the telephone. "Miss MacGowen? How good of you to return my call."

"Are you all right?"

"Yes. Thank you for asking." As always, his manner was very formal. "I have some information that might interest you. Might we meet?"

"Of course," I said. "When?"

"As soon as possible. This weather has rather changed my circumstances. As soon as I am asked to leave this establishment, I do not know where I will go next."

The car's radio gave a steady update on closed roads. Driving across the L.A. Basin was probably impossible. But the trains were still running; I had seen them as we drove down Mission Street.

"You have a dollar and some change, Mr. Tam?" I asked.

"I have a little money."

"Can you get yourself to a Blue Line train stop?"

There was pause before he said, "I can. The line is not far."

"Take the train into downtown L.A., go all the way to

Metro Center, then transfer to the Red Line east." I looked at my watch; the trip should take him an hour plus walking time. Mike was already saying his good-byes; I could see him at the open door. "I'll meet you at Union Station in ninety minutes."

He agreed, and we said good-bye.

I called Guido next because I was worried about him. Guido lives in a little gem of a house in the rugged hills behind the Hollywood Bowl. During summer evenings, music fills his canyon, rising and falling with the breeze. In winter, only occasional car sounds and howling coyotes break the silence of his wooded retreat. Ten minutes from Hollywood Boulevard, he lives in eerie seclusion. During heavy rains he can always count on some part of his canyon to shed its face. Guido was working at home that morning, and I needed to know that he was all right.

"You staying dry?" I asked him when he finally answered.

"At the moment," he said. "I'm trapped, Mag. Mudslide has my road blocked at the north end, and the bridge at the south end is ready to wash out. It may be gone already."

"Will you be okay? Your house isn't going to slide down the canyon, or the canyon isn't going to slide down on your house, is it?"

"I'm all right for now," he said, though his tone lacked its usual cocky macho. "Caltrans has dozers working on the slide. As soon as they have the road clear, I'm out of here."

"Mi casa es su casa," I said. "You know where the spare key is if we're not home when you get there."

"Thanks. I'll take you up on it. Think Bowser will freak if I bring my cats?"

"He might, but he'll get over it," I said. "San Francisco is still on for this weekend. Are you coming with us?"

"Yes," he said. "Definitely. If it isn't raining up north, I'm going."

The last call was to Arlo Delgado. I gave him the social security number I had taken from Pedro Alvaro's autopsy report and asked him to find out anything he could about the dead man's family and friends.

When Mike got back into the car after booking Tina, he was in a foul humor. He argued with me about my plan to drive to Union Station, as I knew he would. But he didn't put much energy into it. "Do what you have to do. At least there's no traffic to speak of; anyone with any sense is off the road." The last was a dig.

The terrain along Mission Street between the Golden State Freeway and the Los Angeles River is a wide, shallow bowl. When Mike neared the flooded bottom of the bowl, his car hydroplaned, slid across all four lanes, and spun a hundred and eighty degrees before the front wheels reconnected solidly with asphalt. Good thing there were so many sensible citizens; we had no one to collide with. I gripped the armrest and waited, silently, watching the ugly backside of the railroad yards flash by, until Mike had control of the car again.

"Well done," I said.

He shook his head, his face set in grim lines. "We'll go right past Union Station here in a minute. Makes no sense for you to come back this way in an hour. There's a lunch counter inside the terminal. Let's get a bite and wait for your buddy to show."

We ate tuna sandwiches on white bread and tomato soup heated out of a can, seated at a polished table facing the tunnels that led to the tracks. The old terminal, moribund until commuter trains began running a couple of years ago, teemed with life. The click, click of hard leather heels on the marble floors echoed off the high, vaulted ceilings, the noise rising and falling with the arrival and then dispersal of each load of passengers.

When Mike laid a ten and two ones on the lunch check and folded his napkin under the edge of his plate, one hour and five minutes had elapsed since I spoke with Tam on the telephone.

Mike stood. "Ready?"

"Ready." I gathered my jacket, bag, and umbrella and walked out with him to wait at the Red Line terminus.

Five minutes later, Minh Tam emerged, struggling

under the weight of two canvas duffels, the fabric stained dark by water. He saw me and smiled, veered off from the other exiting passengers to meet me, but stopped suddenly, balked,when he saw Mike beside me.

I always wonder about people who can immediately recognize a cop in plainclothes for what he is. They have a history with the law, I suspect, some experience that informs them. And Minh Tam knew right off, even though Mike's proverbial cheap suit was hidden under the handsome raincoat the kids and I gave him for Christmas.

I stepped forward and gripped Tam's elbow, drew him out of the traffic stream. "Mr. Tam," I said. "Meet Mike Flint."

When Mike put out his hand, Tam set down one of the duffels so he could accept it. I picked up the bag, taking a hostage, as it were, in the guise of being helpful, so that Tam would not run off.

"So," Mike said, taking the handle of the second duffel from Tam, a gracious gesture motivated, I was sure, by the same impulse I'd had. "You're a friend of Khanh. Ever eat at Khanh's restaurant? It's a real nice place. We were up there this winter." He was fast-walking, and fast-talking the whole time to make us keep up with him. "You expect it to be all chili-hot raw fish, rice, and noodles, but it's mostly French. Big surprise to me when she brought out pâté and crackers instead of egg rolls."

By the time he mentioned egg rolls, we were out of the traffic path. At the first pewlike row of oak benches, Mike stopped and set down the duffel he carried. He took the duffel I carried and set it down, too. He asked me, "What's your plan?"

"Depends on Mr. Tam," I said. I turned to Tam. "Would you like a cup of coffee?"

With a wicked smile, Tam held up his hands, showing us how they shook. "For the price of a cup of coffee, I can stay out of the rain. As you can see, I have had enough coffee since the rain started last night that I won't need to find a place to sleep for a very long time."

"You have no place to stay, Mr. Tam?" I asked.

He shrugged. "There will be more shelters opening tonight because of the rain."

I saw some calculation in the look he gave me. I asked, "Have you eaten?"

"I have eaten a little, yes. But I have not slept."

From Mike I heard a warning that sounded like a low growl, the same sound he made when Michael brought a stray cat home from school over the holidays. I put my hand on his arm.

"We could get a hotel room for Mr. Tam," I said. "I'll list it on the budget as an interview venue—it's done all the time."

"Just for tonight?" Mike asked.

A sort of longing passed across Tam's face.

"We'll play that by ear," I said. There were three storms backed up across the Pacific, each waiting its turn to slam onto the coast. Most good hotels give the studio a corporate rate. Though cost wasn't a big factor—Lana's production office probably spent more for designer water in a day than the room would cost—I wondered if we could get a break on a weekly rate for a room.

Mike said, "The Intercontinental Hotel is right there by Metro Center. If the subway isn't flooded, you can take the Red Line back downtown. No need to be out on the street."

I picked up one of Tam's duffels again. "Let's get you dry."

Mike saw us off on the subway before he headed back to Parker Center in his car.

The hotel desk clerk glanced at Tam, but was a paragon of courtesy. May have been his training, or the Gold Card I handed him along with my business card. He gave me a city view room at the discounted corporate rate, and let me put a daily limit on the amount of room service and laundry that could be charged. There was no hint that Tam in his saturated, unlined windbreaker was in any way out of place. But, after all, this was L.A., the megalopolis perched at the edge of a desert. Who has raincoats?

When I opened the door to the room we were assigned, Tam smiled very wide and for once with no hint of sarcasm. I had the sense as he walked in that he felt as if he had come home after a long absence.

All of his possessions were soaked. I called room service and the valet while Tam showered. Twenty minutes later, when he came back into the sitting room, wrapped in the enormous terry robe the hotel provided, the table was set for his lunch and his clothes were out being laundered.

Tam sat down to hot lobster bisque, rare roast beef sliced so thin you could almost see through it, and Caesar salad, double anchovies. I gave him some time to eat, filling space with idle conversation. When he was finished with his meal, he leaned back in his chair and caressed his concave belly.

He said, "Thank you for being a good Samaritan."

"Your cousin Khanh would do the same for any member of my family in distress. The only favor I ask from you in return is that you call Khanh and tell her that you're all right."

"I will," he said, but his tone lacked conviction.

"Yesterday, after we spoke, I went back down to your camp to talk to you." I poured myself a second cup of coffee and settled into a deep velvet chair. "But you were gone. And so was your camp."

"Vandals." His thin lips curled with disgust. "Delinquents. They think because we have no homes that we don't have bank accounts. They think we have our little bits of money hidden away somewhere. They go looking for anything they can steal so they can put another needle up their arms. It is endless harassment when you have no door to lock."

"Kids tore apart your camp while you were eating lunch?"

He dismissed the incident with a disdainful shrug. "I am fortunate I was not there at the time, or they would have torn me apart as well."

"How awful," I said, though I thought he was lying. Wouldn't thieves have carried off the duffel bags that were now safely resting on the closet floor? Wouldn't they at least have flung anything they didn't want in an arc too wide for Tam to have gathered it all up so quickly that there was nothing for me and Guido to see? Tam's story didn't hold water.

I said, "When you called, you said you had something to tell me."

"You have done me such a favor, and now I feel embarrassed. After thinking things through, I am certain it was nothing."

"Why don't you tell me anyway?"

"I thought for a while that I was being followed."

"Followed by whom?"

"FBI, CIA, Immigration: They all look the same."

"Are you a wanted man?"

"Not at all."

"Who would want to follow you?"

He waved away the question, smiling as if he had been frivolous to have brought up the notion in the first place. "I am certain that I was wrong. The power of suggestion planting strange ideas: I imagine how it must have been for Khanh when Bao forced his way into her house. I think how surprised she would be to see him after so many years, and then I think how very frightened she must have been when it was her old friend and colleague who was treating her in such a manner. How confusing that is, you see?"

"Yes, I do see."

"Also I think, what reason could Bao have had to do this thing? And then it occurs to me that whatever reason he has to assault Khanh, he also has to assault me."

"What is that reason?"

"We deserted him. We left our country without him."

"You think Bao wants revenge?"

Tam shook his head. "He wants his share. Khanh and I were able to take a few items with us. Nothing of immense value. But the value is not the point. Whatever we had, a portion rightfully belonged to Bao."

I said, "You filched some things from the museum."

"Why not? After all the risks we took, should we

leave behind everything precious for the Communists?" He grew quietly fierce. "I made great sacrifices for my country. Was I not due some reward?"

"I'm sure you were." I told him what Arlo had learned about Bao Ngo's cargo of forged artifacts. His reaction was very similar to Khanh's.

"Bao would know the difference between a genuine piece and a fake, Miss MacGowen," he said. "He would know better than anyone. You see, as curator of the museum, Bao regularly sent items from the collection to Paris for restoration. In the process, he would order a duplicate to be made. Now and then, the original would be sold and the duplicate would be placed on exhibit, and no one would be the wiser."

"No one except who? You and Bao and Khanh?"

He bowed. "Our government salaries were very small and our family obligations were very large. A little amendment was necessary to survive."

"What would have happened to you if you'd been caught?" I asked.

"Caught by whom? The president, Mr. Thieu, had an official salary of no more than six hundred dollars every month. How do you imagine he lived so well? How do you imagine he continues to live so comfortably in exile? Surely not on savings taken from his government check."

"As I recall, Thieu left the country with a suitcase full of gold."

"Do you think that is all he had set aside for a rainy day?" Tam glanced at the window, at the sheet of water pouring down the glass. "The small amount that Khanh and I took was nothing in comparison. Nothing."

I got up and walked over to the window. The outline of the Citicorp Plaza high-rise across Seventh Street was visible only as a block of deep gray studded here and there with lights from office windows. The sky was as dark as night.

Tam yawned and I thought I should leave him so that he could get some rest. I had more questions for him, but he wasn't going anywhere until the rain stopped.

I wrote my home number on the pad beside the telephone. "Call me later."

He promised that he would, though I had not trusted much of anything Tam had told me so far.

"Get some rest," was the last thing I said as I walked out the door.

Chapter 10

Pedro Alvaro's sister and brother-in-law lived in Little Salvador, a neighborhood west of downtown, near MacArthur Park.

Arlo located their address for me on a recent booking slip: Pedro had a fender bender just after Christmas. When he blew 1.2 on a field Breathalyzer, driving his sister's without a license, the cops at the scene hooked him up and took him in.

Pedro spent a night in jail sobering up, entered a guilty plea at an early morning walk through court, and drew sixty days, which would mean about fifteen days of actual time inside. The judge, for all the best reasons, I'm sure, gave Pedro a sentence deferment so that he could take care of some personal business. Pedro promised to show up at the jail on March 1. Only, he didn't live long enough.

I wondered if the judge would ever know that his kindness had cost Pedro his life.

I took the subway to MacArthur Park and came up on Sixth Street, across from Langer's Deli. The deli seemed nearly deserted—the lunch hour was long over, dinner was still hours away—but the lights were on and I could see people moving around inside. It looked like a haven, the windows glowing golden and warm against the darkness of the day. As I walked away, I kept checking back to make sure that my path to the deli was clear. MacArthur Park, rain or shine, isn't a neighborhood anyone should be walking around in alone.

The streets were essentially deserted; a few souls shrouded in makeshift coverings now and then dashed past, every one of them in an obvious rush to find shelter. Rain beat a steady tattoo on my umbrella, but the downpour was lighter than it had been all day. In the sky, there were patches of white among the black clouds, a promise of clearing.

Pedro's sister lived in a 1920's-era, mission-style stucco fourplex; two units up, two down. A rank of buildings of the same style lined the block: arched doorways, narrow windows, a flat tarpaper roof fronted by a low parapet that was crowned with a single row of red clay tiles to suggest the Spanish origins of the builder's intentions. The tiny patch of front yard at number 114, no more than four feet wide, had been cemented over a long time ago. Weeds grew through the cracks.

I walked up a dark, narrow stairway and knocked on the door to my right.

"Momento, por favor." I heard a female voice call from inside amid the racket of clattering pans and water pouring. *"Esperate."*

I glanced at the notes I had taken during my last phone conversation with Arlo, made sure of the name he had given me before I called out, "Mrs. Ruiz?"

She must have dropped a pan on a bare floor. There was some muttering, and then the door was opened. She looked at me with huge brown eyes, looked me up and down. I tried not to be obvious as she was as I studied her. She was short and round, sturdy Indio stock with beautiful mocha skin and hair that was as long and straight as a horse's tail. According to the coroner, Pedro had been five-three. He would have towered over his older sister.

I said, "Meixia Ruiz?"

"Si?" She was wary about me. Even though the door chain was on, when I said her name she closed the open space a few more inches.

"May I talk with you about Pedro Alvaro?"

"Pedro." Tears rose between her heavy lids. "You are police?"

"No." I handed her my card. "I just want to talk to you."

Mrs. Ruiz's big eyes grew impossibly wide. I heard a quick intake of breath. And then she said, with barely subdued excitement, "You *America's Most Wanted*? You want to find those killers?"

"Something like that." Close enough. She slipped the door chain and let me in, so I didn't bother to refine the explanation of my presence.

Her living room was surprisingly spacious. There had been a time, before the last world war, when this was a fairly good address. Before the freeways, an earlier version of yuppies had commuted to downtown from here: Young lawyers, actors on their way up, mid-level government workers had started their families in apartments like this one.

Carved detail work over the three doors that led to other rooms was nearly obliterated by perhaps seventy years' accumulation of paint. But I could still see the potential. If the house could be moved to a better neighborhood.

The roof leaked. The clatter and water I'd heard through the closed door had been Mrs. Ruiz emptying one of the galvanized buckets she had set under any of the four or five ceiling drips. The old flat roof above just could not contain the hundred-year storm.

All the time we talked, the steady plink of leaky ceiling punctuated our conversation. The room was cold and damp and smelled of mildew. We had been in a long drought; there must have been other, older sources of water leakage than the rain.

When I complimented Mrs. Ruiz on her English, she told me that she took English as a Second Language classes at Belmont High School during the evenings after working all day cleaning houses. I found out right away that I couldn't use slang if I wanted to be understood, but we got along well otherwise.

"Pedro was the youngest of my brothers," she said. "We are ten in our family. Five older, from my father and my mother, and five younger from my father and his second wife after my mother died. Pedro was a little spoiled because he was the baby."

"What did the police tell you about the way he died?"

"Oh!" She clutched the neck of her starched blouse. "It was terrible. Those girls said they wanted to be friends with Pedro. But all they wanted was his money. He would give it to them. Why did they have to kill him?"

"Where did Pedro get his money? He had at least two hundred dollars on him."

"He was a gardener. He worked for some big company. After work and on weekends, he mowed lawns for some people. Mostly apartment houses. Pedro worked hard and he saved his money like crazy. In Mexico, he has a wife and children. He sent them money every week. And still, he saved to have enough for them to come north."

"For a man who was saving to bring his family north, he was very generous with his money. He bought beer and paid bus fare for those girls."

"The policeman told me he did that." Mrs. Ruiz got up from the sofa to check the water level of her buckets. "Pedro was a little lonely. He has a room in a house over there by the Coliseum. Every night after work, he goes there alone and he thinks about his wife and his children. I don't know what he was doing with those girls. But men, you know, they can't be alone very much or they get themselves into trouble. He should never have left his wife in Guadalajara. I try to tell him, but he says he knows how to take care of himself."

"He got into trouble when he drank."

"*Si. Indio estúpido.* He has one beer, then he has six more. Or twelve more. He can't stop. The first one makes him think about his family, the second one makes him forget."

"Forgetting? Do you think that's why he went home with those girls. They were very young, you know. Just children."

"Children here." She tapped her head. Then she grabbed one ample breast. "But not children here. The policeman says they were not innocent, those girls."

"Which policeman did you talk to?"

"Big guy." She stretched one arm as high as she could to show me how tall he was. *"Uno taco de ojo."*

Taco for the eye, she said; eye candy. Handsome. LAPD prides itself on the hard bodies of its boys and girls in midnight blue. I assumed she was talking about some sweet young thing in uniform. But she went to her purse and pulled out a business card and handed it to me.

"Mike Flint?" I said, loud enough to startle her when I saw the name on the card. "You think he's cute?"

She grinned and preened. "He is so nice. *Muy guapo.*"

I gave her back the card. *Taco de ojo,* indeed. Charm sometimes works magic on the eye.

I said, "What arrangements have you made for Pedro?"

"The coroner, he said we can have Pedro on Saturday. We want to take him home to Guadalajara, but there is not enough money. The priest at our church will say a special mass Friday night and ask for help, but he said we will be lucky to get enough money to bury Pedro in a cemetery here."

She swept a hand through her long ponytail. "I watch the news on Galavision and I hear about those men who own the cemeteries. They take all your money for a piece of ground, then they dig up the grave when it is still fresh and they sell it again to someone else. I do not want that for Pedro."

"Those men have been arrested," I said.

She raised her hands to show that I had missed the point. "I want to bury Pedro next to his mother in Guadalajara where no one will disturb him."

"I hope you find a way to do that," I said. I asked her if she would talk to me again on camera.

Mrs. Ruiz looked around her living room as if deciding whether it was sufficiently presentable, and then she asked, "Do you pay money?"

"No, we don't. But a contribution might be made to the church.

She smiled at that, and agreed to talk with me any time

I cared to come by. When we said good-bye, I folded a bill into her palm, hoping she wouldn't be offended.

When I came out of the Ruiz house, there was only a light drizzle falling. The streets were still inundated, but they were quickly draining. There were larger, brighter patches in the sky than I had seen all day, a faint promise of clearing. I decided to take a chance that maybe He had decided against the forty-day flood this time, and pulled out the address list Arlo had left on my e-mail.

I had a couple of choices. One of the Customs agents who signed the documents allowing Bao Ngo to bring his load of fakes into the country lived in Simi Valley. From a phone in the subway, I called the number listed. An old man's voice invited me to leave a message on his answering machine. I gave my name and office number, and wrote myself a note to try him again in the evening.

Next I called Khanh and told her machine that Minh Tam was safely resting in a downtown hotel and that I hoped he would call her.

I rode the train back downtown, came up at Flower Street and caught a Dash bus back to Parker Center. With luck, Mike would be finished for the day and we could go home before it started to rain heavily again.

Mike was sequestered in an interview with another of his baby murderers, a gang-banger nicknamed Pen. I remembered Tina mentioning how Pen had helped Shannon hold Pedro so that a kid named Snoop could use him like a punching bag. I wanted to hear Pen's version and appealed to Cecil to get me inside. My camera was downstairs in the van and Cecil thought there wasn't time to get it before Mike had finished with the kid, but he would ask about that, too.

The lieutenant came out to the hall from his office cubicle and gave me the word. "Mike's on a roll," he said. "You go in there and make a fuss setting up cameras and Mike could lose his edge. It's okay if you want to listen in, but that's it." End of discussion.

Cecil ducked his head into the interrogation room,

said a few words, then gestured for me to come. I slipped inside, took a seat in the far corner so that I could watch both faces. Mike glanced my way, but said nothing. The kid looked at me a couple of times out of the corner of his eye, but that was all the interest he showed in this newcomer.

Pen was lanky, underfed-looking, too young to grow decent whiskers, though he was trying. He wore baggy denims, an oversize polo shirt, heavy high-top basketball sneakers. His head was buzz-cut up the sides, leaving a long tuft sprouting from his crown. Over his left ear, he had razored *DM2* into the short hair.

Mike looked at some notes in front of him. "So, Zeema's mother came home from work. Do you know the mother's name?"

"I know her. Arzeema Porter, Senior. See, it's the same name as Zeema, cuz she's Arzeema Porter, Junior. Like the way you call a boy after his father. Like me, Ronald Ward, Junior."

"Mrs. Porter was at the house when you came back?"

"Yeah. Shannon calls me up and he says, Bring me a gun. So I took him over a .22."

"Where'd you get the .22?"

"Belongs to my grandmother."

"What happened when you took the gun over?"

"Shannon meets me at the door and he says, You bring it? I say, Yeah. I show him the gun and he snatches it right out of my hand. I follow him inside the house cuz I want to see what he planned to do. It was my grandmother's gun, see. I didn't want Shannon doing something that might come back on my grandmother."

"Where was Mrs. Porter when you gave Shannon the gun?"

"She was on the porch."

"Did she see you hand the gun to Shannon?"

"She musta'. She was real mad. She kept saying no one listens to her and she wants all the shit cleaned up that's inside the house or she's gonna call the police."

"What did you see when you went into the house?"

"Nothing." Pen, all innocence on his young face, spread his arms wide, exposed his wrists the way a magician would; nothing up his sleeves. "I saw nothing but someone's feet all tied up. Then I went out onto the porch and after about five minutes, I left."

"Where was Mrs. Porter when you left?"

"She had left already."

"What did you do?"

"Went over to the park for a while to shoot some hoops."

"Weren't you interested in what was happening inside?"

"I was only interested in getting out of that house."

"After you left the house, did you see Shannon again that day?"

"About dark time, I see Shannon and Snoop pushing a cart at about a slow jog. They're going to the high school. I turn around and went home."

"Did you see what they were pushing in the cart?"

"I seen what they have in there movin', so I had a pretty good idea."

"You knew they had a man."

"That's what I guessed."

"You gave Shannon a gun. You must have had some idea what was going to happen. Weren't you concerned?"

"I was concerned, but I didn't want to get into it."

"You didn't see who shot the man?"

"No, I did not. Later, Shannon gave me the gun back. He says get rid of it. I took out the grips, the cylinder, the hammer, and the firing pin and tossed 'em. Then I put the frame back where my grandma kept it."

"Why did you do all that?"

"I didn't want my grandma to get in no trouble. Shannon said you couldn't put nothin' on us if I took that gun apart."

"Did you ever ask Snoop and Shannon what they did with the man?"

"We was at a party over across the street later. Shannon came in and I said, What happened to that man? He said, I shot the motherfucker. We don't have to worry about him anymore."

"He told you he shot the man?"

"Yes, he did."

Mike set his notes aside and leaned in closer to the kid. "I've heard this story a couple of times now, and the way you tell it just doesn't go with what everyone else is saying."

"It's the truth. What I say is every word of the way it went down."

Mike used his pen as a pointer. "What's that carved into your 'do?"

"That's me, Dee Mac two. You know, my gang name. You pass a gang name down like you name your son after you. Kind of like junior, like we was talking about earlier. Like Dee Mac one, he jumped me in. After me, there's three more. Five Dee Macs."

"You're from the Trey-four posse?"

Pen flashed a gang hand sign.

"You're the only Dee Mac two, is that right?"

"Uh-huh."

Mike slipped a Polaroid across the table. "This is a picture the coroner took of Mr. Pedro Alvaro. What is that symbol carved in his abdomen?"

Pen paled. He checked the door real fast, as if maybe he flashed on bolting.

Mike slid the Polaroid my way. *DM2* was clearly carved into Pedro's skin just under the breastbone.

"Did you do that to Pedro, Pen?"

"Yeah." The kid had been caught out and he knew it. "I cut him."

"You told me that you dropped by the house only long enough to give Shannon the gun. The others I've talked to say you were at the house for quite a while. The others say that you helped Shannon and Snoop beat Pedro Alvaro. They also said you helped put Pedro into the cart and wheel him over to the high school. This is all going to go easier on you if you start telling me the truth."

"I didn't shoot him, man." Sweat ran down Pen's dewy face. "I swear, I didn't shoot nobody."

"When you brought the gun over, did it occur to you that someone might get shot?"

"You never know what Shannon can do."

"So it occurred to you someone could get shot?"

He collapsed down into himself. "It occurred to me."

Mike had Pen start over. This time the boy told about being inside the house for hours, beating Pedro, making him drink bleach mixed with Cisco, carving and burning him. The only change he would not make in his story was confessing that he had been with Snoop and Shannon at the time Pedro got shot.

When he had finished his tale, Mike asked him, "Where is Shannon now?"

"I don't know."

"When did you see him last?"

"Yesterday morning when he heard you all was going through the house and taking out Mrs. Porter's knives from her kitchen and taking out the rags and stuff we cleaned up with. Shannon heard that, and he took off."

"Where would he hide?"

"I don't know."

"Does he have family that would take him in?"

"Shannon?" Pen scoffed. "He ain't got no family. I don't know where he would go."

"Okay." Mike thumbed through his notes. "How old you say you are?"

"Seventeen."

"Seventeen." Mike gathered his notes and forms and the coroner's Polaroids and made a neat pile of them. Then he stood. "Let's go."

Pen stayed in his chair. "There going to be a hearing? Am I going home or the CYA?"

"Youth Authority? You're seventeen now, Pen. This is a capital case you're involved in. Sheriff's going to transport you over to the Hall of Justice Jail to wait for arraignment."

"HOJJ?" Tears and snot started flowing. "No, man.

They do me bad over there. I can't go to HOJJ. I'm not eighteen."

"You just graduated." Mike grabbed him by the biceps and hauled him to his feet. "Welcome to the big time."

Chapter 11

Casey and Michael arrived home before Mike and I. All day I had restrained myself from calling their schools to check whether their campuses had washed away, taking small comfort knowing that if there were major problems, someone would call or we would hear something on the news.

We found them both ensconced in the living room doing homework in front of the fireplace, Michael stretched out on the sofa, Casey curled up in my grandmother's wingback chair, the dog on the floor at her feet. Except for the heavy metal music blaring from the CD player, it was a lovely scene.

A nearly empty basket of popcorn, a carafe of hot cocoa and dirty cups showed that they had been home for some time.

Casey looked up at me over the top of her biology book, a sassy grin taking form as her glance moved from my damp hair to my sodden socks. "Have a nice day, Mom?"

"I'm glad to be home."

Mike used Michael's cup and poured himself some cocoa from the carafe. I went to stand with my backside to the fire. Steam rose from my jeans.

Mike asked, "Have any problems with the car, son?"

"The car made it fine," Michael said. He pulled up his feet so that his father could sit down. "Did you hear what happened at my college?"

My stomach dropped, Mike froze halfway down to the sofa.

"The gym roof collapsed."

"Anyone get hurt?" Mike asked, dropping down onto the cushion.

"No. The coach saw the ceiling start to bulge and cleared everyone out in time. Ceiling in my bio lab leaked and the first floor of the social science building flooded, but that was the worst of it. They canceled all the afternoon classes and told us to go home."

"Casey," Mike said, "your school have any flooding?"

"Just the teacher's parking lot. When Michael picked me up at lunchtime, everything was okay."

I was still sorting through possible responses to that nugget of information when Mike turned to his son, head cocked, eyes narrowed. "You picked up Casey from school early?"

"Had to." Michael shrugged, matter-of-fact. "The way it was raining, I thought I'd better go get her while I could."

"Casey," I said, "the school released you to go home?"

"Everybody was trying to leave. We had to give Mrs. Langston, my English teacher, a ride home because her car was swamped. The whole faculty lot was covered in two feet of water."

I said, "Thanks, Michael. Good thinking."

Mike set down his empty cup and yawned. "I don't suppose these perfect, genius children, while they were sitting around all afternoon in front of a nice warm fire, thought to make their poor old, hardworking, wet as hell parents a nice hot dinner?"

"Grandma made stew before she left," Casey said. "It's in the oven. We can eat anytime you want."

Dear old Mom, I thought. Mike wore an enormous grin. He said, "That's what mothers are supposed to be like. She could write the book."

His own mother had been no Donna Reed. She ran off with a trucker when Mike was in the third grade and came back pregnant when he was in the fourth.

I peeled off my socks. "Any possibility I can have a hot bath before we eat?"

There was a consensus that I could be indulged.

"I won't be long. Mike, are you changing out of your wet things?"

"Yes." He reached out to me for a hand up. "I'll be there in a minute."

I went upstairs. One of the best things about the old house we rented was the master bedroom. Originally, there had been only one upstairs bathroom. It was big enough for a whole family to use at once, and grand enough to suit a czar. A claw-footed tub held center stage, placed right in front of a small fireplace with a granite hearth. I lit the fire, filled the tub, picked up the morning paper, and settled in for a soak.

Mike came in when I was laughing over the daily "Only in L.A." column in the *Times*. He handed me a glass of red wine and sat down on the edge of the tub. Ever since we moved in, the tub had been where we talked over our days.

"Climb in," I said. "Water's fine."

"Later maybe. Cheers." He tipped his glass against mine and took a drink. "You had a long day. How are you feeling?"

"I'm fine, Mike. How are you?"

"Good. Another day down, sixty-seven to go."

"You already told me that. But who's counting?"

He got up to fool around with the log on the grate. Something weighed heavily on him, made him thoughtful and quiet. He put the brass poker back in its rack. "I'd better change and go down. Casey's setting the table. How do you feel about a salad to go with the stew?"

"A salad would be nice." My answer sounded oddly formal. But so had his question. He patted me on the head and left me alone.

I dressed in sweats and went downstairs.

Vivaldi had replaced hard rock on the living room CD player. Mike, wearing sweats and thick running socks, sat in Grandma's chair now, with his feet up, his eyes closed, hands folded across his stomach. I left him to his repose and went on through to the dining room.

The table was set with the good china, candles were

already lit, the salad served. In the kitchen, Michael held the heavy porcelain tureen while Casey ladled in Mom's beef stew—Mom would prefer it be called pot-au-feu, but she wasn't around to correct us.

Candlelight, beautiful music, a congenial air all about, the aroma of good homemade food, a wild storm shut out of the tight, warm house. Everything around me was oddly perfect, a rare moment to savor.

Perfection, like a straight line, does not occur in nature. It has to be manufactured. That is, it seemed to me that this moment of harmony was the result of a lot of effort. Losing the pregnancy had affected us all. The simple act of putting dinner on the table was a series of quiet gestures of affection from every person in the house. I knew the moment would pass, but I would hold the sentiment behind it forever.

Casey garnished the top of the tureen with a sprig of fresh basil. "Five more minutes, Mom. We'll call you."

I poured myself a second glass of wine. "We'll be in the living room." I went in and watched Mike pretend he was dozing.

Without moving, he said, "I can't find Shannon. I put word out at every shelter in town, and no one has seen him. No known associates have copped to hearing from him. We sent black and whites to every house he has ever been known to visit, and all we got for our trouble was a boxful of junk he left behind somewhere and some attitude."

"What's in the box?"

"Dirty clothes and photo albums. He left it a long time ago." Mike drew in a long breath. "I don't know where to look next."

"You've checked hotels and airports?"

"He killed a man to get twenty bucks. Where would he find money for a hotel or an airplane? Besides, Shannon has never been farther away than the Youth Authority camp in Sylmar. He's here; he doesn't know how to get out of town."

"You'll find him, Mike. Someone knows where he is. Someone always knows."

"Mike?" Casey stepped into the room. "Telephone. Mom, dinner's ready."

Mike took the call in the kitchen while I helped the kids carry hot dishes into the dining room. I heard him say, "Nothing?" "No report?" "No record?" and assumed the call referred to the missing kid named Shannon.

"Maggie?" he called out to me. "What was the date of the robbery at Khanh's?"

I told him, he repeated the date into the telephone, had a few more words, and then he hung up, looking thoroughly puzzled.

"What?" I asked him.

"Khanh never reported the robbery to the police."

"She must have."

"Should have. But didn't." Mike pulled out Casey's chair and held it while she sat. "Could be a cultural thing, fear of the police. My guess is that if something was taken, it was something she didn't want the authorities to know she had. Did she ever say what was stolen?"

"She suggested that a piece of jade sculpture was taken. Generally, she was enigmatic."

"Enigmatic?" Mike laughed as he sat down. "Casey, that's one of your mom's Berkeley words. Out here in the real world, we say, the woman kept her mouth shut. Maggie, I think you need to call your friend and ask her what's going on."

"After dinner," I said, "I will."

Guido and his cats appeared at the door just then, looking half-drowned and pathetic. The cats set up a mewling that made Bowser retreat.

Casey took the cat carriers from Guido, saying, "I'll put George and Gracie in my room until they quiet down." We heard her talking to the cats as she walked up the stairs.

I poured Guido a glass of wine. "I was getting worried about you."

"I was getting worried about me, too. Caltrans took forever to clear the road. I wasn't sure we were going to get out." He glanced at the table. "Sorry to intrude. Sit down. Eat."

"Go get dry." Mike took another dinner plate out of the sideboard and put it on the table. "We can wait a few minutes."

Ten minutes later, when we started dinner all over again, Guido raised his glass. "Bless you, friends."

"And pass the stew," Mike said.

Guido laughed. "And pass the stew."

While we ate, we talked about the planned trip to San Francisco. Originally, we were going to drive up on Friday morning, stop at a couple of wineries north of Santa Barbara, take our time, picnic along the way. But bad weather in the southern half of the state would spoil the scenic part of the trip.

I asked, "What shall we do?"

"I may have to stay home and work my case over the weekend," Mike said. "Especially if I get a line on Shannon. Can't Uncle Max fax down the offer on the house?"

"I can't go anywhere." Michael sounded very firm. "I have a lot of studying."

"But you promised we were going, Mom. No fair." Casey pushed out a pouty lip. "I called all my friends. We made plans for the whole weekend."

Guido put down his fork. "If it's okay with your mom, Casey, you can fly up with the crew."

"What crew?" I asked.

"When you said you were going up north this weekend, I told the crew to scratch the New Year parade in Little Saigon because we were going to Chinatown." Guido seemed way too happy. "Fergie made reservations for the whole crew to go up. If the rain doesn't hold us back, I have every intention of being on a scaffolding on Grant Street Saturday night, filming the dragon."

A perfect moment can't last forever. Here was the proof.

I said, "I have the offer on the house to take care of

by Monday, so I'll be flying up sometime this weekend. Casey, you can go early with Guido or wait for me."

"Okay." Casey was mollified. Mike was not.

After dinner Guido and I ran through the tape of Tina's interview and talked about how the film would be restructured now that Bao Ngo had been included. The process was something like throwing the pieces of several big jigsaw puzzles into one pile and trying to make one coherent picture out of the mess. I had a fair idea what that picture should look like. The problem was finding the right bits and then making them fit.

Guido worked with me on storyboards, but it wasn't long before he started nodding off. A long and trying day, good wine, the warm room: He couldn't stay awake. I helped him make a bed on the sofa in the workroom, turned out the light, and went upstairs.

Mike was reading in bed. He looked at me over his glasses. "Casey is worried about her dad. Linda still hasn't heard from him. I told her we saw him, but she's upset. The Four Seasons doesn't have him registered."

I checked the bedside clock: a little after ten, not too late. I called Arlo Delgado.

"I don't think there's anything to worry about," I told Arlo. I explained the situation to him. "But is there any way you can find out, at the very least, where Scotty is using his credit cards? Whether he's alive or dead?"

"Any particular preference?" Arlo asked.

"Yes," I said. "But I won't say which."

Arlo promised to call me as soon as he knew anything.

I stripped off my sweats and slipped under the covers beside Mike. I snuggled into him, as I always did. He put his arm around me, but there was a hesitation in his touch, a lightness when he held me. I knew he was afraid of what might happen in bed if he let down his guard. He felt guilty for the pain I had been through.

With my head against his chest, hearing him breathe, I fell asleep.

Deep in the night the telephone rang.

I reached out a hand and groped for the receiver,

mostly asleep, but still conscious enough to run through the essential list: Casey, Michael, Mom, Dad . . .

Mike, with a longer reach and with the conditioning that comes with his job—most murders happen in the middle of the night—found the phone first. He mumbled, "Flint," and then he listened. With his face still smashed into the pillow, he asked when and where, said, "Thanks. I owe you," and rolled out of bed.

I sat up and turned on the light. "Is it Shannon? Did someone find Shannon?"

"No." He yawned, scratched his butt with one hand, drew the curtains back with the other, and looked out the window: It was raining. "Go back to sleep."

"Who called?"

"Paula. You know her, sergeant, Hollenbeck Division."

"The weightlifter?"

"Yeah. Paula. She brought in my dad."

Chapter 12

"Hey, Mikey? You remember that place down on Valley Boulevard we used to go? You know the one, open all night. Served the worst damn pastrami, but they was open all night. How many's the time we ate pastrami for breakfast, huh, son? But damn if I can't remember the name of the place."

Oscar Flint scratched his forehead around the edges of his bandage. The bandage wasn't big enough to completely cover the cut over his left eyebrow, a clean split made by a flying beer bottle. He looked grizzled and confused and plain worn out. Now and then I saw something in a gesture or the way he canted his head that reminded me of Mike. But years and buckets of alcohol had wiped out most of the resemblance.

"Mikey used to eat half a big old pastrami for breakfast and save the other half for his lunch. I'd say to him, Little boy, you eat enough of that shit, it'll make you stink." Oscar laughed. He wore dirty green work pants and a clean white T-shirt that had come out of Paula's police station locker. Wadded at Oscar's feet: an old blue ski jacket, a plaid shirt, and wet sneakers redolent of vomit and barroom floor. He looked at the pile, and something occurred to him that made him grow thoughtful. He turned to Mike. "Why'd you eat so mucha' that shit pastrami, boy?"

"After I paid your bail, there wasn't any grocery money."

"Oh, yeah." Oscar threw back his head to laugh, but he bumped it against the wall hard enough to make him flinch. He felt for a knot, talking all the time. “We had some good times, didn't we, Mikey?”

After that, Mike said an occasional “Uh-huh” or “Sure, Dad” as his father rambled on. He was courteous to his father, but he wasn't listening.

“Glad you got here so fast this time, Mike.” Sgt. Paula unlocked the cuff from around Oscar's right wrist, the restraint that kept him on the bench. She spoke to Mike as if Oscar couldn't hear. “Lately when Oscar has a few he gets pretty aggressive. Pretty destructive. You and I go back a long way, Mike. Last thing I want to do is throw your old man in the tank. But it's a challenge anymore to contain him when he gets like this. I thought you had him in rehab.”

“He skipped.” Mike took off his Christmas-present coat and wrapped it around Oscar's hunched shoulders. “This last place I had him in was the end of the line. They won't take him back in the condition he's in. No facility can hold him when he gets thirsty, and he doesn't show any sign he's giving up the juice anytime soon.”

“That's tough, Mike. Really tough. Can't blame a place for giving him the boot when he's drunk. I can't handle him.” Paula owned the women's regional record for the clean and jerk. If she couldn't hold him. . . . “You have my sympathy.”

Mike gripped her muscular shoulder. “Thanks for calling me, Paula. I appreciate your keeping this one off the books.”

“No problem.” Paula slipped a business card into Mike's shirt pocket. “I told the bar owner you'd cover the damages. You can call him tomorrow.”

“He's not pressing charges, then?”

“Not this time.” She shrugged. “But next time?”

Mike took Oscar by the arm and guided him to his feet. Oscar seemed confused. “Where we going, Mikey?”

“Home to sleep it off.”

“Oh.” Oscar thought that over.

Paula aimed a finger at Oscar's bundle of fouled clothes. “Burn them?”

"Burn them," Mike answered.

"So, Mikey." We were walking out the back of the police station. Oscar padded on bare feet.

"Yeah, Dad?"

"You remember that place we used to go to down on Valley Boulevard? Worst shit pastrami I ever ate, but they're open all night. You want a bite, son?"

"Not tonight, Dad."

When we got home, the mantel clock said five. Mike cleaned up Oscar while I made a bed on the living room sofa. The sun was just coming up when we tucked him in. We closed the curtains, but nothing, certainly not the pale gray light of that drizzly dawn, would have wakened him.

Mike stood looking down at Oscar, a confusion of feeling in the expression on his face; something like looking down on a sleeping child who has kept you awake all night.

"We'll call around again," I said. "I'm sure we can find a bed in a rehab somewhere."

"He looks so old, my dear old Dad." Mike pulled the blanket up over Oscar's shoulder. "When I was a kid, I used to get hold of the Sears catalogue and cry my eyes out. I'd see all the pretty people in there and think, boy, that's what normal looks like. I'd pick out the man and the woman I wanted for my parents and fill out the order form for them. If I'd ever had a stamp, I would have mailed it in. Pretty stupid, huh?"

"If I'd known you when I was about fourteen, I would have sent you my mom and dad. Gladly."

He smiled. "I would have taken them."

"For all of his shortcomings, Oscar raised one hell of a fine kid." I took Mike's hand. "You know he loves you beyond all things."

"Yeah. Except for his booze." There was no self-pity in his attitude. Mike had grown up in the real world where seeing things as they are was the means to survival. And he was a magnificent survivor. He squeezed my hand. "Thanks for coming with me."

"Thanks for asking me." I kissed his cheek. "How about some coffee?"

We went into the kitchen and found Guido, looking pale and exhausted, sitting at the table with half a pot of coffee in front of him.

"Can't sleep?" I put my hand against the pot. It was still warm enough. I took two more mugs out of the cupboard. "You feeling okay, Guido?"

"I heard you leave." Guido pulled his old flannel robe tighter around him. His face was backlit by the light over the stove so I couldn't see his expression. I knew him well enough that I didn't need to. He dropped his chin an inch, turned his head slightly to his left as his shoulders came up. The two or three times I've seen Guido cry, and maybe half-a-dozen other times when he came close, Guido held exactly that posture. I know Guido: He was worried. "Maggie?"

"We're fine, Guido." I went behind him and wrapped my arms around him, patted his flat chest. "Mike's dad had a little problem we needed to take care of. We brought him home and he's sleeping in the living room."

He put his hands over mine. "I thought, maybe, complications or something. Leaving in the middle of the night like that." He didn't finish the sentence.

Mike glanced at me, a question in his frown. I knew what he was asking, so I shook my head. I hadn't told Guido about Saturday night.

As if reading the silence in the room, Guido said, "Liam Farrington told me. He bribed a nurse at Cedars to get the scoop."

I pulled away from him. "Who else has Liam told?"

"I don't know."

"It's nobody's business," I said.

Mike drew a deep breath that ended in a yawn. The hard light made him seem years older than he had just the night before. He looked at me. "How soon can you pack a bag, Maggie? Let's get the kids and get in the car. Let's go now. We can be in San Francisco by lunchtime."

"What about Shannon?" I asked. "What about your case?"

"Fuck it. What are they going to do if I drop the ball? Fire me?"

Chapter 13

We couldn't leave town Thursday morning. Instead, we went about business as usual: Michael had a chem lab quiz, Casey had a ballet workshop, Mike had a solid lead on Shannon, I made contact with a man who had arrived on the same boat as Bao. And Oscar was sleeping it off in the living room.

Thursday was one of Michael's early days, leaving Casey to take the city bus to school. Guido offered to drive her, but she declined; several of her best friends took the same bus and they had things to talk about.

Mike boxed up everything in the house that contained alcohol—a couple of bottles of beer, three bottles of wine, some cooking sherry, half a bottle of mouthwash, some aftershave, and the vanilla extract—and locked it all up in the back of his car. Before he kissed me goodbye, he said, "I'll call around for a new place for Dad. But it might take a while."

"There's no hurry," I said.

"You'd be amazed how much of a hurry you can be in once he gets his hands on some booze. And he will. There's nothing to keep him from walking over to the store." Mike's face was set in grim lines. "I'll ask around, call Social Services. Maybe the VA has forgotten what happened last time they had him and they'll take him back."

"You do that, and I'll call the bar and see what the owner wants."

"Thanks." Mike tried to smile. "That'd be a big help."

When we backed out of the driveway, headed in opposite directions, the sky was black and threatening, but there was still no rain.

Guido and I drove out to Westminster, a bedroom city on the western edge of Orange County. We left the freeway at Bolsa, the exit marked Little Saigon.

Arlo had found a recent address for Mr. Ralph Yuen, a refugee who had shared a cabin with Bao Ngo on the cargo ship *Manatee* on the trip from Saigon to Long Beach.

Mr. Yuen had traveled on diplomatic credentials. I expected to find him living in one of the better tract house developments, one of the thousands of cookie-cutter stucco palaces that spread out from the freeway as far as the eye could see. But our Thomas Guide took us into a leftover zone, an undeveloped triangle defined by the freeway, a cemetery, and the Navy Weapons Depot railroad.

"Used to be nice down here," Guido said, looking for street names as he drove. "We used to drive to the beach down this way. The whole area was farms and fields back then. Lima beans and strawberries."

I looked out at featureless cracked-stucco houses with broken-down cars pulled up onto hard-packed front yards, a stretch of curbless, potholed asphalt that was a long way from being new. Then I looked at Guido. "You're not that old, Guido."

"No, really. That's what this all was. Just farms and farmhouses."

I checked the map. "I think you passed the street. We have to go back two blocks."

"No problem." Guido braked and started into a U-turn. There was a blast of horns and tires squealing. A white car swerved off onto the muddy shoulder to keep from hitting us broadside.

"Oh Jeez," Guido muttered. "I didn't even see him. Where'd he come from?"

The other car was okay. The driver may have been swearing, he should have been rattled. But he kept going, pushed the accelerator when he bumped off the shoulder back onto the road. A near miss, but a miss.

Guido finished his U-turn. I asked, "You okay?"

"Yeah. I guess. Sorry. You?"

"I'm fine. This is your street."

He turned up a street that dead-ended at the tracks. "What was the number?"

The address Arlo gave us took us to the last house on the block, an old two-story wood-frame with faded, peeling paint that stood alone among vacant lots. Brown weeds grew through the torn mesh of a pair of screens discarded on what had once been a front lawn.

The yard sloped down to a gully, an irrigation runoff ditch lined with concrete. At the edge of that long gray gash, filled with roiling brown water by yesterday's rain, a few scrubby live oak and eucalyptus trees managed to survive, giving a little green relief to the dismal beige landscape.

Beyond the gully, the railroad tracks and more undeveloped land. Attached to the Cyclone fence on the far side was a sign: Choice Industrial Site, and an 800 number to call.

"Like I said," Guido gloated as he parked at the side of the street. "Old farmhouses."

I heard chickens when I got out of the van. I reached for the 35mm camera I keep in my bag and snapped off a few frames of the house and the yard against the deep gray of the clouds. The scene was spooky enough for Halloween.

Guido gave me an optimistic smile when a voice responded to my knock on the front door. He said, "Let the games begin."

Heavy footsteps inside, then a mammoth shape behind the dirty screen, a woman well over six feet tall. Even her blue-black hair, a huge, kinky, Medusa-like tangle, gave her volume. Her calico muumuu was worn threadbare over her unrestricted mounds of breasts and belly. I was disappointed. My guess, she was Samoan. Not that it mattered, except that she definitely was not Vietnamese.

In a deep voice, the woman demanded, "What you want? You Child Protection?"

"No," I said, slipping my card into the crack between the door and the jamb. "We're hoping to find a Mr. Ralph Yuen."

With her doughy arms crossed over her wide chest, she wasn't giving an inch. "You don't say what you want. You from his job?"

"No," I said. The woman was nosy, that's all. Why we wanted Yuen was none of her business. "Where can I find Mr. Yuen?"

"Around back." She extended a thick thumb toward a patched side gate. "Don't let the chickens out."

"Thanks." I grinned at Guido as we went down the front steps. "Every day, something new, boys and girls."

Guido shooed chickens away so that I could close the gate after us. The latch was a loop of wire that hooked over a bent nail hammered into the side of a two-car garage.

The backyard was better tended than the front. There were trellised winter squash, and navel oranges hanging ripe from well-trimmed trees, a manicured lawn. Along the back fence, grape and berry vines, pruned for winter, were just beginning to show some green.

"Nice hooch," Guido said, indicating the garage. "Not quite up to code, though."

I hesitated before knocking on the door. If this was Ralph Yuen's home, it was quite a come-down for a man who had come over on diplomatic credentials.

"What are you thinking?" Guido asked.

I shook my head. "We've come this far. Let's see this story out."

When Guido knocked on the door, the old paint left white chalk on his knuckles.

The door was opened by a small, thin woman with a beautiful face and hair long enough to sit on. She glanced shyly at Guido, who gawked, and then looked straight at me.

"Yes?"

"We're looking for Ralph Yuen," I said. "Does he live here?"

The woman bowed slightly, then backed into the gloom beyond the door. Almost immediately, a man appeared, holding a sleeping baby against his shoulder. He smiled, but he was cautious. "You have come to see me?"

"I am Maggie MacGowen, and this is Guido Patrini." I gave him my card and he gave us the usual wide-eyed going over. "We want to speak with you about your trip over from Vietnam. About a man named Bao Ngo."

"So long ago." Yuen frowned, patted the baby's back when the child began to stir. "What could I have to tell you?"

"That's what we're here to find out."

"Please, come in." Gently swaying and patting the baby all the way, he led us into the relative warmth of the garage. As he passed the woman, he said something to her in Vietnamese. She nodded and moved soundlessly, gracefully, into the corner set aside as the kitchen. At the stationary tub that was the kitchen sink, she filled a kettle and put it on the two-burner stove.

I looked around. The converted garage was clean. The only furniture was a Formica table with four chrome chairs, a cradle, and an old sofa covered with a chenille spread. Tatami grass mats covered the concrete floor. Against the wall there were rolled-up beds: futons. Unpainted sheets of drywall petitioned off the far end of the room.

The woman set teacups and a pot on the table, then took a Sara Lee cake out of the freezer section of an ancient Frigidaire.

"Please." Mr. Yuen gestured for Guido and me to sit on the sofa. He squatted on his heels, cradling the baby. Beside him was a plastic baby bottle shaped like Fred Flinstone.

"How old is your baby?" I asked.

"Six months. He is my grandson, Eric. This is Trinh, my daughter-in-law."

We exchanged hellos and bows with her.

"I am baby-sitter when Trinh goes to college." He put his finger in the baby's tiny fist and smiled into his sleeping face. "Eric has a little fever from his vaccination. But he will be fine. However, if his mother does not leave soon, she will be late for her class. And that will not be so fine."

Smiling at the dig, Trinh bowed. "Thank you, Father. I am leaving."

"What school do you attend?" I asked her as she picked up her book bag.

"University of California," she said. "At Irvine."

"It's a good place," I said.

"My son is finishing his doctorate," Yuen said with a quiet yet obvious pride. I looked around at that shared garage home with new appreciation. College, even in the tuition-free state system, is expensive.

After the door closed behind Trinh, Yuen laid Eric in his cradle. He came back to us with tea and cake, and served us.

"I have a small idea of what you want to talk about," he said. "Will you wait here for one moment?"

He went into the area behind the drywall partition. We could hear him moving things around.

Guido leaned in to me. "Any guesses what he's got back there?"

At the sound of Guido's voice, Eric began to wail.

"Now you've done it." I went over and took the baby out of the cradle and held him against me. He quieted right down. His head was warm in the crook of my neck, his hair softer than down. I hadn't held a baby for a long, long time. For no good reason, I was having trouble breathing.

Then Eric looked up at me, didn't know me, opened his mouth, and howled, showing three sharp little teeth. I nudged his bottom lip with the nipple of his bottle. Still snuffling, still eyeing me with suspicion, he closed his mouth so he could drink his juice.

Yuen padded back into the room carrying a plastic folder. He smiled when he saw me with Eric.

"This is what you have questions about," he said, pulling out a weathered and torn booklet that had faded to sepia. There were three titles on the cover. One in phonetic Vietnamese, one in French, "La Musée de Tourane—Les Beaux-Arts du Pays Ancien." And, "The Museum of Da Nang—The Art of Ancient Champa."

A little trill of adrenaline passed through me when I saw the catalogue. I reached for it just to make sure it was genuine, and, with my free hand, awkwardly turned the pages. The caption under each photograph was printed in three languages, the schizoid legacy of Vietnam's last century.

I rocked Eric in my arms as Yuen showed me the contents of the catalogue and explained some of the more important pieces that had been in the museum collection. There were more ancient jade and stone figures than anything else, most of them dancing girls. But there were also rare porcelains from China, some gold jewelry, glass beads, bracelets with pearls, bits of centuries-old ceremonial garb—some buckles and two-headed earrings—hammered bronze plates and pots, a jewel-hilted saber. It was interesting. Exotic and unusual. The intrinsic value of the stuff was beyond measure. But the market value?

I caught Yuen watching me, met his eye. "Did you know Bao Ngo before you boarded the *Manatee*?"

"Oh, yes. I was on the staff of Mai An. It was I who called and told Bao to evacuate the museum in Da Nang."

"Mai An?" Guido said. "Who is Mai An?"

"The wife of the president. Madame Thieu. Before we called Da Nang, she had already sent the collection from the Saigon Museum to Canada under the care of General Quang." Yuen handed the catalogue to Guido.

I asked, "Did you stay behind in Saigon to wait for the trucks from Da Nang?"

"Not specifically. Mai An had her own collections of jade and diamonds that needed transport out. She had also ordered sixteen tons of gold to be sent to her from the Bank of Saigon."

"Hooh!" Guido blurted, startling Eric. "She took sixteen tons of gold out of the country?"

Yuen shook his head. "We could find no one to carry it. Swissair said at first that they would help her with personal items, but when they came to the palace and saw the pallets stacked on her bedroom floor, they changed their mind. Something about not wanting to breach their neutral status by removing a nation's gold reserves." Yuen shrugged.

"Ly, who was Mai An's brother-in-law, bought space allotments from a few Canadian embassy personnel who were being evacuated. That's how he managed to get a number of crates aboard the *Manatee*. He bought passage for myself and for Bao Ngo as well. Whatever Ly could carry, he took with him to France."

"The gold stayed behind?" I asked.

"Most," Yuen said. "Not all. President Thieu had at least a suitcase full of gold."

"The stuff that got out," Guido said, "where is it?"

Yuen laughed. He took Eric from me when the baby began to fuss. "If I knew where there was any part of sixteen tons of gold, do you think my family would be living in a garage? Trust me when I say, I do not know."

"Okay," I said. "But tell us what happened when the *Manatee* reached California."

"What do you want to know?"

"Were you there when Bao Ngo went through Customs?"

Yuen furrowed his brow as he thought. "Yes. All cargo going on to Canada, and all possessions of passengers traveling under diplomatic passports, were sealed and left aboard. Cargo entering the United States was picked up by bonded courier and carried by truck to the Customs warehouse for inspection."

"Did you know that the collection from Da Nang was fakes?"

"Most of it was." He nodded. "But not everything. There were, for instance, some especially fine jade pieces, temple dancers."

"Was Bao very upset?"

"Upset? Not one bit." Yuen walked over to the cradle and laid Eric down. He reached for a bottle of children's Tylenol and gave the baby a dropperful. As he talked to us, he rocked the cradle. "You see, Bao needed the paperwork, not the artifacts. Provenance, you understand? He had the originals stashed away somewhere in the world. But the only way Bao could sell those pieces on the open market was to have Customs stamp his paperwork.

"Ironic, isn't it?" Yuen said. "Bao had to smuggle fakes so that he could sell the genuine articles."

"It's not ironic," Guido said. "It's corrupt."

"Perhaps." Yuen bowed. "I cannot make that judgment, not knowing Bao's intentions. Museums have qualms about displaying items that have no pedigree, even when those items are donated. Private collectors are not always so careful."

"You think Bao was going to hand all this stuff over to some museum?" I asked.

"That is what he told me." Puckishly, Yuen grinned. "If you want confirmation, you will have to ask Bao Ngo himself."

"I'd love to ask him," I said. "But where the hell is he?"

"The last time I saw him, he was driving a U-Haul truck north on the Long Beach Freeway."

We had been there long enough. Eric needed attention and I needed to think over what we had just learned. I had one last question:

"Mr. Yuen, according to the records, you traveled on a diplomatic passport."

He nodded.

"Were you exempt from a Customs search?"

The answer he gave me was a bow and a mysterious smile. And nothing more.

Chapter 14

We were on the freeway headed north toward downtown Los Angeles when I saw the white car again, two lanes over, three cars back. I said, "Guido, would you please change lanes?"

He looked at me as if I had lost it, but he complied. In the sideview mirror, I watched the white car move over one lane, too.

"Do it again, please," I said. When the white car changed again, I said, "We have a tail."

"Cool." Guido started watching the rearview mirror more than it was probably safe to do. "Which one is it?"

"The car that almost hit us in Westminster."

He thought about it. "Think they want to get even for me making them stop short? Gang-bangers needing to get their mojo back?"

"Gang-bangers would have shot you by now, Guido," I said. "I'm seeing short hair, short-sleeved shirts, and ties. White guys. My guess is FBI or a close cousin."

"Like?"

"Customs. DEA. ATF."

"What do they want with us?" he asked, all scandalized innocence.

"It isn't us. It's what we've wandered into."

"Want me to dust them?"

"Not yet." I reached into the back for the camera bag. "Let's get a better look at them."

"Whatever you say."

I snapped a telephoto lens onto my 35mm and checked to see how many shots were left on the roll:

eighteen. Guido found the slot for his maneuver, changed two lanes, and slowed, putting us within a car length of our pursuers. I was on the floor, on my knees facing backward, braced against the seat, with the lens just at the level of the open window. I didn't let the end extend out: Someone might think it was a weapon and panic. Worse, the men in the car would see it before I finished my business and would disappear.

The van bounced too much for me to see clearly through the long lens, but I set the auto focus, aimed at the white car's windshield, and snapped off eight frames.

"Can you get beside them?" I asked. "I want to shoot into their side window."

Guido put a truck between us and the white car, hoping the car's driver would use the truck as cover to drop back so he could get behind us again. We were in good position. Guido slowed, let the truck move ahead, leaving nothing but ten feet of open space between my lens and the driver of the white car.

I snapped three frames and said, "Go."

Guido hit the brakes, slipped behind the other car long enough for me to get the license plate, and then sped off the freeway at the next exit ramp.

"They didn't see me." I got back up on the seat and finished the roll taking extreme close-ups of Guido. "They were too busy trying to figure out what you were doing."

"But you got them?"

"Oh, yeah." End of the roll, the auto rewind began its whir. "Unless I'm very wrong, we've seen them before. The two bozos hanging around the marina Tuesday watching us talk to Minh Tam? Ring a bell?"

"No." He drove a zigzag down side streets to make sure we'd lost the tail. "Who are they?"

"They made a fuss about where they were seated. I thought all they wanted was a table with an ocean view. Now I wonder if they just wanted to be closer to us."

He shrugged. He didn't remember them.

"Look at Minh Tam's interview again. If you did any

crowd shots, you probably got them." I took the film out of the camera. "I'll see what Arlo can turn up from the license plate."

Guido checked his rearview mirror and then relaxed against the van's plush seat. He reached over and patted my knee. "That was kind of fun, kid. Be more fun if these characters were any good at their work. They've made themselves awfully damned visible."

"Maybe they want us to see them," I said.

"Assholes," was his final evaluation.

Guido parked at the curb in front of City Hall among three news vans and put a press card in the windshield. Then he walked across the street to the underground mall and left the film at a one-hour processor.

Guido stood in line for coffee while I called Mike.

"I'm across the street," I said. "How's it going?"

"The VA won't take Dad, not after what he did the last time. There's a place out in Trona that Social Services says has a good program for hard-core cases."

"Where's Trona?"

"Out in the desert. As long as Pop doesn't wander off, there isn't much mischief he can get into out there." Mike cleared his throat. "Problem is, it's damned expensive. Medicare won't cover half the cost. I don't know where I can come up with that kind of money."

"We'll think of something," I said, hearing a click in my brain: Sell the damn house. "There's always a way."

"We'll keep it as a fallback. I also heard about a halfway house in Reseda. I'm going to check it out tonight."

"I called the bar owner and he's being reasonable," I said. "He says he knows you from when you used to work Hollenbeck street patrol."

"That was a long time ago," Mike said.

"The guy says you helped him out a couple of times and he figures he owes you. He says his insurance will cover the pool table Oscar ruined and whatever he did to the plumbing, but the owner would appreciate it if you covered the deductible."

"How much?"

"Five hundred."

"Ouch." Mike pulled in some air and blew it out. "Still. That's more than fair. I have a feeling, though, that the cop who's calling in a debt is Paula. I don't remember the bar, and I don't remember patrolling that particular neighborhood. Of all the boys in midnight blue who must have passed through his dive over the years, how do you suppose he would remember me?"

"So, I'll tell him okay?"

"Yes. If you don't mind calling him back, tell him I'll drop by tonight with a check."

I said I would. "Can you meet me and Guido for coffee right now?"

"Can't. I'm bringing in Shannon. Seems he got wet and cold enough that a dry jail cell started sounding pretty good."

"You're going to let me sit in on the interview, right?"

"Sure. Give me a couple of hours to get him processed through upstairs. I'll page you when we're ready to talk."

I called the bar owner and gave him Mike's message, and listened to his story about his own dear old dad who died of cirrhosis at the age of thirty-eight. Quite a fraternity Oscar and Mike belong to.

Guido and I drank our coffee and then killed time until our pictures were ready by reading funny cards to each other in the stationery store next door to the photo shop. As soon as I had the shot of the license plate in my hand, I called Arlo. He had an answer for me in less than two minutes.

"Number goes back to Hertz," he said. "Take me a little more time to get the name on the rental agreement. I'll page you when I have it."

Next I called Minh Tam to make sure he was in. "I have some pictures I want you to see."

We went back to the van and drove across town to Tam's hotel, parked in the covered lot, and went up to the room the studio was paying for.

Minh Tam was growing sleek on the studio's nickel.

He had a fresh haircut and a manicure, and pressed slacks under his terry robe.

Guido looked around the room appreciatively. "Not bad. I could camp out in a place like this and be fairly happy."

"I haven't left the room even once," Tam said, grinning. "I am afraid that I am getting used to this treatment."

"Khanh Nguyen asked me to tell you that you are welcome to stay at her house," I said. "Have you ever been there? It's quite a castle."

"We spoke," he said. Revealing nothing.

I showed him the Polaroid of Ralph Yuen holding Eric that I had taken when we said our good-byes. I asked Tam, "Do you recognize this man?"

Tam studied the face, his brows knit with the effort to remember. All he said was, "Nice baby."

"The man's name is Ralph Yuen and that's his grandson," I said. "He worked for Madame Thieu and he knew Bao."

"Sorry." He handed back the snapshot. "Maybe he has changed very much. It has been a long time."

"How about these two?" I gave him a snap I took from the van, aiming into the driver's side window. The driver was in profile, his passenger's face three-quarters full on.

Tam nodded. "I saw them several times. First, they observed when you videotaped me two days ago. Then, I saw them yesterday. These are the men I told you I thought were following me."

He took the next picture from my hand, a windshield shot with the two faces seen fairly clearly behind the reflections on the glass. "I was not being paranoid, after all, was I?"

"They're following somebody, that's for sure. I think we'll have an idea who they are very soon."

"Was there anything more?" Tam asked.

I gave him a quick recap of our talk with Yuen, and asked Tam for his opinion.

He said, "I think this Mr. Yuen may be very correct.

Why else would Bao carry such a cargo? There was much danger getting out of the country with only the shirt on one's back. But to risk taking crates of cargo, there must have been high stakes indeed."

"How difficult would it have been for Tam to sell the original artifacts?" I asked.

"Not difficult. Asian art is highly prized right now," he said, donning the mien of the art historian he was trained to be. "Many private collectors want only to accumulate. They do not care what road an item followed before it reached their hands. Museums, however, are somewhat more careful. There have been successful lawsuits, you see, from individuals and countries who claim that items were removed illegally. Lawsuits are very expensive and the result can be very embarrassing when some treasure is taken off exhibit by the authorities and sent abroad. Donors don't like to underwrite such misadventures."

Tam picked up the Polaroid again and studied it. He nodded. "Bao cared nothing for politics nor for material wealth. He cared only for the land and the people. I believe it is most likely that Bao wished to preserve the Cham collection in a museum, if that was the most feasible solution."

"An honorable man, you say."

Tam bowed. "A scholar."

My pager had been vibrating all morning. Because the hotel room's telephone bill was on my tab, Tam said he wouldn't mind if I made a few calls. I carried the phone over to a chair by the window where I could watch the first rain of the new storm gathering over the ocean.

Tam dialed up a Pay-per-View movie and he and Guido got comfortable while I took care of business.

Lana Howard, my producer, was on the warpath about something. I could't figure out what the issue was, except that maybe she felt left out. Guido and I had spent very little time in the studio all week. Normally, we were her chief source of entertainment. When

Lana signed me on to do independent films, she hadn't counted on my being quite so independent.

To make amends, to keep her happy, I invited Lana to join us in San Francisco and help us film the New Year parade in Chinatown Saturday night. She seemed somewhat mollified.

Scotty had called three times. He left a local number, meaning either he was still in town or he had a locally franchised cell phone in his pocket. Looking out for Casey's interests, I called him back.

I asked him if he had ever known Ralph Yuen, but he brushed aside my question. Instead, he asked me, "Did you have time to think over what I said?"

"What did you say?"

"I want the opportunity to match any offer you get on the house."

"I don't know," I said. "It took me a long time to get our financial affairs disentangled, Scotty. Let's just keep things uncomplicated. There are plenty of houses you can buy, and you never liked San Francisco anyway. So why go through this?"

"All cash. No strings."

"Wait until I see the offer," I said.

"When?"

"I'll call Uncle Max sometime today and have him read it to me."

"Why don't you and I get together tonight for dinner and see where we stand? It's for Casey, Maggie. If you get the right price for the house, Casey can write her own ticket to college."

"That argument doesn't work, Scotty. If you have cash to buy this house, then you have cash to pay for your daughter's education. If I sell to a third party, then Casey will have two cash-rich parents."

"That's naive, Maggie."

"It's simple arithmetic."

"Have dinner with me tonight. We'll go over the possibilities."

"I'll get back to you," I said. Honest to God, the hair stood up on the back of my neck. Dinner with Scotty?

Alone? That prospect was about as close to a waking nightmare as I could conjure up.

On the TV screen, Jean-Claude Van Damme was kicking his way through a legion of armed terrorists. Even with Scotty on the far end of a telephone wire, I had some idea what the character in the movie, were he real, must have felt: outgunned.

I called Khanh and asked her what she knew about Yuen, and got as little help from her as I had from Tam and Scotty. She said she was curious about the man and would be eager to see the Polaroid when we got together Friday morning.

There was some routine film business to take care of, and I dumped it all on Fergie. She complained that she was bored and that she missed us. I knew she was misstating whom she missed. Fergie and Guido had had an office fling during the fall that had chilled by winter. At least, had chilled for Guido. Fergie still carried, if not a torch, then at least a spark. It was Guido's sweet face she missed, not mine.

I was sitting with my feet up watching the storm curtain roll onshore, remembering how little Eric had felt in my arms. It was a nice feeling, but awfully confusing. I was thinking it wouldn't be hard to be a grandmother, when Mike paged me.

"He's ripe," Mike said.

"Shannon's ready to talk?"

"I don't know about that. I was referring to the way he smells. Hasn't had a bath since we started looking for him. I sent him downstairs to booking for delousing and a shower before I'll sit in a room with him. I'll have him back upstairs within the hour."

Guido wanted to stay and see the rest of the movie. "Better than waiting in the hall at Parker Center while you have all the fun."

He said he would take a Dash bus over to the Civic Center if the movie finished before the interrogation ended. I left the two of them ordering lunch from room service.

Chapter 15

"Even if I'm found innocent, I'll do time." Shannon's shoulder-length dreads, still damp from his delousing shower, left damp patches on the shoulders of his orange jail jumpsuit. On his feet he wore rubber jail-issue sandals. He was smaller than I expected him to be, no more than five-six. Tina, his partner in crime, outweighed him by at least twenty pounds.

"If you're found innocent," Mike said, "you're innocent."

"That's why I was scared to come in, cuz I was at the house."

"Just because you were there doesn't necessarily mean you're an accessory. Depends on what you did. Now, tell me about Pen and the gun. How did the gun get to the house?"

"Someone called Pen. Maybe Tina or Zeema. I don't know."

"Why did they need a gun?"

"See, Tina says the man should be shot. I say let him go, but they say he knows their names and he could go to the police. I've got nothing to say on that. They called Pen for the gun."

"When he got to the house, who did Pen give the gun to?"

"No one. He kept it in his pocket. He came one time, looked around, saw the man. When he came back, he came back with a gun, a small .22. He showed Tina and Snoop and them the gun, but he kept it himself all day. Then at night, when they took the guy over to the school, he gave up the gun."

"Who called you to come over to the house?"

"Tina did."

"On your pager?"

"Yeah. I call her back and she says come over, I need you to do something. And I'm pussy-struck so I went over there."

"We're all pussy-struck." Mike glanced my way, suppressing a smile. "What happened when you got over there?"

"The man was in the room with the girls."

"What did Tina tell you?"

"She says he has six hundred dollars and they going to jack him for it. They going to tell him they give him sex and get his pants off him. Then they going to jack him.

"When I got there, Tina was kissing on the dude and then he was on top of her trying to take it from her, but she didn't want to give it up."

"She was masturbating him when you got there?"

"Yeah. But she was just pretending she was going to give him sex. He got on top of her and that's when I hit him."

"You were protecting your girlfriend?"

"Yeah." Shannon brightened at the suggestion. "Like that. I was protecting her."

"You told me Tina was a prostitute."

"She won't go out with you if you got no money."

"So, what were you defending? Looks to me like Tina had things well in hand, so to speak."

"He had her under him. I hit him. Then Pen and Snoop show up. Then I kick his ass for getting on top of her. Zeema tied his hands with an extension cord."

"Did he have his pants on?"

"He was nekkid when I popped him. They let him put his pants back on. Tina started in beating him with a big old belt buckle cuz she was mad he licked on her when she was kissing on him. Zeema beat him with the extension cord. Then Pen and Snoop come in and hit the dude. I was just watching."

Mike shot him a skeptical frown. "All you did was watch?"

"I hit him the first time to get him off Tina. That was the only time. Pen and Snoop got their licks in, then Tina came in with a knife—like a steak knife—and she burned her name in him." Shannon grew more and more excited as he talked about that day. "Snoop was going, 'Ah, ah,' so he put a spatula on the fire and start to burn the man all over. Touch him all over; goes *ssss ssss*."

Mike sat as far back in his chair as he could, as if the story poured a bad odor into the room. "Why did they do all this stuff?"

Shannon shrugged. "Just to do it."

"Did you ever see the six hundred dollars?"

"No. Tina got the money and left."

"You got no money?"

"No, man. Nothing."

"Now, the knife you say Tina used to cut Pedro. Did you wash that knife?"

"No. I never touched the knife. It was still sitting on the counter when you guys came by and went through the house."

"The tip of your thumb was on the knife. How did your print get on the knife? That's fairly significant, isn't it?"

Shannon thought for a while. Twice he started to say something, seemed to change his mind. All he said was, "I don't know."

"Did you ever touch the gun?"

"No."

"Did you ever touch the bullets?"

"No."

Mike looked bored, but hard. "Who took Pedro over to the school?"

"Pen and Snoop and some other guy. I was way behind. Standing on the other side of the street."

"Why did they shoot Pedro?"

"Because the man said Tina's name. Everyone in the whole house says they got to kill him cuz he said the name."

"Whose idea was it to take him to the school?"

"Snoop says it. He says they can't take him to the park because a lot of people work there and a lot of people could lose their jobs. So they went to the school."

"What people was he talking about?"

"Some friends of his. Like, this gang abatement program they have over there. You know, this job program."

"In the park?"

"Yeah."

"Who took Pedro?"

"I didn't see who all, cuz I wasn't there."

"Who pulled the trigger?"

"I wasn't there."

"Who pulled the trigger?"

"I didn't see." Shannon grew agitated. There was more sweat than shower water darkening his jumpsuit. "I wasn't over there where they was at. Last I saw, Pen had the gun."

"Who put Pedro in the cart?"

"All of them. Zeema put him in the laundry bag."

"She had help."

"Yeah. I say the bag is too small. She says she can put three or four loads of clothes in it."

"You're saying you helped put Pedro in the cart?"

"Everybody did."

"You knew where they were taking him?"

"I wasn't there."

"Who fired the shot?"

"There were three people over by the gate. Pen, Snoop, and a third guy I don't know. I was across the street."

"How many shots did you hear?"

"Three."

"But you weren't there?"

"No, man. I swear, I wasn't there."

"After the shooting, then what?"

"Everybody goes to a party across the street from Zeema's house."

"At the party did anyone talk about what had happened to Pedro?"

"No."

Mike put his pen down on the table and folded his hands over the reports.

"You tell a good story, Shannon. Probably a large portion of it is true. But a large portion of it isn't true." He made eye contact with Shannon. "Unfortunately for you, Tina and all the rest of them have already copped out. Every one of them has told me what happened, and every one of them has been fairly consistent with what you did. These people aren't lying to save themselves, because they all copped to what they did.

"For me to believe your story, it has to be pretty close to theirs. You did a whole lot more than pop Pedro a couple times. I know what you did. I know what everyone did." Mike leaned in closer. "Because they all told me. Tina cut her initials in Pedro. Snoop burned him with a spatula. Pen went over and got his grandmother's gun. Zeema put Pedro in her laundry bag. Now, you want to try it one more time and tell me what you did?"

"I'll tell you." Shannon seemed chastened. "I did more. I beat him. I burned him. I gave him Cisco with bleach in it. But I never shot him."

"Who did?"

"I don't know."

"You can't get that past me, Shannon. You were partying with these same people the very day you spent nine hours torturing a man. You were in that house for two days after. There's no way everyone didn't talk about it. They talked to the neighbors, they talked to each other. And everyone says you pulled the trigger."

"I didn't do it." Shannon's voice rose, but he caught himself, came back down, stayed controlled. "They can't put it on me, and I ain't no snitch."

"I didn't ask you to be a snitch, because they've all told me what they did. If you didn't pull the trigger, did Pen do it?"

"I can't say that."

"Pen pushed the cart; he told me he did. Then you shot Pedro three times. You went back to the house and Tina says you left prints on the cart, to go get it. So you go back." Mike's voice dropped to a church whisper. "Pedro was still alive then, wasn't he? He had three bullets in him, but he was still moving around."

"Uh-huh."

"So you dumped him out of the cart and brought the cart back to Zeema's house."

"Pen dumped him. Me and Pen were hanging after the dude got shot. Some of our friends come by real nosy. Snoop been talkin', takin' people by to look at the body."

"Do you remember saying to Pen, this guy just won't die?"

"I was fuckin' scared. I never saw a guy shot who didn't die. Scared shit out of me."

"Did you think he might live and tell the police?"

"That crossed my mind. Tina says go back and cut his throat. Pen said I should go shoot him in the throat."

"You did shoot him in the throat."

"I didn't shoot him. They say go cut him, I say no. I ain't takin' no chance on that cuz the fuckin' police come and I'd be really fucked." Shannon began to cry, but he wasn't very convincing. "I didn't shoot the man, dude. I don't want to go to jail on this. They're all trying to put this shit on me. They all had time to put this all together."

"The last thing I want this late in my career is to put an innocent man in prison." Mike did not acknowledge the kid's show of distress. "And Shannon, I gotta tell you, in my twenty-five years, this is one of the easiest cases I ever assembled. Something you forgot to tell me. I know you handled the gun, and I know you unloaded the gun at some point, because I have your prints all over it."

Shannon gave up on the tears routine. "I was playing with the gun, unload it, cock it, dry fire by the man's head."

"Was the man scared?"

"He says he wants to go. I say, I can't let you go, man."

"Did you explain to the man why you couldn't let him go?"

"Yes."

"You told him he had to die?"

Shannon sucked in air.

"You understand that based on what we know already, who did the actual shooting isn't a big deal. The fact he was shot is as important as who shot him. You've just told me you had foreknowledge. The fact that you won't admit to what you did makes it look like you're hiding something." Mike tapped the table in front of Shannon. "The gun thing, Shannon?"

"Yeah?"

"It's going to come back and bite you in the ass." Mike sat back, folded his arms across his chest. "I know you shot him. You're the leader here, the only one with the guts to do it. All the rest of them are followers. The gun thing right now is the only thing still hanging us up."

"I'm going to jail."

"Yes, you are. I'm going to book you right now. There are a lot of people going in with you. They're all going to pay. It would be better for you right now to tell me the truth. Because if you don't tell the truth right now, it taints everything else you've said."

Shannon considered. "Even if I did shoot the dude, it's not going to change shit."

"The only thing telling the truth will do is show the judge and the jury that you're sorry for what happened."

"I'm going to get my life taken. You're going to recommend the gas chamber."

"I don't recommend anything. That's up to the DA. All I do is get the facts together." Mike held up his hands. "I know you shot the guy."

No preliminaries, Shannon spilled. "Yeah. I shot the dude."

"You shot Pedro Alvaro?"

"Yeah. I shot him."

"Okay." Mike stood up. "Let's go."

The interview was over.

Shannon, at nineteen, wasn't a juvenile. I was able to film him all the way through the booking procedure. He had been in jail before and went passively through the procedure like an old hand.

Once, while he was waiting for some paperwork to be finished, he turned to me and tried to start a conversation.

I said, "I can't talk to you."

"I was just wondering," he said. "It's my girlfriend's birthday coming up. Can I give her the tape of the interview for a present?"

I said, "I'll see what I can do."

Chapter 16

I needed to be with my daughter.

The impulse to connect with her normally hits me several times during the school day. Most of the time I manage to suppress the urge, in the interest of her budding independence. But after listening to Shannon's strange version of the way the world works, I needed to see Casey's sweet face. Immediately.

What a good idea, I thought, to videotape the first rehearsal of *Cinderella*. Casey's dance teacher thought it was a good idea, too.

At three o'clock on Thursday afternoon, I was in the main dance studio of Casey's school, camera on my shoulder, a parent-voyeur.

Casey is a wonderful, talented, hardworking dancer. But nothing she could do, no quantity of practice or conditioning, would fix her essential flaw if she wanted to make a career out of ballet: Casey is too tall. Six-foot ballerinas have no one to partner them. She was head and shoulders above the rest of the troupe, a standout like a swan among goslings.

At five-thirty she was a tired, wilted swan, and happy to have a ride home with dear old mom. As she gathered her school materials and soiled dance clothes, she only mentioned once that she thought it was time she had her own car.

We walked out to the parking lot arm in arm, both of us with loaded bags over our shoulders. It was nearly dark, and the heavy skies made it seem later than it was. Other dancers and their rides and some teachers were also leaving, most headed, as we were, toward the parking lot. The lot lights were just coming on.

"I'm doing a solo," Casey said, her feet light under her. "Mr. Andreavich is rechoreographing a pas de deux for me to dance solo. He said not to let it go to my head. There aren't enough good boys to cover all the parts. And there is, like, no one who can dance with me."

"A solo is a solo," I said. "Think of the bragging rights Grandma and Grandpa will get out of the show."

"I suppose the whole family has to come." She tried to make a face as if displeased by the burden of family. But she wasn't convincing. Performers need an audience.

"Your grandparents have come to every single performance you've been in since you were the spout in 'I'm a Little Teapot' when you were three. Now that you're the exalted soloist, you know they'll be here. Get used to it."

All of a sudden Casey wasn't listening. She pulled me toward her. "Mom?"

"What?"

"Those men." She dipped her head toward the parking lot. "I saw them this morning when I got on the bus. Leon asked if they were friends of mine."

"Who is Leon?"

"The bus driver." She gripped the front of my raincoat. "Who are they?"

The white car was parked next to the van. This time, there were three men inside.

I handed Casey the camera and my cell phone. "I intend to find out who they are. You stay here. If I look like I'm in trouble, scream like bloody hell and dial 911."

"Okay."

Chip off the old block, Casey put the camera on her shoulder, aimed it at the white car, and started the tape.

A light drizzle fell. As I approached the white car, the driver snapped on his dome lights. It was a showy thing to do, something like training a single spotlight on a figure in the middle of a dark stage. The three men inside looked straight ahead until I was abreast of the driver's side door.

The driver turned his pale, close-cropped head on a thick-muscled neck and looked me over. Wordlessly, he challenged me with sun-faded eyes.

Fresh from the war zone, I thought, meeting his stare. I have seen soldiers when they come in off the field of battle. There is a stone-hard fierceness about them that time and adjustment to civilian life tempers. From the look of him, this man—maybe fifty, white squint lines etched across the corners of his flat cheekbones—he hadn't come in yet. But where was his war?

I felt off guard, because I had misjudged him. Or, rather, failed to really notice him. The scene in the marina restaurant had seemed buffoonery to me. Now I understood: He wanted my attention.

I rested one hand on the roof of the car and spoke down to him. "Did you want to speak with me?"

He winked at the man beside him before he answered. "I'm not much of a talker."

"I seem to see you everywhere I go. Now my daughter tells me she sees you, too. We could talk about stalking laws. Or you can tell me what it is you're up to."

"Stalking? Kind of full of yourself, aren't you? Why would we want to stalk *you*?"

"That's my question." I took one of the freeway pictures out of my pocket and flipped it into his lap. I lied: "The LAPD has the rest of them, and a videotape from the marina on Tuesday. Now, who are you?"

"I leave the heavy philosophical questions to my partner here." The driver dropped the picture into the lap of the man beside him. "So, Bowles, who *are* we?"

Bowles only shrugged as the third man leaned forward from the backseat, his round, pale face a sharp contrast to the leaner men on either side. He propped his forearm along the back of the driver's seat as if he wanted me to see the puffed, jagged scar that cut a path through his dark hair from his wrist up his biceps, disappearing under his sleeve. I recognized the challenge here, a warning maybe: He'd already survived something damned horrible. But when he looked up at me, he had long lashes that made him effeminate and ruined his air of malice. "Show the lady some ID, Elwood."

"Mrs. MacGowen?" Casey's dance teacher, Mr. Andreavich, was walking toward me. "Is there a problem?"

I heard the driver snicker. Mr. Andreavich had thrown on a short jacket over his flesh-colored leotards. He looked frankly ridiculous, less than imposing if I did have a problem. But dancers are formidable athletes. If I needed backup, Mr. Andreavich would be a good choice.

"We're okay," I said to him. "But if you don't mind, would you please keep Casey company for just a few minutes?"

Mr. Andreavich took another hard look at the men in the white car before he turned away to join Casey.

I said to the driver, "You were going to show me some ID."

"Sure." He flipped open a new-looking wallet and passed it to me. A not-quite-focused color photograph of the driver in the center, the signature of E. P. Dowd, Field Investigator, Department of Fish and Game, on the bottom.

I handed the wallet back. "Your mother had a sense of humor, Mr. Dowd."

The passenger said, "Who says he had a mother?"

"Whoever the hell you are," I said. "I don't want to see you around me or my family again. *Capisce?*"

"You won't see us unless you go fishing without a license." The passenger seemed to think it was a good joke. "Or poaching for rabbits."

Dowd started the car and began to back out. "Catch you later."

I walked back toward Casey, listening to the car's sounds, making sure it kept going away.

Casey walked up to meet me. "Who are they, Mom?"

"I wish I knew." I reached out my hand to Mr. Andreavich. "Thanks for being the cavalry. If you see those men or that car around again, I think you should call the police."

"Count on it," he said.

When Casey and I climbed into the van, simultaneously we hit the door locks.

I used the car phone to call Arlo, put it on the speaker so that I had both hands to drive. "Any more word on that car I gave you?"

"There's been a development, Maggie. You sure you gave me the right tag numbers?"

I pulled out the picture and read off the numbers to him.

"According to Hertz, those tags belong to a 1996 Celica. Green," he said. "The car was rented on a corporate account, and it was turned in this afternoon."

"I saw the car again, a white Ford, not five minutes ago."

"Did you happen to look at the tags?"

"No. I didn't look. I have a name for you to work on, though I have a very strong hunch it won't get you anywhere. Would you find out from the Department of Fish and Game if they have a field agent named E. P. Dowd on their roster? That's Elwood P. Dowd."

Arlo laughed. "This is a good sign, honey. I see your sense of humor is intact."

"I hope it is, Arlo. But I'm not kidding."

"Whatever you say. I'll make the calls. Just promise me, if they send the boys in white jackets after me that you'll come rescue me."

"Count on it."

I clicked off.

"What was that about?" Casey asked.

"The name's a phony. Elwood P. Dowd is a character in an old play. Dowd talks to an invisible rabbit named Harvey. Using the name is someone's idea of a joke. A bad joke."

We picked up Chinese take-out on our way home.

When I was first separated from Scotty, my father got into the habit of dropping by. First, he changed all the locks and put in superlong dead bolts. After that it was little things, like washers in the kitchen faucets and a new cord on an antique lamp. All he wanted was to know that Casey and I were all right. It was very dear of him.

That evening when Casey and I walked into the kitchen, shielding our take-out bags from the rain, my father and my Uncle Max were sitting at the table with a box of crackers and a brick of cheddar between them. Spread all over the table, under a dusting of cracker crumbs, was a sheaf of legal-sized documents.

My dad, tall and gangly, is best described as Ichabod Crane's better-looking brother. He wore professor-wear, a madras shirt with six pens in the breast pocket, good but old slacks, and soft-soled leather shoes.

Max, who is my father's much younger brother, must have been left by the stork at the wrong house. There is no resemblance I have ever discerned between Max and Dad. Where Dad is tall and angular, Max is short and round.

Max is extravagantly handsome and dark in a Gallic way; masses of rich brown hair sweeping down to thick, well-shaped brows. Still, they have a great deal in common. Most notably, their affection for one another.

"Dad?" I set the food on the counter. "Uncle Max? This is a surprise."

"We called," Dad said, reaching out an arm to draw Casey to him, raising his cheek for a smooch. "Talked to that cute little redhead over at the studio. I like that girl."

"Her name is Fergie," I said. "What did you tell her?"

"Max and I thought we might as well come on down. I know you said you were coming up this weekend. But I also know how that goes. Seventy-eight percent of the time you say you're coming, you get caught up in obligations and you can't leave town." Dad handed me a cracker with a triangle of cheese on it. "Max says the buyers want an answer right away on this offer for your house. So we brought the papers down. If you're going to make the right decision, Maggot, you need to take the time to read the fine print. Right, Max?"

"Hi, sweetheart." Max stood up to put his arms around me. He whispered in my ear, "Can a guy get a drink around here?"

"Sorry, no. Mike took everything out of the house. His father got into a situation last night, and Mike decided that as long as Oscar is staying here, we shouldn't have anything around to tempt him."

"I understand." In a stage whisper, imitating W. C. Fields, Max said, "I come all this way only to find there's a terrible drought." He reached for the jacket of his pinstripe suit and pulled a silver flask from the inside pocket, uncorked it, and took a long pull.

"You can wait until we get back to the hotel." Dad snatched the flask from Max, smelled the contents with a disapproving, prudish sneer on his face. Then he took a drag. "Good brandy. Is it mine?"

"Was until I claimed it." Max slipped the flask back into his jacket.

We went through a little family drill, I'm fine, you're fine, we're all fine, while Max gathered up the papers and I set the table for dinner.

Mike called on the phone. "Don't wait dinner. Michael and I are taking Pop to see this halfway house in Reseda. If it's okay, he'll stay there tonight."

"And if it isn't okay?"

After a pause, Mike said, "Trona. I'll drive him up tomorrow. Got Shannon out of the way, and now this happens. I don't know what it will do to the San Francisco trip. I don't want you to be alone."

"I'd hardly be alone," I said. "Casey, Guido, Lana, and a whole film crew will be there with me. But I hate to go without you. Let's put the trip off, Mike. My dad tells me that seventy-eight percent of the time we cancel out on him, so we'll merely be upholding precedent."

"Where did he get seventy-eight percent?"

"Made it up."

"Reminds me. Fergie called. Your dad is flying down."

"He's here now."

Mike chuckled. "Have fun. See you later."

Casey counted place settings. "Where's Guido?"

"He went to check on his house," I said. "If the house is standing, he'll stay there."

She looked disappointed. "Did he take his cats?"

"Not yet."

She smiled. "I think Bowser likes the cats."

I sighed. I could say, Don't bring home any kittens. But it would do no good.

Over Chinese food, Max outlined the offer on my house.

"It's solid, Maggie. The buyer deposited an earnest money check, and it cleared the bank. Top Standard and Poor and Dunn & Bradstreet ratings. If you want to sell, I don't think you'll do better. The only catch may be the short closing." He reached for the soy sauce. "Think you'll be ready to let go in thirty days?"

I turned to Casey. "What do you think about selling our house?"

She studied me. "It'll be okay to sell, Mom. We like it here with Mike and Michael. I know what Mike says about moving into the woods when he retires. But he isn't going anywhere until Michael graduates. And that's two years away, if Michael graduates on time."

"She's a wise child," Dad said. "Listen to her."

"And another thing." Casey pushed aside the bowl of rice that was between us. "Michael says that if Mike gets Oscar into a good rehab, it'll cost so much that Mike won't be able to retire as long as Oscar lives."

Dad raised his eyebrows, looked worried. "Is that true, Maggie?"

It was true. Mike's pension, which would be roughly half his LAPD salary, would barely cover his agreed-to share of Michael's tuition and his own groceries. And then only if Michael continued to live at home. Oscar had never been factored into the budget before.

I thought of my own situation if I left the shelter of a network contract: Casey's tuition, our health insurance, rent—I looked at Dad—my own parents, possibly, in the future.

Lana had been pressuring me to extend my contract and do another set of documentaries. Next time she brought it up, I would ask her to draw paperwork.

My dad reached his long arm across the table and took my hand. "Maggot?"

I squeezed his hand. "Okay, Max. Give me the bottom line. After sales costs and the mortgage payoff, what will I have?"

"You planning to buy a replacement home within twenty-four months, or are you going to pay the capital gains?"

"Give it to me both ways." I looked at the columns of figures Max had computed and groaned. "Mike should be here."

Dad contributed, "You should marry that boy. Think of the tax savings."

Casey said, "If we rent again, can I still get a cat?"

The only time since my divorce that I was ever glad to hear Scotty's voice was right there after the cat comment. Actually, I would have been glad to speak with anyone. But it was Scotty who called and interrupted things.

"You were going to get back to me about dinner tonight," he said.

"It can't be tonight. I have guests. But here's the scoop you wanted." I repeated to him the offer as Max had presented it to me. "You need to do better than merely match what is already on the bargaining table. These people have deposited nine percent in earnest money."

"I'll need a little time to put a package together."

"You have twenty-four hours," I said.

"All right." Sounded like a poker bluff, but he wasn't folding. "Dinner tomorrow then. I'll have my offer together. Pick you up at seven?"

I shuddered to think of being closed in a car with him. "I'll meet you."

He named a restaurant at the far end of Monterey

Drive, down near the Arroyo Seco—translation, the big, dry ditch—and said he would make reservations for seven. He also said he was looking forward to it.

"Here's Casey," I said, and handed her the phone.

I couldn't talk Dad and Max into staying the night with us. If we'd had anything to drink, Max might have. But Dad is always very reticent to stay at anyone's house except his own much past the dinner hour, unless there's a bridge game. If he felt more comfortable staying in a hotel, then it was fine with me.

After good-night kisses, Max asked what time they should come for breakfast.

By nine o'clock, Casey and I had the house to ourselves.

We were sitting in front of the television and I was making a French braid in her long hair when she said, "Are we going to sell our house?"

"What do you want to do?"

"Well, if you had wanted to sell it last year right when we moved down here, I would have been all, like, don't do it. But we're here and it's pretty much the bomb. I mean, when you think how the renter-people have trashed the house in one year, well, what could they do after two years? Kelp in the bathtub. I mean, how gross. Good thing they moved out."

"Exactly my sentiments. But I miss looking out at the ocean, hearing the foghorns at night. No smog. Good public transportation."

"And tourists everywhere all the time up there. It's not like you can ever just go for a walk on the beach by yourself. Or swim in the water, because it's too cold and too rough. All you can do in San Francisco is, like, look at the water. Down here you can actually go into the water."

"I miss being able to drop by and see Grandma and Grandpa."

"As if they're ever not here, Mom."

"You're right." I took the rubber band she was holding and wrapped it around the end of her braid. "Anyway, we're not going anywhere for at least two years. Not until you and Michael are ready to fly the nest."

She leaned back against me and pulled my arms around her. I couldn't see over her head.

"So, Mom. You going to marry Mike?"

"What? And live in the woods for the rest of my life? I don't think so."

She laughed, the wise child.

Oscar came home with Mike and we made him a bed again on the living room sofa. Mike seemed dispirited. When we were upstairs in our room, he told me about the rehab facility he had visited in Reseda.

"I couldn't leave my dad there." Mike looked drained. "It was clean, but that's the best I can say. Marginal neighborhood. The food was all starch. He has diabetes, he wouldn't last long on macaroni and white bread. The brochure says there's a counselor on staff, but it's a grad student trying to build up clinical hours. Drops by three times a week. Dad would chew him up and spit him out. Four men to a small room, can't take any of his own furniture. Difficult cases they put in restraints."

"You think Trona will be better?"

"It has to be. I know two guys who have their fathers there. He'd have a private room and his own TV. No place is perfect, but I want Dad to keep some dignity. I worry that Trona is so far away—six hours in the car." He puts his head in his hands. "So damned expensive."

"Look at this." I sat down on the bed beside him and held out Max's figures.

He looked them over, nodding approval. "If you accept, you'll be set. You'll have money for Casey's college so you can quit the network and go do your own films again."

"Michael said that if Oscar goes to Trona, you won't be able to retire."

"Not for a while."

"Can you live with that? How many more days can you spend with Shannon and Tina and Pen before you lose it?"

"I've done it for twenty-five years. I can do it for a few more."

"Don't re-up right away. Don't sign anything." I put the paper with all the dollar signs into his hand. "We can take care of Oscar."

He seemed confused at first, then he thrust the paper back into my hand. "Forget it. This is your money, Maggie. I can't take any of it."

"Give me a break." I straddled his lap and pushed him over backward, pinning his shoulders to the bed, kissed his face, his neck, opened his shirt and kissed his chest. "And you don't have to pay me back. I'll just take it out in trade."

Chapter 17

Friday morning, the kitchen of our house could have passed for a neighborhood diner.

Max and Dad were knocking on the back door just as I stumbled downstairs for my first cup of coffee. Mike came in from his morning run a few minutes later.

"Beautiful day," Mike said by way of greeting.

"How do you know?" I yawned, taking mugs out of the cupboard. "The sun is hardly up."

"I saw patches of blue in the sky. Maybe it's going to clear up for us." He planted a sweaty kiss on the back of my neck. "Boy, am I hungry."

I counted mouths to feed—no one had been to the market all week. There was a box of Bisquick in the pantry and milk and eggs in the refrigerator. I said, "Pancakes?"

"Don't put yourself to the trouble." Mike excused himself to go shower, taking his coffee with him.

Max put his hand against my back and pressed, impelling me toward the door. "You go get dressed, Maggot. Daddums and I don't have anything better to do. We'll make breakfast."

I was the last one down. Michael was carrying extra chairs into the kitchen from the dining room. He grinned at me. "Morning. Welcome to Denny's. How many in your party?"

Someone had put the leaf in the kitchen table to make room for everyone. Mike and Dad sat together at the laundry room end, the house documents sharing space with their dishes. Casey had the morning paper. Oscar was upright, barely, clutching a cup of coffee with shaking hands.

Guido had dropped by to check on his cats, and had brought Lana with him. Like everyone else, they had stacks of pancakes in front of them.

"Good morning, all," I said, pushing a chair into the gap between Mike and Lana. "What's up?"

"Good morning." Lana, way too hyper for the hour after dawn, pushed a wedge of pancake from one side of her plate to the other. "You look well."

"Sit down, sit down." Max set a plate in front of me. "Eat and be amazed. Someone named Connie called and said she's having car trouble so she'll be a few minutes late."

"Khanh." I kissed his cheek. "Thanks."

"Plane leaves at noon for San Francisco." Guido spoke around a mouthful. "Our bags are in the car. The crew will meet us at the airport. Are you coming with us?"

"Not at noon today." I poured myself some juice. "Maybe tomorrow morning. Khanh's coming over, and I'm hoping she'll agree to talk about Bao Ngo on camera. If she does, that segment of the film will be pretty much set, don't you think? I have all of Mike's little torture killers on tape now. We still need some filler. You get good background stuff this weekend, and we'll be ready to start a rough edit the first of next week."

"Wonderful," Lana said. She drizzled syrup on her pancakes. I had yet to see her put anything into her mouth. "I have such great expectations for this project."

"Yeah," was Guido's gratuitous response to her. He turned to me. "I don't have to go today. Want me to stay and give you a hand with Khanh?"

"Thanks, but I think she'll be more likely to talk openly if we're alone."

Guido thought hard about something. "We can go back to plan A and film the Tet parade in Little Saigon. We don't have to go to San Francisco. Save a lot of money and effort if we don't."

"Bite your tongue, Patrini." Lana swatted at him. "We're going. You've both promised me one hell of a party. As close as the West Coast gets to Mardi Gras, you told me, and I do not intend to miss it. Especially not if you think I can be impressed by frugality. It's my budget, and that's the last I want to hear about staying home."

I was just saying, "More coffee?" to Lana when there was a loud crack outside that made everyone jump.

"What the hell?" Lana bolted to her feet.

"No, she doesn't want more coffee," Guido said.

"Just kids." Mike reclipped the stack of documents, reached back and set them on the dryer. He looked at me. "It's a good offer."

Lana was still juiced. "Mike, what was that noise? Shouldn't you go out and look? It sounded like gunfire."

"What? You want me to go out there and get shot, Lana?" He laughed. "It's just the Lunar New Year bang-up. Kids get their hands on firecrackers and can't wait until the party to shoot them off."

"Wait till you get to San Francisco, Lana," Casey said. "Like, if that little firecracker bothered you, you'd better take ear plugs."

Max chimed in with, "I think Halloween in the Castro District is closer to Mardi Gras than Tet is."

"Never been to Mardi Gras," Dad offered.

Mike reached for the pancake platter. "Yesterday, I saw a guy on the street in Chinatown selling cherry bombs and bottle rockets to kids. Big ones, M-80s. There's a uniformed cop standing right there on the corner, and he doesn't do a damn thing about it."

Casey perked up. "Did you buy me some, Mike?"

"No, I did not buy you some." He took some pancakes and passed her the platter. "People who live in wooden houses shouldn't fool around with firecrackers. Firecrackers aren't just illegal, they're dangerous."

Casey imitated his know-it-all tone. "If you don't let people have firecrackers during Tet, they shoot off their guns into the air. In San Francisco, everyone has firecrackers."

"San Francisco burned to the ground once before, Miss Wiseacre, Junior," he said, grinning at her. "You think it can't happen again?"

"Take your pick, Mike," she said. "It's either firecrackers or accidental lobotomies."

Lana, head bobbing like a tennis match spectator, turned to me. "Aren't they precious?"

"Just darling," I said. She seemed tense. Family life was foreign turf for my boss.

Mike appealed to me. "Who runs the show up there? Is no one in charge?"

"The trains run on time. Isn't that enough?" I thought, and not for the first time, that no matter what he said, retirement would not settle easily on Mike. During all his twenty-five years on the streets, I doubted whether Mike ever stood by passively when there was something happening that he could meddle with. I asked him, with a sort of dread, "Did you say anything to the Chinatown cop?"

"I wanted to say, Get a haircut. The back of his hair almost touched his collar. What is going on when the department lets foot patrol cops wear shorts and Reeboks? Long hair, soft shoes, fat guts. Every one of those guys should be beefed for being out of uniform."

I stood to kiss the top of his well-trimmed head. "The good news is, Mike, come May, firecrackers and fat-bellied cops are someone else's problem."

Michael spoke for the first time. "Unless they burn the house down."

Lana checked her watch, and then she scraped back her chair and rose. The food on her plate had been skillfully arranged to look like table scraps, but I knew that not one bite was missing. I watched my daughter's eye follow that plate and then slide to Lana's skinny behind, and I worried, not for the first time, about the powerful message she might get from it. Ballerinas and Hollywood career women share the same horror: getting fat.

"We should be going." Pointedly, Lana said, "Guido, did you have some business to take care of?"

"Right." Guido picked up his plate. "Michael, you're staying home all weekend?"

"Yeah. I'll be around."

"Would you mind looking after George and Gracie until Sunday night?"

"Sure." Michael shrugged. "No problem. What do I do?"

"Just feed them, one can each in the morning. I already took care of the litter box. Thanks, Michael." Guido stood. "Business taken care of, Lana. Ready when you are."

She seemed annoyed, but kept smiling. "Mike, Maggie, please excuse us. Sorry to run, but I have a meeting to take before we fly out, a conference call with New York. Breakfast was fabulous."

Lana pushed in her chair. Instead of leaving, she hovered, stalled, looking so uncomfortable that I expected her to lower the boom, say something like, Breakfast was fabulous and by the way, you're fired.

She said, "Guido, you can't leave without saying good-bye to George and Gracie."

This was an obvious dismissal. She didn't want to drop her bomb in front of a colleague. Guido, after a pregnant hesitation, excused himself. But his were the only pair of eyes that left the room.

All of us watched her, waited for her to get up courage. In the time it took her, I decided that being fired wasn't necessarily a bad thing. We could live off the proceeds from the house for a while. Then we'd think of something.

Finally, after a deep, reedy breath, Lana said, "Maggie, would you mind stepping into the next room with me?"

"I think I would mind, Lana. Anything you have to say to me, my family should hear."

"If you wish." She looked at every face at the table, including Oscar's. "I am absolutely forbidden to leak any hint of this, so I beg you all—I implore you—to keep it to yourselves. Not a word, even to Guido. Promise?"

A chorus: "Promise."

"The network is putting together a new package to offer you, Maggie. Carte blanche. Content control, artistic freedom."

"And the catch?" I asked.

"They want a long-term commitment."

She went on about how maternal she felt about my network projects to date, but I didn't hear much after long-term. I watched Mike watch me.

"I don't need a decision now," she said, winding down. "I just want you to begin thinking."

From the next room, Guido called out. "Is it safe to come back now?"

"It's safe," Lana called back.

There was a round of air kissing and they were gone.

Michael broke the silence they left in their wake. "Well, well."

"Interesting confluence of events." Dad cleared Lana's and Guido's plates from the table. "Does this offer help you make up your mind about the house, Maggot?"

I was watching Mike. I said, "How long do you think long-term means?"

"She said, total freedom."

"We need to talk," I said.

He nodded. Then he put a hand on Oscar's shoulder. "We're not in a hurry to head out, are we, Pop?"

Oscar, red-eyed and pale, shook his head. "Anytime, son. Anytime."

"Last call for pancakes." Max slung a dish towel over his shoulder and squirted dish soap into the sink. "I'm ready to clean the skillet."

Dad took the butter dish from my hand. "Your mother asked me to ask you whether you had any objections if she redid your old bedroom."

"My bedroom in the Berkeley house?" I was puzzled. "Of course not."

"She thought that if you sold your house you might need to know you still had a room."

"Paint the room, Dad."

Casey leaned toward Mike. "Lyle is moving into Mom's old room at Grandma's house, you know." Lyle had been our San Francisco housemate. Now he lived with my parents.

Mike leaned in and met her, nose to nose. "I don't think your mom needs her old room anymore."

"It's Mom's museum," Casey said. "Lyle will rip down her Jim Morrison posters."

Mike's turn to scoff: "Jim Morrison?"

"I've seen your baseball cards," I said. "And your little cigar box shrine to Mickey Mantle."

"Damn right." Mike puffed up a bit, girding his loins for the offensive. "The Mickster was a genuine, red-blooded American hero. For you to in any way compare him to a needle-freaking, rock-and-rolling lunatic like Jim Morrison is worse than farting in church. Jeez, Maggie, I'm surprised your parents let you hang his posters. What sort of role model was he? OD'd before he was thirty."

"The Mickster OD'd, too, big guy." I took a handful of Mike's shirt front. "His drug of choice just took longer."

"Mom, may I be excused?" Casey had already gathered her share of breakfast dishes and deposited them on the sink. She was headed for the door before I could say, "You may," an answer as ritualistic as the question had been. With three long strides she was through the door.

"What's your schedule for the day?" I called after her.

"Stuff."

"What stuff? What are you doing after school?"

"I told Madame I would talk to her senior classes about the academy in Houston. Alyssum has her mother's car today. We're all going to the mall and maybe rent a movie. If we aren't flying up north until tomorrow, I might sleep over at Rachel's. I'll call you."

"Curfew is . . ."

"I know. I know." I heard her feet hit the stairs, her

recitation receding as she went up. "I know the drill. Don't talk to strangers. Use the buddy system. Grandpa, are you ready?"

"Ready," Dad called out. He fished keys out of his pocket. "Volunteered for chariot duty. I'll help you with the dishes, Max, when I get back."

"Miss Wiseacre, Junior." Mike was watching me again.

I said, "What's keeping Khanh?"

Mike stacked his plate atop the pancake platter and handed it to Max. "So, Khanh's visit is a business meeting?"

"Turned into one," I said. "Started as a holiday visit. We used to go to their house for the big Tet meal every year—I met Nguyen Cao Ky there once. Remember him? The flyboy vice president of South Vietnam. If you're lucky, Khanh's bringing us spring rolls."

"As long as she doesn't bring Nguyen Cao Ky." Ever skeptical. "What's your schedule for today?"

"Talk to Khanh. I've sent a crew down to shoot the park, the house, and the school where Pedro spent his last day. I should check on them, but I don't have to."

"Ever seen Trona?"

"No." I put my hand against his cheek. "But I've always wanted to. I can be ready by noon."

We heard sirens in the distance. Oscar perked up. "That police or fire, Mikey?"

"Can't tell, too far away."

I said, "Maybe some long-haired cop is going to hammer a kid for possession of illegal firecrackers."

"You can only hope." He yawned. "Feel like taking a walk?"

"Sure," I said. I glanced at the mantel clock. "As soon as Khanh leaves."

"Why don't you two go ahead?" Max opened the dishwasher. "I'll wait for Khanh and keep her entertained, if you'll take the dog with you. He's been underfoot all morning, driving me nuts."

I actually hadn't seen Bowser all day. I looked out

the back door and spotted him sleeping on the patio in a patch of sunlight.

"Good idea, Max," I said. If Khanh came on the most direct route from San Marino, I thought, she would probably pass us. If not, well, Max would be good company for her.

When we stepped out the front door, Bowser pulled at the leash for a few paces until he got the message that we weren't going for our usual run. He quickly settled into an easy saunter, checking constantly to make sure Mike and I were still with him. We walked over to Fremont Avenue and headed north toward the mountains, thinking we would browse through a bookstore on Mission and pick up some fruit on the way home for the drive to the desert.

There was some blue showing among the dark clouds hanging low overhead, but the air was cold and heavy. The mountains that rose above the north end of the city wore a dense blanket. The forecast said snow above four thousand feet.

Mike zipped up the front of his windbreaker when we faced into the breeze. "Is Lana true to her word?"

"As television industry promises go, she's better than average. I'll wait to see what the network comes up with, but it could be a good gig, Mike." I looped my arm through his and used him as a windbreak. "At least for a couple of years. Give you time to figure out what your next career is going to be.

"And I've been thinking about it," I said. "As much as I complain when I'm answerable to other people, at least I'm working. Arts funding has dried up so much in the last couple of years that it's scary out there. When I see how many of my colleagues are making commercials and instructional films or doing completely unrelated jobs altogether, I realize how cushy my slot is."

His eyes were narrow. "What's this 'next career' shit?"

"The closest you're going to get to living in the woods for a long time is hanging out in a tree nursery."

He said, "Whatever you say," but his focus had shifted away from me to what at first looked like a street fair up ahead, complete with a light show and streamers. A crowd packed the sidewalk, shopkeepers clustered in their doorways, talking. The general low murmur of voices said this was not a happy carnival.

"Maybe that was no firecracker we heard," I said.

"Doesn't look like it." Mike reined Bowser in close beside him. Black-and-white police cars with lights flashing blocked Fremont Avenue where it intersected with Mission. Yellow crime scene tape marked off a patch of sidewalk and festooned an empty city bus standing with its doors hanging open.

I said, "I only heard one siren."

"Once the guy's dead, there's no emergency." Mike tried not to let on, but he was plenty curious, as I was.

Through gaps in the mass of dark blue uniforms and gray suits inside the taped perimeter, I saw a small, covered mound lying on the sidewalk. Too tiny to be Casey; an automatic reaction.

A couple of days a week, Casey caught the bus at that corner. But Casey had gone to school with her grandfather that morning. The message Max delivered to me from Khanh said nothing about her taking the bus. That's why the size of the body rang no alarms once I decided that it could not be my daughter; something like having no available disk space.

I pulled on Mike's hand. "Let's walk around the block the other way." But Mike had begun moving in closer. "Busman's holiday," I said, keeping up with effort, grousing all the way because I did not want to go down there. "You can't stay away, can you, Mike? You have to tell the South Pasadena Police Department how it should be done?"

"Not hardly." His attention was on the crowd, not the crime scene. He studied the ever-shifting throng of curious neighbors with method, section by section. I leaned in to him, trying to define his field of vision.

Our next-door neighbor, Steve Lesick, emerged from

the cluster of people watching from the sidewalk patio of a cappuccino bar. Steve was somewhere in his seventies, a big, barrel-chested man, a retired schoolteacher, an old navy man. The bamboo cane he needed to walk uphill in no way diminished his air of command.

"Mike, Maggie," Steve said, extending his hand to Mike. "Hell of a note, isn't it?"

"What happened?" Mike asked, his eye drawn to the coroner's van coming from the direction of the freeway.

"Random shooting, it looks like. Fred at the dry cleaners says he thinks it's a little girl. He saw it happen out of the corner of his eye. Says the gal was just stepping off the bus when he heard the gunshot, and then he saw her go down."

Steve snapped his fingers. "Just like that, Fred said. Boom, and she fell. Never had a chance. Didn't even have time to scream. Fred was the one who called 911. He's over there talking to the detectives now."

"It sounded like a firecracker," I said. "We heard it."

"I heard it, too," he said. "This time of year, we hear all sorts of racket, don't we? I was out front waiting for my ride; Friday is my day to tutor English as a Second Language up at Para los Ninos. All the years I've lived in this neighborhood, I never thought I'd see anything like this. Never. This is right up your line, Flint. What's your opinion?"

"You said, little girl?"

"That's how Fred saw it."

Mike still had me by the hand and he tugged it gently as a signal that he was ready to go. "I think we should stay out of the way and let these people do their work."

I said, without putting much thought into it, "Steve, bring Phyllis by for a drink one evening next week."

"A drink?" Steve gave my shoulder a paternal pat. "A drink of milk, maybe. Phyllis tells me congratulations are in order, dear."

I felt Mike's reaction, an almost painful squeeze on my hand like sharing a bolt of lightning.

"I'll call Phyllis," I said, and, huddled closer to Mike, walked on down the street.

Mike put his arm around me, dropped his head close to mine. "Who all did you tell?"

"No one. Just family. Amazing how news travels. I hope the grapevine sends out an update, because I don't like bearing bad news and I hate fielding sympathy."

"Mizzes MacGowen?" A uniformed officer, excruciatingly young, stopped us before we had gone far. Beside him was a plainclothesman. "Remember me? Clayton Terrell. I walked Casey home from the bus a couple of times."

"Oh sure, Clayton," I lied. I thought he was too young for a uniform until he said he knew Casey. If he was in uniform, he was way too old for her. "How are you?"

"Fine, thank you."

My God, he was solicitous. I'd had no idea there were so many people who were familiar with Casey's daily routines. Maybe it was time for Casey to start driving herself to school.

"I'm assigned to the neighborhood, routine street patrol," Clayton said. "Homicide asked me to give them a hand this morning because this is my 'hood, so to speak. Detective Mareno here wants a word with you. Detective, this is the Maggie I told you about."

I said, "Hello," shaking the hand Mareno extended. He was a tall, dark, bald man with a beak nose and a protruding Adam's apple: the Scarecrow in a cheap gray suit. I began to feel queasy, stole another look at the bundle on the sidewalk, but it was still just too small to be Casey.

Clayton dropped back a pace to direct sidewalk traffic away from us.

"Mrs. MacGowen," Mareno repeated formally. "People call you Maggie?"

"Everyone but my mother," I said, queasiness giving way to something stronger, more like borderline panic.

Mareno made a note on a form clamped on his clipboard. He glanced up and pointed the end of his pen Mike's way. "You Mr. MacGowen?"

"Only the dog here qualifies for that honor," Mike said, the flash of a wry smile creasing his cheek briefly. "Neighbor says a little girl was hit."

"A female, yes," Mareno said. "We have tentative identification on the victim; now we're trying to determine what her business at this location might have been." Mareno talked while he secured the edge of a plastic evidence bag to his clipboard. There was a slip of paper inside the bag. "Officer Terrell suggested the possibility that you might be able to help us understand the significance of this list."

A list of errands with eight stops. The first item was Maggie, the second was a bakery in Chinatown. The last was Los Angeles airport to meet a 2:15 flight. As soon as I saw the scribbled note, I knew, and so did Mike.

"Jesus," he said.

"Khanh Nguyen," I said, though I could hardly get the name out of my mouth. My relief that Casey had been spared curdled instantly into guilt. "Khanh was coming to see me."

"What was the purpose of her visit?" he asked.

"We're friends. I thought that she was probably dropping off something. Holiday goodies of some kind."

"Presents?" Mareno asked.

"Tokens of affection," I said.

Mareno had a second plastic bag to show me, this one containing an untidy tissue-wrapped lump about the size of my thumb, with *Maggie* written in pencil on one side. If this were meant to be a present, Khanh hadn't gone to her usual trouble with fancy wrappings. I reached out and squeezed the lump. Hard as a rock.

"Recognize it?" he asked.

"No," I said.

"Any ideas?"

"None."

Mike edged forward. "Any reason you can't give Maggie a look inside? Might move this line of questions forward."

Mareno studied Mike before he gave a little shrug of his narrow shoulders. "Can't see why not."

It was awkward business, juggling the clipboard while trying to unwrap the little package without tearing any of its tissue paper. When he was finished, Mareno said, "Hold out your hand."

Into my open palm, Mareno placed a cold piece of translucent white jade that was carved into the shape of a dancing woman. She was a tease. Bare-breasted, smiling wickedly, she had one leg raised as if poised for flight.

"Ring any bells?" Mareno asked.

"In a way, yes," I said. "I saw similar figures in a museum catalogue yesterday. Looks to me like a Vietnamese temple dancer. An apsaras, it's called."

Mike cupped my hand and raised it so that he could get a better look. "Cute," was all he said.

Mareno eyed Mike. He said, "I didn't get your name."

"Flint. Mike Flint."

"Your relationship to the deceased?"

"She poured me tea once." Mike looked up from the little figure to Mareno's angular face. "How do you see this shooting going down?"

"On first look, it could be a drive-by or a stray bullet," Mareno said. "Maybe, maybe not. A lot of people have guns, too many people use them, especially this time of year. Any ideas what the victim might have been involved in?"

"Khanh Nguyen," I said again because it offended me when he referred to her as the victim. She had a name. I told him about the raid on Khanh's house and spelled Bao Ngo for him. I still had the picture of the white car's license in my coat pocket from the day before. I gave that to him, too. I told him about the restaurant Khanh and Sam owned, and about their four children coming into the city for Tet. And about how I had met her through my former husband. Just about there, I started to lose it.

Mareno gave me a minute to get control again before

he asked, "Why did a restaurant owner need a high-power lawyer like Scott MacGowen?"

"Because this world is a complicated place to navigate," I said. I found an old tissue in my pocket. "Ask Sam."

Poor Sam. I felt hit hard. Khanh, dead? Mike was again patting my back.

"When you think about what Khanh survived—she spent her whole lifetime in a war zone until she came here. And this is how she dies, stepping off a bus?"

Both Mike and Mareno mumbled platitudes: Fate, you never know when your time will come, at least she didn't suffer. What was there to say? What could I possibly say to Sam?

Mareno gave me time to collect myself when I choked up, but he was still all business. Hawklike, he never took his little black eyes off either of us. A good detective, I thought, reserving my estimation of the man. After a few quiet moments, he zoomed his beady eye on me. "Are you with me?"

"I'm all right," I said.

"Glad to hear it, because I'm going to ask you to do something that's just damned hard for anyone, even us old vets." He took a deep breath. "The toughest part of my job is notification of next of kin. It's a visit I never have the heart to make. Before I do it, I want to make sure the message is an accurate one, because I don't want to deliver grief, then have to take it back. I'd sure appreciate having a visual verification of the victim's identity from you."

"You want me to look at Khanh?"

"Think you can handle it?"

I was never Khanh Nguyen's best friend. It did not feel right for me to be the one to make a formal identification. I agreed to do it, though, because I needed to make sure for myself.

Mareno looked at Mike, expecting, probably, some protest. He got none.

Young Officer Terrell reached for the dog's leash.

"Let me walk Bowser home. He doesn't need to be down there."

Bowser was confused at first when Mike handed over the leash, but he went with Terrell, with his tail between his legs. Maybe he remembered Terrell, who knew him by name.

Mike and I walked up to Mission Street with Mareno parting the crowd in our path. The procession was uncomfortable for me. Every shopkeeper and neighbor that we passed tried to pump us. "What did the police say to you, Maggie? Mike, who was it? What is this world coming to?" Beyond morbid curiosity, they showed real anger that their peace and well-being had been violated, as well as relief that, this time, the victim was not them or theirs. I could only respond with a shake of the head or a passing touch of the hand. It was not enough. I knew there would be phone calls and visits all day long.

Mareno squatted beside the covered body and raised the drape away from the face. I thought it was odd that he kept his eyes averted from the corpse. Just the same, proximity made him pale, made sweat glisten on his shiny dome. I was afraid the old vet, as he called himself, would pass out on us before the task was done. Mike, on the other hand, knelt right down close and leaned in.

Khanh did not leave this life with peace in her heart. Her face was frozen in terror, her eyes bulged, her mouth drew back for a scream she never had time to deliver. Maybe she died before she felt the bullet. But she certainly had time to know what was going to happen.

I stood behind Mareno, making him a buffer between me and my friend's remains.

"No question," I said. "This is Khanh Nguyen."

"You're certain?" Mareno asked.

"I'm certain."

"Thank you." He had to wait for Mike to get out of the way before he could recover her.

Mareno stepped away, put his back to us and Khanh, and got busy writing a field report of our conversation.

I whispered to Mike. "What did you see?"

"Through and through head wound. Went in over her left eye, blew out the back. Like Steve said, she must have been standing just about the bottom step of the bus when she got hit." Discreetly, he pointed. "The open door caught most of the spatter, but the bullet continued through into the side of the bus. I can see daylight through the hole. Whatever is left of the bullet is probably loose inside the bus."

I felt my breakfast rise. Khanh's blood, bits of shattered skull, her brain, sprayed the Plexiglas window in the open door and blew past its edges, leaving a long, stenciled frame of deep maroon around the bullet hole.

"Gunman was probably right there at the corner." Mike went on, defining the bullet's path. "If it was my case, I wouldn't let all these shop owners hang out here swapping lies with the locals. Their testimony will be polluted before they give it."

I heard irregular breathing behind me, sounded like impending hyperventilation, and turned. A big man wearing a Southern California Rapid Transit District bus driver's blue uniform held on to a utility pole. He stared at Khanh's covered body with eyes that did not seem to focus. If black men can turn white as a ghost, he had.

"You okay?" I asked, walking over to him. The name embroidered over his shirt pocket said *Leon*.

"I don't know." Leon hardly had breath to speak. "I just don't know."

"Were you driving the bus?" I asked.

When he nodded, his eyes began to stream. "I been held up seven times. I been hit in the face and stabbed in the back. I been vomited on more times than I want to count. But I never saw nothing like this before, not since I did my time in Vietnam." He added a syllable, Vi-Et-Nay-Yam, turning one word into a whole paragraph of distress and anger.

"Pretty rough." Mike moved in closer. "How do you see it going down?"

"I didn't. The little lady, she ax me for a transfer, and

I give her one. Then she goes to get off and I'm turned the other way, scoping out the traffic coming up on my left side, you know, seeing where my slot is going to be. I see it. I got my signal on. As soon as the passenger is away, I'm going to slide in. I hear the pop, I turn my head, and she is already down. I think at first she fell on the step, and I'm going to spend all the rest of the day filling out forms. Then I see all the blood."

Leon tweezed a bit of his trouser fabric between his thumb and index finger, showing us a spray of tiny brown flecks.

"You know what this is?" He sucked in air, his pallor changed to a vivid flush beneath his dark skin. "This is the lady's blood."

I was afraid he would faint. He was a big man and I knew I couldn't hold him if he went. But he wiped his face on his sleeve and composed himself. After he drew a long breath, he smiled at me.

"I know you," he said. "You're Casey's mom."

I said, alarmed, "How do you know Casey?"

"She rides my bus all the time. How's she doin'?"

"She's fine." I was nonplussed. What happened to the Don't talk to strangers drill?

"She still dancin', isn't she?" he said.

"Still dancing."

"She get that part she wanted in that show she auditioned for?"

"I don't know if she got the part she wanted, but she got a part."

"Well, good for her. I'm not much for ballet, but I've never seen a six-foot-tall ballerina before. Maybe I'll have to go and see her."

"Please do. A dancer needs an audience."

"Your girl is real proud of you." Leon smiled, began to look like a survivor. "Those movies you make? She always tells me when to be watching for them on the TV. I like that one about the old people best. *Aged and Alone* it was. I started calling my mother every single day after I saw that."

I think I probably blushed. I have long considered my

years in front of the camera as a sort of purgatory I had to suffer through before I earned the right to hide behind the lens. I don't like being recognized by strangers. It scares me.

"Nice to meet you, Leon." I offered my hand. "I'm Maggie. This is Mike."

We three were old friends in a big hurry. Leon was telling Mike how I sometimes followed Casey from a distance to make sure she got safely on her bus, when Mareno remembered us. He passed me his hand-written field report, asked me to check it for accuracy and then to sign it.

Mike read over my shoulder and made some corrections—my name is not short for Margaret, for one thing—told me to initial the changes, and to leave no space between the last word Mareno had written and my signature.

When I handed the clipboard back to Mareno, he listed Clayton Terrell, Leon Williams, and Mike Flint in the spaces labeled "others present." After he crossed the *T* in Flint he paused with his pen over the page and thought something over. Absently, an aid to memory I suppose, he reached back and grabbed enough of the sparse hair that straggled over his collar to make a stub of a ponytail. Then, slowly, he turned his head and settled his dark hawk's eye on Mike. He said, "Occupation?"

"Civil servant," Mike said. "Almost retired civil servant."

"Age?" The way Mareno said the word, it sounded like an accusation.

"You have a space on the F.R. for the age of every also-present on the street? I don't think so."

"You're young to be retiring," Mareno said.

Mike ran a hand down the side of his craggy cheek. "I'm old enough. When are you eligible?"

"Two years ago," Mareno said, suddenly chummy, a colleague, a brother in blue, as it were. He had outed Mike. "I have twenty-seven years on the job. And you?"

"In sixty-five more days on the job, I'll have my twenty-five."

"Mike Flint, huh?" Mareno wore a tooth-sucking grin as he gave Mike a careful going-over. "LAPD. I know who you are. Anything you want to contribute, Detective Flint?"

"Yeah," Mike said. "One thing. Get the guy."

Chapter 18

"Do you have to take Oscar out to Trona today?"

A sudden rain, whipped by a bitter wind, pelted our backs as we walked toward home.

"The sooner the better," Mike said. "Pop can behave himself for only so long."

"But he's been great, Mike. One more day won't make a difference, will it?"

"When he wants a drink, one more minute is too long." Mike shielded his eyes with his hand. From the rain or from me? "You don't understand how it is."

"If you can wait until Mareno finishes with me, I still want to go with you. He said it would take a couple of hours to go through the mug shot books."

"It's late already. I should have headed out first thing this morning." He checked his watch. "Staying clean over Friday night might be asking too much of Pop."

As it turned out, staying clean all of Friday morning was asking too much. I don't know when Oscar slipped out of the house and bought his booze, but he was loaded by the time we got back home at just past ten-thirty.

"Mikey, boy." Oscar, so quiet at breakfast, had come to life. "Had a little accident in the other room. But don't you worry about it. I'll get it fixed right up. Hey, honey, Mikey ever tell you about the body shop I had me? Nice place. It was a real nice place, wasn't it, Mikey?"

"Until the law shut you down." Mike peeked into my workroom, sighed, closed the door. "Where'd you get the money for booze, Pop?"

Oscar furrowed his brow. "I musta dropped my wallet. I went inside there looking for it, but the damn thing didn't turn up. I found some of my money, though, up there on the little girl's dresser. Don't know how it got all the way up the stairs. Musta been walkin' in my sleep again."

If Mike had been a hitter, Oscar would be dead. He clenched his fists and backed up, put himself out of striking range. "You went into Casey's room?"

"Good thing I did, cuz someone put my money up there."

"How much did you take?"

Weaving on his feet, Oscar struggled to keep his balance while he fiddled around trying to get money out of his front pocket. He pulled out a wadded dollar bill and some change. "This is all that's left. Where'd you put the rest of my money, Mikey? I want to go out for a while, see some friends of mine. I don't have any walking-around money on me. Suppose you could spot me a little something? Tide me over?"

"It's raining, Pop. I'll drive you. Why don't you go wash your face and get ready."

"Thank you, boy. Nice of you to offer." Oscar shuffled off toward the downstairs bathroom. "Won't be but a minute."

Mike, chagrined, began looking under chairs and sofa cushions as soon as Oscar was out of the room.

"I'm so sorry," he said. "Ask Casey how much Pop took from her room and I'll pay her back."

Tucked behind a throw pillow on Grandma's wingback chair he found an unopened bottle of Wild Turkey. He handed me the bottle and got down to reach under the sofa. "He tossed the workroom looking for money, but I don't think he broke anything. You want to go up and check Casey's room for damage? God, I can't believe he went in there."

Mike's arms were longer than Oscar's, but he still had to stretch to reach out the second bottle, this one half gone. I wondered if Oscar might have kicked it there when we came in and surprised him.

Mike repeated, "I'm so sorry."

"It's not your fault, Mike."

He looked around the room, assessing hiding places, I supposed. "Do you know how much money Casey had in her room?"

"Couldn't have been much."

Mike's face was red. He held that half-full bottle like a cudgel. "I should never have brought him here."

"What was the alternative, sweetheart?"

"Sometimes I think I'm doing him no favor when I bail him out." He turned away from me. "Maybe I should just leave him be."

"Whatever you think is best."

He took a big breath and let out a long sigh. "I better help Pop get his things together."

I poured the Wild Turkey down the kitchen sink and then packed a lunch and a Thermos of coffee for the car. Mike wouldn't be able to take Oscar into a restaurant on the way out to the desert. Too risky.

Oscar seemed happy when he was belted into the passenger seat of Mike's Blazer. His time-worn suitcase lay flat on the backseat. A few changes of clothes, that's all he had left. Anything of value that came his way tended to get "lost" and ended up in the window of a pawnshop.

"Have a good trip, Oscar," I said. "Take care of Mike for me."

"You bet, honey. Too bad you can't come along. Boy, we could have us some fun."

I kissed his cheek and he pinched my butt. I hoped Mike hadn't seen, because he didn't need another beef to hold against his father.

"Don't look for me before midnight." Mike embraced me. "If you have any problems with Mareno, call my partner, Cecil."

I said I would.

He promised to call. He promised to be careful driving in the rain. And he promised not to blame himself for Oscar's weaknesses.

The neighbors started calling, four of them before

Mike left, six more before my appointment with Detective Mareno. I told them all the same thing: No one saw the shooter, but police were looking for a white Ford driven my a man with a short dark crew cut and pale blue eyes.

At the appointed hour, I took a stack of videotaped interviews and Arlo with me when I drove over to the South Pasadena police station, a small building only a block from the murder scene. Mareno didn't seem to like the idea of an extra party in the bull pen until Arlo started talking.

"It's real strange." Arlo pulled computer printouts from his briefcase and laid them in front of Mareno. "Maggie called me when she thought some a-hole was following her. I ran the numbers, but the tags on the Ford were phonies all the way. A dead end."

He pulled one sheet out from the middle of the pile. "But the name she gave me came back."

"The name's a phoney, too, Arlo." I reached for the sheet. "A lot of people over the years must have called themselves Elwood Dowd. He was a character in a big James Stewart movie."

Arlo had his smug grin in place when I looked at the mug shot in my hand, as if he had successfully pulled off a card trick. "That's your man, isn't it, Maggie?"

E. P. Dowd, looking quite a bit younger than he had sitting under the dome light of his car last night, took a fair picture, both full-face and profile. The bar under the picture read, "Metropolitan Police, London."

Mareno chewed his bottom lip while he studied the mug shot. "This is the man you talked to?"

"Looks like him," I said. I pulled out the snaps I had taken on the freeway and found the best shot of the driver. I laid it next to the mug shot; a dead bang match. "Who is he, Arlo?"

"Jean-Claude Steinmetz. Trafficker in bootlegged antiquities. He's the chief conduit between Mideastern and Asian grave robbers and the marketplace. Need Imperial Roman coins? Syrian marbles? He'll find 'em. He'll also smuggle the stuff out of the country of origin and get you whatever documentation you need to bring it home.

"I'm surprised he's in the country," Arlo said. "FBI wants him. But so do a lot of agencies. There must be something big going down if he would risk showing himself."

I told him about the missing collection from Da Nang and the invasion of Khanh's home a week ago. While I talked, I scanned the dossier that Arlo had downloaded from Interpol.

Several nations wanted Steinmetz for questioning in situations that ranged from theft to murder. Greece charged him with treason in absentia for smuggling out of the country a fifth-century B.C. Athenian bronze that was now on exhibit at the Getty Museum in Malibu. Steinmetz was charged, but never caught.

I kept going back to the first section of the document, Steinmetz's early career. He was drafted into the U.S. Army in 1969, and then—and this is where I got stuck—worked as a Southeast Asian specialist for the United States Agency for International Development. Scotty had spent two tours in Vietnam under the aegis of USAID. Everyone knew the organization was a front for the CIA, and other nefarious activities.

I stood up and started to pace. "It makes sense that Khanh Nguyen and her friends are somehow involved with this Steinmetz. He may have brokered the treasures they lifted from the Da Nang museum, if that's what he does. But why is he following me around? What can I possibly have that he wants?"

"He made no demands?" Mareno asked.

"Nothing. He seemed happy just to spook me."

"Your only connection to the museum was the victim, Mrs. Nguyen?"

I had to mull over that question before I was ready to answer. There had been times when I would have given just about anything to have my ex-husband disappear off the planet. I never wished him ill. I simply wanted him to go away. Far, far away. Here was my big chance, and I couldn't bring myself to mention him.

Tabloid TV: "Prominent attorney, former husband of filmmaker Maggie MacGowen, shown here with his teenage daughter, was implicated today in a brutal murder."

No way. I had been in the business long enough to know how that scenario played out. Casey didn't need either the attention or the pain that came when your face was a news lead-in, a sound bite on three channels at five, six, and eleven.

I stonewalled Mareno on Scotty. I wouldn't even give him an oblique entrance by suggesting he call the Nguyen family attorney. I merely shrugged my shoulders and said, "As far as I know."

My dad said that seventy-eight percent of the time I change my plans. I thought his figure was high, even if he included plans that changed more than once. That is, I had accepted Scotty's invitation to dinner Friday night, then had decided to go with Mike to the desert. And in the end I stayed home to talk with Mareno. In between, I never called to cancel with Scotty. We were still on for seven o'clock. I decided that this was an appointment I needed to keep.

"Detective Mareno, I need a favor," I said. "Steinmetz knows where my daughter's school is and he knows what she looks like. If I go get her, I'm afraid he'll try something. Can you help me?"

"We'll pick her up, sure," Mareno said. "Do you want her taken home?"

"Home wasn't safe for Khanh," I said. "Casey wants to go to San Francisco this weekend. Now's the time."

I located my father by having Uncle Max paged by his office. They were in an antiquarian bookstore in West Hollywood, haggling over the price of an early edition of *Huckleberry Finn*.

"Did your mother put you up to this?" Dad asked.

"Of course not," I said. "Why would you think so?"

"A minute before you paged, I called and asked her how much we have in the checking account. She wouldn't tell me."

"I need your help. There's been a shooting in the neighborhood, and after those men last night, I want

Casey out of town until things cool off. I'm being over-protective. Indulge me."

"Indulge *me,*" Dad said. "Under the circumstances, I want my little girl to blow out of town, too, until things cool off. I want you to come with Casey."

"I'm waiting for Mike to get home. I'll see you tomorrow."

"Seventy-eight percent of the time. . . ."

"I'll see you tomorrow," I said. "Come hell or high water."

Chapter 19

Khanh's wake started without her. The county coroner wouldn't release her remains until after an autopsy. A week, the coroner told Sam Nguyen. Maybe two. Prayers began immediately: A violent death during Tet left the deceased's passage into the next world especially difficult, and the family especially vulnerable.

I tried to reach Minh Tam at the hotel because I thought he should know what had happened to his cousin Khanh before he heard the news on TV. There was no answer in his room, he wasn't in the hotel's dining room, bar, or coffee shop. Even the barber hadn't seen him. I wasn't worried about him—almost no one knew how to reach him—but I asked Mike's partner, Cecil Renfrew, if he would send someone over to check. Cecil promised he would go himself.

Arlo drove me to the Nguyen home in San Marino. There were more guards, and this time uniformed policemen stationed on the grounds, and no one was allowed to drive through the gates. Arlo let me off in front, and waited while I showed a picture ID and let the rent-a-cop run a handheld metal detector over me and the gifts I carried.

"Miss MacGowen." Khanh's elder son, Sean, greeted me at the door, very formal as he bowed. He wore the white muslin hood of mourning.

I had known Sean since he was in grade school, and now he was finishing his master's degree in business administration, preparing to move into the family businesses: restaurants and liquor stores. Though he was somber that evening, I could still see in him the playful little boy who used to have water balloon wars with Casey. I returned his bow when my impulse was to hug him.

He said, "My father will be pleased to see you."

"How is he?"

"He has been very quiet. I think he doesn't realize yet what has happened."

"What happened is beyond comprehension. I will miss your mother. I know she loved you very much."

"She always spoke well of you." Sean took the flowers and the basket of fruit I had brought with me. He hesitated before he asked, "You saw her?"

"Yes."

"How. . . ." He struggled to maintain composure, and could not finish his question.

"It happened very quickly, Sean." I touched his arm. "She felt no pain. When I saw her, the police had covered her and were protecting her modesty. She looked very dignified."

He nodded, though I don't know whether my answer fit his question. "My father is inside."

Sean led me into the living room where perhaps three dozen friends, relatives, and business associates milled around, many of them familiar to me from the old days. The air was heavy with burning incense. Taped temple chants played in the background.

An altar set up against the near wall was covered with offerings, mostly baskets of fruit and flowers. Sean set my basket among them and I added the flowers I brought, a lei made of plumeria blossoms—frangipani, Khanh called them, her favorite. I had also brought a framed photograph of Khanh, a picture that I had taken several years ago, but I held on to it because the family had already placed a large formal portrait of Khanh on the altar.

I followed Sean's lead and bowed to the portrait—an old, studio-made black and white that showed Khanh, who always found things to laugh about, with a stern face, her black hair sculpted into a stiff pageboy. Khanh would have laughed at the portrait. As I bowed to her, I silently reminded the spirits she believed in that here was a truly good woman and they should receive her.

When I stepped back, the family waited in a formal receiving line. Beginning with an elderly aunt, each bowed to me in turn.

Sam seemed devastated, shell-shocked. He moved like a robot when he reached for my hand, and bowed. "It is kind of you to come and pray with us, Maggie."

"Khanh was always a good friend."

Sam bowed again.

"I want you to have this picture of Khanh," I said. "This is how I remember her." The snap was a color close-up of a very lively Khanh, a wide smile showing her straight, white teeth and the mischief in her dark eyes.

Sam ran his hand across the protective glass, smiling through his tears. "I never saw this before, Camera Lady."

"I took it years ago, up in the Muir Redwoods," I said. "Scott and I had recently separated and I was feeling sad. Khanh flew up one day just to tell me that she was a friend and not community property. We went for a walk among the redwoods and I took this picture. I think it captures her well."

Sam had mist in his eyes, but he smiled. "Life is ephemeral. It is better not to hold on to it. Will you light some incense for my wife?" He gave me three joss sticks and helped me light them from an altar candle.

When new arrivals came, I excused myself so that Sam could greet them. I noticed that he held the Muir Redwoods photograph of Khanh tight against his chest all the time I was there.

The room was hot and airless. I wasn't sure how long it was appropriate to stay, or how social I needed to be. A uniformed maid passed among the guests with a tray of drinks. I took a glass of wine, steeled myself, and looked around for a friendly face among Scotty's associates.

"Maggie, sweetie." The voice I dreaded, Sheila Rayburn, the wife of Scotty's law partner. "Didn't you get my message? I called you this afternoon. Mortie and I had dinner with you-know-who last night and when he said you were in town, I vowed that you and I were going to get together. Do you realize how long it's been?"

"Hello, Sheila."

We pressed cheeks. In a room dominated by sleek Asian women, long tall Sheila had the presence of a Clydesdale at a cat show. Big, flame-colored hair, clunky platform shoes, a dark green suit with deep cleavage and out-to-here shoulder pads, she would have fit in better at an old show-girls reunion. Making up for lost time, according to Sheila, the daughter of a Pentecostal minister.

"I can't believe it." She hunched down to place her stage whisper closer to my ear. "You saw her. Was it awful?"

"It wasn't nice. Better that I saw her than a stranger."

"And she was coming to see you. It's so weird, isn't it?"

"More scary than weird," I said. "How did you hear about Khanh?"

"Sam called Scotty, Scotty called Mortie. They were supposed to have lunch together today. And then, of course, we were coming here tomorrow for the big dinner as usual. But that's off." Just about then she decided I must feel slighted about being left off the dinner list. She tried to fix things. "You're better off. You know how boring those dinners are. All the men talking shop." Then she blushed, realizing she had merely put her foot in it again and now she had insulted the deceased. She took my glass from my hand and downed its contents in a gulp. "Oh, hell."

"How are you, Sheila?"

"Older, sweetie. Not wiser, just older."

I chuckled. "Where's Mortie?"

"He and Scotty have their heads together at Mortie's office. Some crisis or another. They'll be here later."

"How much later?"

"Oh." She checked her watch. "I don't know, sweetie, but if you don't want to run into a certain bastard, you might start saying your good-byes before too long. He has a dinner thing later, so I imagine he'll be right along."

"Scotty doesn't scare me." I didn't mention that I was the dinner thing.

"Good for you, but why risk getting into something? We don't want to turn the wake into a boxing match. Poor Sam already has more than he can handle."

"If there are people around, Scotty won't start something."

"It's your neck." She caught the eye of the maid and snapped two glasses from the drinks tray, then handed one of them to me.

"To Khanh," I said, tipping my glass against hers. "May she rest in peace."

"To Khanh."

We talked about Sheila's son, who was a college sophomore, and about Casey. She told me I seemed pale and I told her she looked fine. I was busy with my job, she with her charity work. After that there was an awkward lull. I knew her too well to bring up the weather, but no longer well enough to share anything very personal. I never mentioned Mike, though I'm sure the gossip circuit kept her informed without my adding anything. I felt that I was fair game as a lunchtime topic for the old gang. Mike was not.

Sheila finished her third drink. "Nice turnout on such short notice, isn't it?"

The room was packed, people coming by twos and threes in a constant stream. I decided that it was time to say good-bye.

"Walk me out," I said, taking Sheila's arm. I said good-bye to Sam and to his sons, and promised that I would come back after the weekend to sit vigil.

Dread walked out of the house with me, a feeling as heavy and invasive as the scent of incense that filled my nostrils and billowed up from my clothes whenever I moved.

"Want to talk about it?" Arlo asked as he held his car door for me.

"I do. But I don't know what to say."

Arlo is a considerate soul. He slipped Mozart into his tape player and waited for me.

The green perfection of San Marino slipped by the car window as we drove down Huntington Drive to Monterey Avenue. Most of the houses were set back from the street on their acreage and were nearly hidden from view. Over the hedges: Rooflines as large as European country hotels, multiple gables, multiple chimneys, could be seen.

I said, "How much do you think a place like Khanh's would sell for?"

"More than I'll ever see in a lifetime."

"How much do you think it costs to open a big restaurant in a good neighborhood?"

He chuckled. "Anything else you thinking of buying?"

"A liquor store."

"The answer's the same. It costs plenty."

"The first time I met Sam and Khanh was at their house-warming party. They had just moved into that beautiful house. They had been in this country for four years, and they already had their first restaurant and liquor store."

"Major bucks," Arlo said. "Major."

Sam and Khanh were entitled. They paid their dues, probably enough dues for the next three generations. Born to a privileged class, they met in Paris where Sam studied at Escoffier, as Ho Chi Minh had a generation before, and where Khanh was an art student. They went home to Da Nang to chart their future together—in a war zone.

Surrounded by a landscape created by wealth, I began to suffer feelings I can only explain as guilt. Survivor's guilt that I was still breathing and Khanh was not, and that I might be in some yet unexplained way responsible. And something else, a sense that I had not paid my dues.

As soon as Scotty and I found out I was pregnant with Casey, we moved from his bachelor cottage across the

Bay in Sausalito to our house in the San Francisco Marina District. I loved the house for its ocean view and tall, skinny, eccentric design, the third-floor loft, and the wickedly steep street that ran in front. As soon as I saw it, I refused to look any further.

How ironic, I thought, that Scotty should want the house now, because when we bought it, he argued, long and loudly, to buy an estate-sized property down the Peninsula in Hillsborough, a neighborhood similar to San Marino.

Back then, I was still anchoring an evening news broadcast from a station South of Market in San Francisco. I hated the idea of commuting out of the suburbs every day, leaving my baby behind in the clutches of nannies. I also hated the idea of being isolated in the woods on the four nights out of seven Scotty was out of town or working late. The other thing was, I wanted a mortgage and upkeep that I could manage on my own if something happened to Scotty. To the end, we argued about moving, he pro, me con.

Scotty built his second wife a glass palace in the foothills above Boulder, Colorado, when he moved his practice to Denver. I wondered how it was for Linda, on top of her hill with three acres of ponderosa and two babies for company.

Arlo broke my reverie. "You want to go home, or you want me to take you somewhere?"

I looked at my watch. "Home, please."

Cecil told me that Minh Tam wasn't in his room, but his duffel bags were still in the closet and he had ordered, and eaten, room service breakfast. He was out when the maid made up his room at eleven, and the room remained as pristine as she had left it. There was a message at the desk for him to call Detective Mareno.

The hotel staff agreed to keep an eye out, and to call Cecil when Tam returned.

I took a long shower and then stared at my closet for a while trying to decide what to wear at dinner with Scotty. I didn't want to look seductive, I didn't want to look dowdy, and I didn't want to look as if I cared in the least about how I looked for him.

In the end, I chose a creamy white silk blouse, a straight, mid-calf-length black wool skirt, black tights and boots, and a black velvet jacket. Not dressy, not casual. Frankly, not much of anything. I added my grandmother's long string of pearls, didn't like the way they fell into my cleavage, took them off and wrapped them like a choker around my neck.

I felt nervous. I felt as if I were betraying Mike. All afternoon, while I was in the company of Scotty's friends and business associates, as I thought about what our life together had been, I remembered that it had not all been bad. In fact, there had been times when it was damned wonderful.

Chapter 20

The Gabrieleno Restaurant was only a few miles west of the house I shared with Mike, down where Monterey Road crosses the Arroyo Seco.

The Pasadena Freeway runs through the Arroyo on stilt-like supports, carrying the moving lights and noise of traffic high above the canyon floor. Below the freeway, the terrain is uncivilized, a maze of dead-end streets and flood plain filled with tangled undergrowth. Snow melt pouring out of the San Bernardino Mountains had been redirected underground, but the Arroyo remains untamable in big storms. Most of the flood path is now the Ernest Debs County Regional Park; a notoriously difficult golf course makes use of the treacherous terrain.

The Gabrieleno Restaurant overlooks the fifth green of the golf course. I had been there years ago with Scotty. What I remembered was how dark it was around the park at night. And how isolated.

I left a message telling Detective Mareno where I would be, and then called Arlo and asked him to call the restaurant at eight and have me paged. I thought that an hour was long enough for Scotty to make his pitch and his rebuttal.

Before I left, I accounted for everyone.

The rehab center in Trona passed Mike's muster. He said he would stay for a few hours and help Oscar get settled in before he headed home. Casey was at her grandparents' in Berkeley, helping Lyle strip Jim Morrison from my childhood bedroom. Michael had taken Guido's cats and gone to his mother's house in the Valley for the weekend. Dad and Uncle Max were playing bridge with the neighbors. Guido, Lana, and the film crew were camped out in my Marina District house; they complained there wasn't enough hot water.

Minh Tam still had not returned to his room at the hotel.

A light but steady rain was falling when I drove away from the house. At the first intersection, the van's steering seemed stiff and the car felt slushy. For another block, I told myself that the problem was wet streets. When I turned onto Monterey, I heard the back tire flap and had to admit what I had known, or should have known, as soon as I backed the van out of the driveway. I swore, pulled over to the curb, and got out.

The right rear tire was flat. I ran my hand over the treads but didn't feel anything like a nail. Could be a slow leak, I thought. Or, most likely, someone messing with me. I don't like to be manipulated.

Soaked, hair flat against my head, I got back into the van, swore a little without much energy, and moved the van into the corner strip mall lot and parked it under the lights in front of a 7-Eleven.

If the flat was a warning, it was duly noted. If the flat was meant to keep me from meeting Scotty, or meant to leave me stranded in the Arroyo, then I didn't want to hand over a victory too easily. The restaurant wasn't far away. Using the car phone, I called Information for the number of a local cab company. I dialed the number and waited on hold all the way through two golden oldies playing on the radio. I was still on hold when an RTD bus pulled up beside the lot and honked. I looked up, recognized the driver, rolled down my window.

"Leon?" I said.

"How you doin', Maggie?" Leon got out of the bus, leaving his two passengers inside. "What you doin' out here?"

"Flat tire," I said.

"I can see that. You waitin' for the triple A?"

"I have an appointment, so I'm calling a cab. I'll get the tire fixed later."

"Where you goin'?"

"The Gabrieleno Restaurant."

"I know where that is." He glanced back at his passengers, two men with their faces buried behind newspapers. "You might as well come with me. No tellin' how long it'll take a cab to come all the way over here."

"Is the restaurant one of your stops?"

"Not usually." He grinned. "But I have a feeling I'm going to get lost tonight and end up over by that way."

Before I hung up on the cab dispatcher's hold music, I asked Leon, "Will you get in trouble?"

"After what I went through today, anyone try to get in my face, I say call my lawyer cuz I'm ready to go off the deep end. Fool with Leon at your own risk." He reached for my door lock through the open window. "But we gotta go. Can't make my fares any later than they are right now."

We shared my umbrella and dashed to the bus. I took the seat right behind Leon.

When we were back in traffic, I asked him, "Are you working double shifts? Is that legal?"

"I volunteered. I thought if I drove this way enough times, something might come to me, you know, about what happened. And what else am I going to do? All this adrenaline running through me has got to get out somehow. And sitting at home thinking about that poor lady and how she got hit right there beside of me just ain't the way I'm going to start feeling any calmer."

He laughed, a roll from deep in his abdomen. "I get time and a half. Besides, most of the other drivers called in sick when they heard what happened on my morning run."

"And has anything come to you?" I asked.

"Only this: When the little lady got hit, I never saw a car goin' by. I've been driving this bus long enough, I have like a sixth sense about where cars are and where they're going to and where they're coming from. If that lady was hit from a moving car, then it was some kind of ghost car."

Leon pulled up to his first stop and one of his passengers got off. "That Detective Mareno keeps asking, did I see a white car. I keep saying, I saw no car. Not at the very time I heard the noise and the lady fell."

I pulled one of the shots I had taken of Steinmetz out of my purse. "Ever seen these men?"

Leon studied the picture before he shook his head. "Mareno showed this to me. I never saw them. But I'll keep an eye out. Tell you this: I know the car before I know who's driving it." He slipped the picture into his ID frame so that everyone getting on the bus could see it.

"Thanks, Leon," I said.

"Any time." Looking at me in his rearview mirror, he winked and gave me a thumbs-up. "It's nice to be with someone who knows what happened. I don't want to talk about it. I don't want to be alone with it, either."

Two more stops, Leon let off his last passenger, and then doubled back to make the turn into the Arroyo.

"Leon's limo service," I said. "Nothing like it in the city."

He cocked his head. "I'm not crazy, you know, goin' off my route and drivin' you out here like this. The thing is, it makes me so damn mad, them shooting at my bus the way they did. Anybody coulda been hurt. They can't get away with that on *my* bus."

"I'm mad, too. But don't go looking for trouble."

"I'm not looking, but if I find trouble, I'm not running away, either." Leon turned up the park access road, a dark expanse lined with a high oleander hedge. Beyond the bus lights, the road disappeared into blackness. "You want to tell me how your tire happened to go flat?"

"I've thought about it. And what I thought scares me."

The restaurant sign came up on the left, and Leon turned into the circular drive. "How you getting home?"

"I can have the maître d' call me a cab, or I can call a friend."

"The one-ten bus stops right by the driveway every half hour, at twenty after and ten to. The last run is just before midnight; picks up the busboys and kitchen help.

I don't know who's driving the route tonight, but I'll put out a call to be watching for you."

"Thank you, Leon." He drove me right up to the door in his big city bus. Before I stood, I pulled one of my cards out of my bag and handed it to him. "Keep in touch. Let me know how things are going for you."

He looked at the card before he slipped it into his shirt pocket. He pushed the door release. "You have a nice dinner, Maggie."

"Good night." I kissed him on the check before I got off the bus. He didn't drive away until I opened the restaurant's massive front door and walked inside.

Garbrieleno exuded a quiet, comfortable gentility. In the lounge, sofas were arranged around a huge tile fireplace. The motif was meant to be Early California: adobe walls, Mexican clay pavers on the floor, rough-hewn beams in the high ceiling. This wasn't a trendy restaurant, but a place that catered to a regular, well-heeled local crowd. It was Friday night, and the house was full, neighbors and old friends sharing a rainy evening out. Scotty and I had eaten here a number of times with Khanh and Sam, and Mortie and Sheila Rayburn, whenever business brought us to L.A.

It was awkward to be in a place that belonged to my former life, to see people who had once called me by name now look right through me. I wondered if this was the way the prodigal felt when he dropped in for dinner after a long absence, a living ghost from the past.

Because Khanh had brought it up, I imagined how damned awkward it must have been for Linda, Scott's newer wife, to walk in my footsteps. How many times, standing at Scotty's side, had she heard some knucklehead say to Scotty, "And how is Maggie?" I felt sorry for her, knowing that a ripple of gossip followed her every time she turned her back, just as it followed me.

I looked at my watch—I was five minutes early—and hoped I had time to order a drink from the bar before Scotty arrived. A Kir Royale, I thought. A little champagne to take the edge off my jitters.

Scotty was already at the bar, waiting. He rose from a

seat near the door. As he walked over to meet me, he carried a small, elegant leather attaché case, his offer to buy the house, I supposed.

"You look beautiful, Maggie." He held me by the shoulders and bussed me on the temple, the way a fond uncle might. Familiar, but not forward. Not sexual. "Is it still raining?"

"Sprinkling." I was nervous. It had been years since I had been in a room with Scotty unchaperoned. There were good reasons why I avoided situations exactly like the one I had just walked myself into. As those reasons occurred to me, I knew that if my car were out front in the lot, at that point I would have turned tail and driven myself away. Far away.

I looked at Scotty, trying to decide how devious he could be, and how perceptive. If I were Scotty and I didn't want someone to run away from me, how far would I go to clip that person's wings? Would he mess with a tire? I realized that I had never known him well enough to be able to answer the question. Maybe that was the problem between us: We didn't bother to find out what we needed to know about each other.

"I missed you at the Nguyens' this afternoon. Sheila said you had just left," he said. "Poor Sam looked like hell, didn't he?"

"I thought he looked like a man whose wife had been murdered."

Scotty tsk'ed. "What is this world coming to?"

Looking at him, really looking at him up close, for the first time in about four years, I saw that the attractive lines in his face were etched more deeply than I had realized. The last four years had been hard ones for him. Gone was the young man I carried in my mind's eye.

The maître d' glided up. "Are you ready to be seated, Mr. MacGowen?"

"I believe we are." Scotty took my arm. Apparently no one expected me to speak.

"Nice to have you back, Mr. MacGowen." The maître d' preened for Scotty as he guided us across the dining room.

"Nice to be back, Philip."

Heads turned, people stared, then pivoted back to their companions to share some tidbit. I overheard scraps of their conversation as we crossed the room, "first wife," "together?" "so surprised." Surprise was the general current among vaguely familiar faces. Gossip was the undertow.

Philip seated us at a booth in a quiet corner. Floodlights on the lawn created an irregular strip of green against the black, moonless night.

Philip pulled out my chair for me, so he must have know I was present. He had yet to acknowledge me or speak directly to me, never took his full attention from Scotty. As I sat down, he spoke over my head to Scotty. "Martini with an onion and a Kir Royale, am I right?"

"Thank you, Philip." Scotty sat down and Philip vaporized.

"You're having two cocktails?" I asked.

"It hasn't been so long that I don't remember what you like. I ordered for us."

"Maybe tonight I feel like sherry."

"You hate sherry, Maggie." He wove his fingers together and rested his chin on them, vaguely amused and superior. Condescending. "But if you want sherry, I'll tell Philip when he comes back."

Scotty made me feel like a tongue-tied adolescent. I remembered why I hated him.

"Drinks aren't the issue." I sat back in my chair and spoke softly, forcing him to lean my way, to do all the work. "In truth, there is no issue. We have a little business to discuss, so let's get to it. There is a solid offer to buy the house at home waiting for my signature. I'm willing to hear your counterproposal if it reaches the criteria I gave you."

Drinks appeared, Kir in front of me, martini in front of Scotty. And a silver basket of rolls in the middle of the table.

"Let's eat first." Scotty put a roll on my bread plate before he served himself.

"Why wait? I'm ready to hear your pitch right now.

Shouldn't take more than a minute or two to tell me whether you can better the offer on the table."

A pale radicchio salad with pine nuts and a tiny pink shrimp was placed in front of me by an ancient silver-haired waiter. The plate was a pastel work of art. I said to the waiter, "I believe this belongs to another table. We haven't seen the menu yet."

The waiter looked at Scotty for guidance. Scotty said, "Thank you," to the man. When the waiter was gone, he said to me, "I ordered off the menu. The chef is making us something special."

"Scotty, for God's sake." I moved the salad, the bread, and the cocktail to the side of the table and smoothed the space in front of me. "Either you have it, or you don't. If you don't, you can't buy me off with a meal, so quit stalling and lay out your offer."

Scotty pressed his napkin to his lips as if he were stanching a hemorrhage of words. He knew that he had to proceed with caution or I would walk right out. With some effort, he reassembled his smile. He reached down for his attaché, pulled out a legal-size manila file folder, and placed it on the table in front of him. There were several sets of documents. After some thought, he chose one.

"College for Casey, if she goes to a private school, will cost around twenty-five thousand per year. I have opened a trust account for her, with you as the sole trustee." He slipped a printed three-by-five card from inside the stapled document. "This is proof to you that I have arranged monthly direct electronic transfer from my checking account to the trust account in the amount recorded. The first deposit has been made." There was a receipt.

"You can understand the tax advantage to you, of course. By the time Casey graduates, a total of one hundred thousand dollars will have been made available."

"What protection does Casey have if something happens to you and you can't keep up the payments?"

He handed me a paid-up term policy on his life, in an amount sufficient to cover Casey's college if Scotty died, and a second policy that covered the same amount if he should be unable to earn a living because of disability.

I said, "You're coming up short, Scotty."

He handed me a couple of computer-generated pages of figures and two thick legal documents. "I am assigning to you the equity in my Colorado home. Conservatively, this figure." He circled a number at the bottom of a page.

"Colorado is a community property state," I said. "Half the equity belongs to Linda."

He shook his head. "The house was excluded in the prenup."

"The two of you have kids. What's their share?"

"Maggie." He said this through clenched teeth. "I don't need you to worry about my family."

"Equity is too nebulous for me. Potentially risky. I prefer cash."

"Capital gains on cash will kill you." His paper tower was moving from his side of the table to mine, one stack at a time. "And I'm asking you to carry back a second mortgage on the San Francisco house in this amount." Another circled figure.

"You can see the tax advantages this offer gives you over a cash deal, Maggie. If you accept, I will ask you to quit-claim your title to me—a simple legal transfer. We'll label it final disposition of community property, and you will not be liable for capital gains penalties nor will you have reportable income as a result of the transaction."

"I see the tax advantages to me. I can't miss the advantage to you if you're cash poor right now, Scotty, but there is just one problem."

"What's that?"

"You're short by half."

Under the table, I felt him tap my knee and I heard paper crinkle. I reached under and touched the sharp corner of a large envelope. I took it, felt it, brought it up to my lap.

Scotty snapped my napkin open and handed it to me,

clearly intending that I should use it to cover the envelope on my lap.

"The envelope isn't going to explode, is it?" I asked.

"Take a look, but don't put it on the table."

I opened the envelope, saw that it was currency, a lot of currency. "I don't like the way this deal feels. I would prefer a nice tidy cashier's check."

"I'm willing to pay for your qualms." The last sheet he handed me was a tally, figures only. A person who hadn't heard our conversation wouldn't know what the numbers meant. The amount of tuition, the total income from a second mortgage at eleven percent with a five-year payoff, his calculation of the value of the equity in his new home, and a last, large number. I touched that last number with the tip of my bread knife.

"Is this what I'm holding in my lap?"

"Yes."

"Where did the money come from?"

"Bonuses. Scottish thrift. Luck at the track. Don't worry about it." He finished his martini. "Money doesn't smell."

"But this deal does. Tell you what, if you get to me an affidavit that I can show the IRS explaining where the case came from, then I'll give the rest of your package to Uncle Max and see what he thinks."

"How soon do you want it?"

"Tomorrow."

"Give me two weeks, Maggie. If I can't pull the deal together by then, you can go back to the other buyer."

"The other offer expires close of business Monday."

"I'm sure they'll wait."

"I'm just as sure they won't." I took a sip of water. "Look, the other offer is clean. Yours has strings attached for the next five years. I think we should shake hands right now and say good-bye."

"I want the house, Maggie." A few heads nearby turned. He leaned in closer to me. "The house means a great deal to me. My little girl grew up there. How can you sell it out from under her?"

"Nice touch. Not convincing, but creative." I stacked

all the papers together, tidied their corners, and handed them back to Scotty. "The answer to your offer is no."

Under the table, hidden by the long, starched cloth, I extended the cash back toward him.

Scotty kept his hands folded on top of the table, refusing to accept the proffer. "I'm sure we can find a way to make us both happy. Is the cash the only hang-up?"

"The hang-up is, I feel the patsy in a shell game. I'm not a gambler like you are, Scotty. I have a sure thing in my hand, and I'm going to accept it. Now, reach under and take this envelope back."

"Don't be in too big a hurry to say no, Maggie. You can fax the documents to Max tonight and have an answer right away. Max is a quick study. He'll see the merit here."

I dropped the envelope. It bounced off Scotty's knee and hit the floor. His face turned red. I felt relieved, as if some enormous, hairy beast had just climbed off my lap.

"Salmon étouffée." The ancient waiter, with a flourish, set dinner in front of us.

Scotty made a show of dropping his napkin and dove down to retrieve it from the floor. I heard the crackle of paper before he came back up.

I would never have admitted so to Scotty, but the meal looked beautiful and smelled like heaven. All day our meeting had hung like doom over me, and now that it was finished I felt a whole lot better. It occurred to me that I hadn't eaten since Uncle Max's breakfast pancakes. The drive-through burger I would have after I called a cab to take me back to the van, and after the triple A had fixed the tire, would simply not equal this meal I intended to walk out on.

I caught the waiter's eye as he refilled my water glass. "Please take my meal back to the kitchen and box it for me. I'm leaving now."

The waiter seemed confused. "But there is dessert ordered. Chocolate-raspberry flan. The pastry chef just took it out of the oven."

"Put my dessert in the box, too." I pushed my chair

back to stand. "Leave it with the maître d', please. I'll pick it up on my way out."

The waiter looked to Scotty for advice, but got nothing. Scotty's head was bent over something he was writing.

"Do you want the dessert in a separate box?" The waiter was nonplussed, reluctant to go away. "Maybe we should use three boxes: salad, entré, dessert."

"Whatever you think is best."

I couldn't decide whether the waiter was upset because I had dared to speak, or because I was leaving. It didn't matter, because in the end he picked up my meal and went away.

Scotty handed me a sheet of his letterhead: a promissory note for an amount equal to what he said was in the envelope, to be paid by cashier's check within ten working days.

"Do this, at least." Scotty stuffed all of his documents back into the attaché, added the promissory note, and offered it all to me. "Fax these documents to Max tonight. I'll be at the Four Seasons. Call me there tomorrow."

"Max will get back to you." I accepted the attaché from him.

"One more thing." I took a picture of Dowd and the man he called Bowles out of my purse and showed it to him. "Do you know these men?"

He said, "No," but I knew he was lying.

"They approached your daughter at school. If you do know them, I suggest you call them off."

He furrowed his handsome brow. "You saw them?"

"I saw them. Talked to them. Reported them. The police investigating Khanh's murder put them at the top of their most-wanted list. If you know them, you might want to steer clear."

"I told you, I don't know them."

"Then, that's it." I offered him my hand. "Good-bye, Scotty."

Standing straight, trying to seem haughty, I walked

out through the gauntlet of curious eyes. Passing a table of four, I heard, "She didn't even have her dinner."

My bravado began to slip before I reached the ladies' room, the emotional letdown from a horrendous day accumulating all at once. Khanh, Oscar, a face-off with Scotty. All of it together was too much. I wanted to go straight home, climb into bed, and pull the covers over my head, and stay there until Mike got home to pat me on the back until I feel asleep. The best I could manage was to lock myself into a stall until I could breathe regularly. After about five minutes, I blew my nose and walked out.

If Leon was correct about the schedule of the one-ten bus, then the next bus wasn't due for another twenty-five minutes. I called a cab company from the phone in the ladies' lounge, and was told that a cab would arrive within twenty minutes. Either way, I had a bit of a wait, and I didn't want to run into Scotty while I waited. I told the dispatcher that I would be at the street, told myself I would get into the first conveyance that arrived.

I spent maybe ten minutes more in the ladies' room, hiding out. When I thought it was nearly time to start looking for my ride, I went out, gathered my dinner from the maître d', whose comment was, "Hope you enjoyed your meal," and walked out into the chill night air.

On the far side of the oleander hedge, the lighted bus shelter was the only bright patch against the dark beyond the driveway. I headed for it, hearing men's voices, some laughter, coming from outside the kitchen service area. When I passed the men, workers in white smocks speaking together in the melodic singsong of Vietnamese, they grew quiet, but resumed again, even louder, when they saw I was no one they needed to worry about. I could still hear them when I reached the street.

The rain had stopped for a while, but the feathery eucalyptus trees overhead still dripped water. As I walked toward the bus shelter, two waitresses wearing the uniform of the golf course grill room, short black skirts and white blouses visible under their open coats, stared at me.

I doubted whether many paying customers at Gabrieleno took the bus unless something had happened, like a fight with a spouse or too much booze. I suspected the waitresses were hoping I had a good story for them. They scooted over to make room for me on the bench, the smoke from their cigarettes hanging like cartoon balloons over their heads, waiting for the punch line to appear.

I said, "Hi."

They smiled politely in response, one a big blonde, the other a young Hispanic woman.

"Are you waiting for the one-ten?" I asked.

"No. The three-oh-five," the blonde said. "It should be here about now."

"Where does the three-oh-five go?"

"Highland Park."

I said, "Oh," in a way that must have shown my disappointment. Highland Park was in the opposite direction to where I was headed.

"Your bus comes right after," the Hispanic woman said, trying to sound reassuring. Then they turned back to their conversation about someone who always left a big mess when it was her turn to refill the catsup bottles.

The evening was quiet. There was nothing at this end of the street except the restaurant, the golf course—now closed—and the freeway above. The few cars that approached turned into the Gabrieleno lot. All was quiet for a moment, the three of us sitting in the bus shelter, water dripping from the trees onto the roof.

A noisy argument spilled out the front door of the restaurant and into the lot. We turned in unison.

"The Harrigans depart." The blonde held her arm up to the light to read her watch. "He was loaded already when the golf course grill closed. And he's been in the bar at Gabe's for over an hour."

The second waitress put her hand in her pocket and pulled out a quarter. "Who's going to win the war of the keys tonight?"

"Quarter on her." The blonde fished in her purse and matched the quarter.

"You're on. He's beat her two nights out of the last three."

"But he's really, really drunk."

The lights of an approaching bus appeared at the far end of the street.

"Dang," the blonde laughed. "The bus is early tonight. Bet's off if it gets here before the fight's over."

The two of them stood up and moved toward the curb, all eyes on the Harrigans as they tussled with each other. There was a car behind the bus; I hoped it was the cab.

The volume from the parking lot argument swelled as the Harrigans reached a red Jaguar parked across two spaces at the end of a nearby row. There was a brief scuffle—pushing and pulling, no blows landed—hands and arms flailing, then the woman shouted in triumph:

"You sorry son-of-a-bitch." She had the car keys held aloft as she staggered to the driver's side of the Jag. She got the key in the lock, climbed in, turned over the motor, and had the car rolling before the man had both feet inside.

"Shouldn't take this from you." The blonde held out her hand for the payoff. "He was too far gone tonight to put up a decent fight."

As I watched the Jaguar speed toward the exit, its headlights picked out a lone man walking from the restaurant toward the street. Scotty, his movements jerky as if he were tense, as if he were looking for a fight.

I stood right up and joined the waitresses at the curb, thinking that my white blouse and black skirt, showing when the wind blew my coat, were enough like the other two women that I would blend in. If Scotty were looking for a fight, chances were I was the target. The whole scene reminded me of a very bad night Guido and I spent in the jungle of El Salvador during the civil war, hoping transport out reached us before a group of right-wing guerrillas found us.

That night, Guido kept saying, Stay low and keep to the trees. Good advice, I thought, watching Scotty pace.

When his face was turned the other way, I moved

from the sidewalk and into the oleander hedge. I wanted to see whoever it was that Scotty was waiting for.

The approaching car sped up, passed the bus on the left, the sound of its horn signaling the driver's impatience. I thought, Here's a cabbie who's hot for a tip. Until the car came out ahead of the bus and passed under the streetlight: a white Ford with three inhabitants. Through the car's back window I could see a thick arm resting along the top of the seat, the white scar writhing as light and shadow played on the unpigmented skin.

A round, pale face appeared over the arm. Eyes shaded with heavy lashes looked directly at me.

Chapter 21

Stay low. The sussurush of the oleander was as soft as a whisper, Guido's warning so clear in my mind that I heard his words in the wind. Keep to the trees.

Eyelashes leaned forward to speak to the Ford's driver. I used that moment to slip into the shelter of the oleander.

I lost Scotty. He was there, pacing, and then he was gone. I thought that he was probably hidden from me by the large trees at the end of the drive. I also thought that the men in the car had come to see him, or maybe even to pick him up. And I was appalled.

What a liar Scotty was. His attaché dangled from my hand, a pocket of lies maybe. I thought about holding it open and letting the wind carry the papers away just as he drove past with his buddies. But to do so, I would have to expose myself.

Instead, I moved deeper into the shrubbery.

The bus pulled abreast of the shelter. The doors opened, illuminating the driver like an angel in a department store window at Christmas.

The blonde stepped right into the bus, but the younger waitress, the Hispanic, called out to me. "You coming?"

The driver, a little guy with a pencil mustache, came to the door to look out. "Who's there?"

"Some woman." The Hispanic waitress shrugged, held up her bus pass for the driver to see. "She's hidin' in the bushes."

I wanted to leave, but I couldn't until I knew what Scotty was up to. I showed myself to the driver.

"Leave, please," I said.

"You sick, lady?"

"Just go."

He started down the bus steps. "Won't be another bus along for a half hour. If you're sick, you might as well come along now."

"I'm not sick," I said. "I'm waiting for a cab."

He shrugged and sat back down. "Cabbie won't go beatin' the bushes for a fare. But if you want to be in there gettin' yourself all wet, who am I to say anything?"

He closed the door and pulled away from the curb, taking his light with him.

Feeling more than a little foolish—so the driver goes back to the barn after his shift and says, Guess what happened to me out by Gabe's tonight? Some woman. . . .

I slipped deeper into the oleander, farther away from the lights of the parking lot that would pick out my khaki coat from the dark all around. I hoped that the pale pink flowers on the shrubs would cover for anything that showed through the gaps in the hedge. My mom, the family botanist, always warned us to stay away from oleander. The bark, the flowers, and the leaves are all poisonous. At that moment, hunkering down among poison plants seemed a whole lot safer than being in the open.

Through the leaves, I looked for Scotty again on the far side of the drive where I had last seen him. The Ford slowed, turned into the drive, and stopped. The front passenger door opened. The dome light was out, but I could see the pale top of a man's head as he squatted in that open door. In the dark, and with the wind shifting my view holes through the shrubs, it was difficult to see very much.

I could hear voices. Sometimes they grew loud. The noise of the leaves around me and the wind, the car's idling motor, made it difficult to hear anything except the occasional word.

The parking lot was ringed by chain-link fence that was disguised by the landscaping. I moved right up to the fence, getting within ten yards of the car, trying to overhear. For maybe a nanosecond, I thought about brazenly walking up and demanding to know what was going on and how Scotty knew these three creeps in the car. Instinct overcame impulse, and I did no more than lurk.

My foot caught on an exposed root and I would have fallen on my face if I hadn't caught a thin branch. I was knocking mud off my boot when I heard the car door slam. Shafts of light pierced the shrubbery as the Ford made a U-turn and headed back down the drive toward the street. I ducked as the car drove off in the same direction it had come.

I couldn't see Scotty, and decided that he must have gotten into the car. I waited in hiding until the red tail-lights disappeared into the night. Then I went back to the bus shelter to retrieve Scotty's attaché, and the boxed dinner I had set down beside the bench.

The box was cracked, and I could smell the food inside. Hungry, I took a slice of radicchio out and snacked on it while I walked back toward the restaurant to call the cab company again.

Every few steps, I turned to make sure the men weren't coming back, but I wasn't overly worried. Puzzled, yes. But not afraid.

A few drops of cold water splashed my cheek. I looked up to see a few stars among the clouds; my dad always told me that when you could see stars, it wouldn't rain. But I was getting wet. Not rain this time. The automatic sprinklers along both sides of the sidewalk sputtered at first and then burst into a shower, drenching the already soaked plants and the long pale strip of sidewalk.

I dashed through the frigid spray, heading for the closest dry patch, the driveway. Twice again I nearly slipped, first in the slimy mud and then the slick sidewalk. Attaché in one hand, food in the other, I kept my balance like a surfer, and somehow managed to keep my feet under me.

I reached the driveway, water sloshing in my leather boots, freezing my toes. My silk blouse stuck to my skin, the wet tendrils of my hair, blown by the wind, stung my cheeks. I started to shiver. Then, I started to laugh.

All day, I had planned how cool I was going to be, hoping to make Scotty eat his heart out. And here I was, skulking around, caught in the sprinklers, looking probably like a boat-lift refugee.

I shook the oleander from my hair, finger-combed the wet strands behind my ears, and then, way too late, I buttoned up my coat; my wet bra was as transparent as my blouse. I squared my shoulders, and walked back toward the restaurant.

There was a black heap of something dumped between two eucalyptus trees near the curb, lying right next to a spewing sprinkler head. At first, it looked like a golf bag dumped maybe by some fed-up duffer. Odd, I thought, that I hadn't noticed the shape before. I had looked right there, because that spot was where Scotty had been standing the last time I saw him.

The dark heap rolled to one side.

"Maggie?" The voice, a whisper as soft as the water falling on the grass.

"Scotty?" Wary, half-expecting him to jump up, I edged closer until sprinkler water pecked insistently on my cheeks and ran in my eyes. "Did you trip? Are you hurt?"

Scotty lay on his back over an exposed eucalyptus root, his chest arched upward as if he were being lifted by the carved ivory handle screwed into his breastbone. Thick black tracings coursed down from that handle, soiling his shirt, spilling into the mud beneath him.

I dropped to my knees beside him, shocked, not believing, and raised his head, cradled it against my chest. He was heavy. I had to move him out of the water, but I was afraid that when I did I would make the knife in his chest do more damage. Unable to comprehend the full horror of what I was seeing, I still half-expected him to be playing a malicious joke. And then I met his eyes and I understood, finally, that he was dying.

I gripped him under his arms and dragged him away

from the sprinklers. When I had him lying on his back on the sidewalk, I took off my coat and covered him. Wiping water from his face, I told him, "Scotty, I have to get help."

He tried to raise his hand to stop me, but could not, and it fell back again onto the sodden concrete. The utter desperation of this gesture held me beside him. We were more intimate at that moment than we had ever been before, adulterers as surely as if we were in bed together.

"I have to get someone," I said, and began to rise.

His fingers curled, gesturing me closer. "Keep the house." He sighed, a dark trickle ran from his lips.

"Oh, for God's sake, Scotty." I blurted the words, a sort of reflex fueled by overwhelming and scattered emotions: love, hate, fear. This was no time to be thinking about the fucking house.

With effort, he focused his eyes on my face. He said only, "Sorry."

That's all, yet it sounded like a deathbed confession, a last attempt to atone for a lifetime of sins. I wanted to say something to offer him gentle passage. "Casey loves you," I said. And then, not knowing where it came from, I said, "I loved you once."

I saw men die in Salvador, I have seen youth die on the streets of the city. Death creeps across the face the way a shadow grows with the setting sun, an extinguishing of the light. That look that is like no other was on Scotty's handsome face.

"Who did this to you?" I demanded. "What do those men want?"

"Hide the babies," he sighed. "Hide."

Death also has a sound. The last breath escapes in a rush and then it is as if all the strings that hold a man together just give up on him all at once. All Scotty's tension, all his anguish, all his future just slipped away with the rush of his last air.

I held Scotty as gently as I would a sleeping baby, finding a delicacy about him in death that I had never seen during his life. He had been a baby once, and someone had held him. For Casey, I wanted him to be handled from this point with dignity.

I pulled my coat up over Scotty's face and rose to get help. I had run only a few steps when headlights from an approaching car lit the driveway all around me. I turned to face the light, wave my arms to flag down the driver.

The white Ford aimed its front bumper at me and accelerated.

Chapter 22

I ran.

The three men had come back, and it certainly wasn't to give Scotty a ride home. As soon as I recognized the car, I said a quick Hail Mary just in case, and then I cursed Scotty for whatever he had gotten me into.

My first impulse was to run to the restaurant, but it was way too far away. Instead, I dove back into the shrubbery outside the parking lot fence. Oleander branches slapped my face, leaving tracks of sticky, flowery sweetness with their sting.

Staying low, I ran toward the cross street, praying someone would come along and get me the hell out of there. No one had left the lot for over ten minutes. Wasn't it about time?

Like a hamster in a Habitrail, I ran along the narrow channel between the nine-foot fence and the oleander that shielded me from the street. The car followed in a parallel line along the curb, a flashlight aimed through a window hitting me now and then.

The three men argued volubly. One of them yelled, "Get out," a couple of times, but their argument was lost to me among the racket I made forcing my way through dense shrubs.

Disc brakes squealed.

"Hey, lady!" Through gaps in the leaves I saw the man called Dowd jump from the slow-moving car. He aimed a flashlight beam into the brush somewhere behind me. "Give it up, lady. No point both of us gettin' wore out. All we want to do is talk to you."

His voice gave me chills just like the mud that sucked

under my shoes. I shuddered: I was cold, but I had a flash of his hands, the hands that might have plunged the knife into Scotty's chest, touching me. The thought made me run faster through the obstacle course of poison oleander, fallen branches, and mud.

"Hey, Dowd, you slut." The man called Bowles shouted from the driver's seat. "She's only one skinny cunt. You ain't hurt bad. Just grab and let's go."

"Fuck you, Arnie." Dowd didn't seem to know exactly where I was, even though I thought I was making a lot of noise. Then his light seemed to get a fix on me. He hesitated for a second before he stepped off the sidewalk and onto the muddy strip. His right arm seemed to bother him as he bobbed and wove, looking for me through the foliage.

His light hit my face just as I turned my head, dazzling my eyes for a moment. I couldn't see the branches that ripped my skirt and tore gashes in the flesh of my legs. I clamped my teeth against the sting and plunged across an open space, hoping to gain some distance. I hadn't run for a week; I was winded already.

Dowd was fast. He flailed through the brush behind me, his strong legs eating up my small lead.

Suddenly, there was quiet behind me, the instant between breaths. I risked a glance back and saw Dowd airborne, then land facedown in the mud, his sore arm pinned beneath him.

Bowles laughed. "Nice footwork, you dumb fuck."

"Shut the fuck up!" Dowd roared as he freed his foot from an exposed root as thick as his shin. He came up running, but he was awkward, babying his arm.

I strained to pull air into my aching chest as I ran. Suddenly he was behind me, so close I felt the push of air he displaced around him. He reached for me, but I arched away and then dropped and rolled under a thick bush. Pebbles in the cold mud gouged tracks in my cheek as I belly-crawled away from him.

"Give it up, sweetheart." The man with the scar called out from the car, calm, amused. He laughed and the arrogance of him infuriated me. "Get the fuck up off the ground, honey. You'll get mud all over my trunk."

Dowd's filthy hand closed around my foot, squeezing until the bones inside my boot ground against each other. It hurt, but no more than the junk that ripped my back as he dragged me into the open.

"You like it rough?" He jumped on top of me, knocking the wind out of me. His muddy, callused hands left patches of heat on my thighs as he groped between my legs.

"Don't mess the bitch up too much," Bowles shouted. "We might want some, too."

I wished I had taken the knife out of Scotty's chest. I bucked against the weight of Dowd's body and nearly puked as I felt his erect penis pushing back. Looking for anything, I clawed the mud until my hand closed around a two-foot-long stick. With the most powerful forearm stroke I ever swung, I slammed the stick against Dowd's sore arm.

He let me go, roaring, "Fucking bitch."

Released from the hot weight of his body, I started to crawl, then to run away from him.

"Enough fun, Dowd." Scar was getting out of the car as I found solid footing. "Someone's coming. Get her into the car. Now."

Big headlights came up the street: the one-ten bus. I had to get the driver's attention. My feet skated over the slick ground and I could hardly stay upright as I ran for pavement.

Broken twigs showered me from behind as Dowd lunged again. His feet shot out behind him, but he managed to catch me by the sleeve. The silk tore as I pulled away, but he managed to shift his grip and get hold of my arm, circling it with his big hand. Pissed now, thinking he was screwing up my only chance, I body-slammed that injured side again.

"Bitch." He kneed my groin and the pain dropped me. I knelt in the muck, nauseous, gasping for air.

A new set of hands snatched me around the middle and dragged me to my feet again like some halfunstuffed toy. Scar grinned into my face, big flat teeth gray in the dim light. I smelled decay behind his breath mints and threw up on his shirt front.

He was not fazed. His fat, feminine hands covered my breasts and squeezed. I had a bad feeling about how this would turn out.

"Hurry up." Bowles stood in the open car door, nervously watching the bus draw closer.

"We'll wait," Scar called back. "Let him go by."

Scar threw me to the ground and pinned me tight against him. The corrupt smell of his sweaty body bled into the crispness of the eucalyptus, soiled the clean night air. When I tried to get free of him, he gripped me by the back of the neck and forced my face down.

"You started this, bitch," he said. "You fucked everything up royal. Now you're going to pay up."

The closer the bus came, the tighter the grid of hands that held me. I wanted the bus to slow down, to give me a little more time for inspiration to hit.

The bus was less than six feet from the car's front bumper. Bowles had ducked down below the window of the open door. All I could see were his legs between the bottom of the door and the curb. Beside me, Dowd and Scar were hardly breathing as they waited for the bus to pass.

There was a quick, short blast from the bus horn, then it veered suddenly toward the curb and with a tremendous explosion of glass and steel, it smacked the car head on, snagging Bowles behind the open door and dragging him thirty feet down the asphalt. Stunned, exultant, I watched Bowles's heels bounce along the pavement like Howdy-Doody performing a weird, drunken dance.

Dowd did a dance of his own beside me. My neck hurt; his hands, like pliers, shook me. I tried to break free before he broke something. Then I realized that Scar, drawn away from me to the crash like a dog offered a better treat, had let go of me.

The bus backed up, grinding wreckage under its enormous wheels. As Scar watched to see what would happen,

I saw fascinated pleasure spread across his face. The bus gears ground and then it started forward again, back toward the smashed front of the car. I heard Bowles, a dark heap next to the car, moan.

"Do something." There was tearful desperation in Dowd's plea.

But Scar held out his hand. "Wait."

"Wait? Shit! That's my best man. I gotta get him."

Scar wasn't listening. He was busy measuring the distance between the bus and the car with his eyes. His face was orgasmic and I could almost see him calculate the angle of bounce Bowles would make if the bus hit him again. When his hand dropped to his crotch, I saw my opening.

I had my feet solidly under me, waiting for the moment of impact.

The bus driver corrected his aim, accelerated, then he rammed that Ford again, obliterating its front end. I was on my feet, sprinting toward the bus when the car door clipped Bowles on the head and spread him out along the pavement. It was oddly quiet after the impact, as metal, glass, and radiator fluid spewed through the air. I ran right toward the middle of it.

"Get her," Scar screamed.

"What about Arnie?" Dowd spat.

"Leave him."

The bus backed up again, and, finally, I saw the driver.

"Leon!" I yelled.

He swerved the bus so close to the curb that the front tires scraped against the concrete as he came for me. He opened the door. "Behind you!"

I could feel someone back there, so I dove again for the ground and rolled, coming to my feet as a hand sloshed through the air past my ear. I saw the white scar out of the corner of my eye, knowing I was in a race against inches whether I got to the bus before Scar caught me again.

He snagged my arm, but I wrenched it free before he had a solid grip. His fingers glanced across my shoulder and then caught a handful of the torn silk that had been my sleeve.

"Come on," Leon urged. Two more steps and I would be on the bus.

I lunged for the open door, hearing the fabric in Scar's hand give. Scar was left off balance beside me with a handful of torn silk.

I was on the bus, both hands on the guardrail, one foot on the bottom step.

"Atta girl, Maggie." Leon beamed at me and began to pick up speed.

That heavy, scarred arm reached out again and caught my ankle above the boot and held on, short nails digging into my flesh.

"Help me," I begged Leon. I couldn't support Scar's weight, and my grip on the handrail began to give. The big man managed to get one of his knees wedged inside, taking a lot of the weight off me, small consolation as I smelled his foul breath.

Still, he held on to me. Blood from my leg ran down his hand and followed the raised line of his scar, as if we had formed some sort of gross merger.

Repulsed, I wanted him off. I raised my free foot and kicked him in the neck. He ducked from the second blow and smashed his face against the edge of the door. I heard his nose go, sending up a vivid fountain of blood. He began to bellow like something crazed and tried to squeeze farther into the bus.

His determination alone was frightening, inhuman. He inched his grip farther up my leg, gouging the flesh as I landed blow after blow with my free foot.

"Hang on," Leon ordered. He bounced over the curb, and Scar's knee, lubricated with his own blood, slipped off the step. His legs waved out the door like laundry flying in the wind.

"Kick him again," Leon shouted.

I tightened my grip on the rail and gave him everything I had left, ramming my foot into the exposed hollow of his throat just as the bus came abreast of a fire hydrant. Scar's shins collided with the hydrant, got snagged on the valve, and he was ripped out of the bus with Leon screaming, "Fucker."

As his hand left my leg, I pulled myself up the last two steps and Leon closed the door. He bounced us back onto the street and sped around a corner onto busy Orange Grove Avenue. When the rocking of the bus settled, I sat on the floor with my back against Leon's seat for support.

All that was left of my blouse was a few shreds that didn't cover any vital territory. Leon passed me the jacket he had draped over the back of his seat. When I had it zipped up, he touched my shoulder. "You okay?"

"I think so." I had some trouble breathing normally, and I had some pretty good cuts and scrapes. My leg throbbed where blood ran in five-finger sets, clotting with patches of caked mud. I pretty much hurt all over, but I was intact, nothing broken. When I closed my eyes, all I could see was Scar's contorted face as he jetted out the door. An ugly vision, but a satisfying one.

Leon cleared his throat. "Who *are* those guys?"

I looked up at him, saw the pallor under the deep brown skin, a fine sweat glowing on his bald head, and felt bad. He had landed in the middle of something that had nothing to do with him. But then, as far as I knew, so had I.

I said, "These men killed my ex-husband."

"Jesus." He swallowed hard. "What, like in the war?"

"No. Tonight. Right outside the restaurant. Unless someone found him, his body is still there."

"Jesus."

We sat in silence for a few minutes. I saw full realization dawn on Leon. When I touched his hand, I could feel it shake.

I asked him, "What were you doing there?"

"Those jerks pissed me off. I got a call from the driver on the three-oh-five. He says he spotted the car and the men I had a watch-out for after he picked up fares at Gabrieleno." He looked down at me. "I had called in a description to the dispatcher from the picture you gave me and the other driver spotted them.

"This other driver, he tells me that he picks up a couple of fares at Gabe's, and starts off west, when this car like the one I said to watch out for starts to tail him. Then it comes up alongside and plays tag with him until the first stop. Then some guy gets on the bus, checks out the passengers, doesn't find what he's looking for. He shows the driver a picture and says call him if he sees this woman."

Leon handed me a Polaroid of myself walking along the Los Angeles River with Guido, just about at the spot where Minh Tam's hovel had been. I wasn't especially surprised; we had seen them at the marina that day.

"I get the call," Leon said. "I meet the other driver to show him the picture you gave me, and he says, sure, those are the guys. I drive on, one more block and I'll be damned if they didn't pull right in front of me and make me stop.

"They come this close." He showed me an inch between his thumb and index finger. "I got a perfect safety record, twelve years and not so much as a dent until yesterday. But I don't think they can hold a bullet hole against me."

I said, "You wouldn't think so."

"So, these creeps push their way onto my bus, show me their picture, and ask have I seen you. I say not me, and get the hell off my bus. Then they start questioning my passengers. When they finish with their business, they don't even bother to apologize for putting me five minutes off my schedule."

Slowly, he started to grin. "So, maybe I help them off a little."

"What did you do?"

"Damned if my foot didn't slip off the brake pedal a little and one of them sort of fell out. Hurt his arm pretty good, from the sound of him. Only it couldn't have been too bad, cuz his friends didn't take any bother about it. They just got in their car and went away."

He hadn't answered the original question yet. I asked, "Did you follow them?"

"Of course not. I had fares on the bus. As soon as I let

them off, I sort of headed back over to Gabe's to see if you might need a ride."

"You're my hero, Leon."

He laughed. "Tell it to my boss. I might be looking for a new line of work real soon."

"Don't clean out your locker just yet." I lay back on the floor of the bus, ignoring how cold I was. "If anyone gives you trouble, I'll put your sainted face on every television station in this country. When I get finished, the RTD won't dare touch you."

"Okay." He smiled. "But maybe I'm ready for something new."

I felt prickly all over from adrenaline wearing off. I longed for a hot bath, and for Mike Flint. I glanced up and caught Leon watching me. I asked, "The guy with the scar, do you think he's dead?"

"Be my guess." Leon had a grim set to his jaw. "If no, I don't want to be around when he wakes up."

I closed my eyes. "Where are we going?"

"The cop house. I already had my dispatcher call to say we was coming in."

"Wonder if Detective Mareno will be there."

Leon chuckled.

"What's funny, Leon?"

"How long have I known you, Maggie?"

"Just since this morning."

"It's been quite a day," he said. "Quite a day. I never had one like it since I left Vietnam."

Chapter 23

"May I go home?" I asked.

"Pretty soon." Detective Mareno wasn't as friendly late Friday night as he had been Friday morning. He looked worn and gray and thoroughly dispirited. He had been a detective in peaceful little South Pasadena for fifteen years, a street cop for a decade before that. He had worked his share of robberies, assaults, and domestic cases. But Khanh Nguyen was only the seventh murder he had investigated during all those years. Until recent budget cutbacks, the county sheriff would normally take over any murder investigation.

Mareno put Leon and me in the police station's assembly room because that's where the coffeepot was. Other than the desk officer and occasional patrol officers coming in on errands, Leon, Mareno, and I had the station pretty much to ourselves. The quiet was eerie, broken only by radio conversation between the desk officer and patrol cars.

Leon wasn't much company. He sat sprawled in a chair and snored.

I complained to Mareno when he wanted to begin again at the beginning. "I've told you the whole sordid story three times now."

"Four."

"Okay, four. I have nothing else to tell you."

"We have bits of clothes and people in little plastic bags all over the place. Enough to keep county Scientific Investigation people busy for a week."

"Excuse me?" The desk officer came in carrying a

large carton. "You want to sign the booking slips for this stuff?"

"Give it here." Mareno set the carton on the table between us. I could smell some of the contents, so it was no surprise when the crushed remains of my boxed dinner were handed out. Mareno flipped the box open to show the congealing remains of salad and salmon and flan. "This belong to you?"

"My dinner."

"Why didn't you eat it at the restaurant?"

"I told you, I was uncomfortable being with my former husband. We finished our business and I wanted to leave." I slouched down, pulled Leon's jacket higher on my neck; my hair made the collar all wet. "I told you already, four times."

Next, he took the attaché out of the carton, opened it, and fanned through the papers. I had dropped everything when I knelt beside Scotty, and hadn't thought about it again until Mareno asked me to go over the evening's events. Like the dinner box, the attaché was soaked. The papers inside curled at the edges, but they were intact. I was glad to have corroboration, because Mareno had seemed awfully skeptical about parts of my story.

"This yours?"

I nodded. "Those are the papers I told you Scotty gave me."

Marino reached into the attaché and pulled out a thick envelope. I hadn't actually laid eyes on it before, but I knew what it was.

"Where did this come from?" Mareno asked.

"I told you. Scotty offered me cash, but I gave it back to him."

I gave him the only answer I could think of. "Scotty must have slipped the envelope in before he handed the case over to me. Does it matter? I told you about the money, and there it is."

"How about this?" He looked in the carton again and this time brought up a twist of stained tissue paper. "Belong to you?"

I leaned forward. "I don't know what it is."

"Déjà vu." He opened the tissue. A little jade dancer, similar to the one Khanh had been carrying that morning, dropped onto the table.

"It's an apsaras," I said. "One of a set of twelve that was on display in a museum in Da Nang until the spring of 1975. It's listed in the museum catalogue. I saw it."

"You think it's very valuable?"

"Probably."

"Then what was it doing in your dinner?"

I picked up the little figure and smelled it: salmon étouffée.

Like hitting replay on a video, I ran through everything Scotty said and did all evening. Scotty had two meetings scheduled, one with me, and one with someone else. I remembered how nervous he had seemed when I watched him from the bus shelter, pacing the sidewalk, checking his watch. My guess was that he didn't want to go into the second meeting with either a wad of cash or the precious little jade lady on him. Ordinary, legitimate business acquaintances don't normally frisk one another, so the meeting probably wasn't either normal or legitimate.

Mareno was watching me.

I handed him back the jade. "Has anyone asked Khanh Nguyen's husband, Sam, about the items that Bao Ngo stole from their house?"

"Funny thing." Mareno rewrapped the jade in the soiled tissue. "You told me about this alleged invasion robbery, but the husband denies it ever happened. Hasn't seen this Bao Ngo in twenty years, he says."

"That's what Sam Nguyen told you?"

"Either he was lying to me, or she was lying to you." Mareno rubbed tired eyes with his fists, the way a sleepy child does. "My first thought was insurance scam. But no claim was filed. Nguyen told me no claim would be filed."

I repeated, trying to make the pieces fit, "You said, alleged invasion robbery?"

"What evidence do you have that it ever occurred?"

"None. Only what Khanh told me. I saw bruises on her."

"Bruises, huh?" Mareno's hand was back inside the carton. "People can get bruises in a whole lot of ways. You've got some honeys your own self right now."

"Has anyone talked to Minh Tam?"

"We're looking for him," Mareno said. "He hasn't been in his hotel room since early this morning. You want to see some bruises?"

A new set of Polaroids was lined up in front of me. Crime scene shots. The one on the far left was a close-up of a face, or what remained of a face. Black eyes, the skin over the left temple burst open like the peel of a ripe grape. A deep gash in the chin showed bone. The rest of the face was discolored, disfigured, reduced to pulp. Over the caved-in right cheek, one colorless eye stared into nowhere.

A second picture, a close shot of a torso with the outline of a car door's armrest just as clear as if a vivid-purple felt-tip marker had been drawn on the poor man's chest. One arm, an unscarred arm, was broken in at least two places. The close-cropped hair was so short that scalp showed through.

"Is this the man called Arnie Bowles?" I asked.

"I'm asking you."

I glanced at Leon, noisily snoring in his sleep, and reached for Mareno's pen and paper. I wrote, "Was he killed by Leon's bus?"

Mareno also looked at Leon, a fleeting smile across his face; Leon didn't sleep cute. He said, "Damn near. And given time, maybe his injuries would have taken him. That's for the coroner to figure out. What killed him was a 9mm slug."

I sat up a little straighter. "He was shot? Who the hell shot him?"

Mareno sorted through the Polaroids and picked out one. It looked like a gob of mud on the asphalt. "Blew off the back of his head."

"No one had guns. I would have felt any guns on Scar

or Dowd." I sucked in air, remembering. "Bowles sure as hell wouldn't shoot himself. Who's left?"

"It wasn't the guy you call Scar. We picked him up right where you dropped him out of the bus. He's in the jail ward of County-USC hospital, pretty banged up. The one you call Dowd hasn't turned up yet. But we'll find him."

"Dowd told Scar that Bowles was his best man and he seemed really upset when the bus hit him. He wouldn't go back and shoot his best man, would he?"

"Would he?"

"Maybe put him down like an injured animal? I don't think so. And if Dowd had a gun, why didn't he shoot Scotty? Much more efficient than a knife."

"Yeah?" Mareno cocked his head, waiting for me to talk.

"And why didn't he just shoot me right there? He had every chance."

"Guns make a lot of noise." Mareno picked up his pencil and doodled on his pad. "Did it occur to you that maybe Dowd didn't want you dead? And maybe he didn't kill Scott?"

"There was no one else around," I said.

"You told me there were kitchen workers outside. Could you identify them?"

"I only heard them talking. I didn't see them."

"You assumed they were kitchen workers. For all you know, the whole Mormon Tabernacle Choir could have been out there."

"True. I also didn't see who stabbed Scotty."

"You said, you lost sight of Scott before the white Ford drove up. Scott could have been lying on the ground already when Dowd and company got there."

"The timing would be tight."

"But possible."

"Scar said something strange to me," I said, trying to remember the exact words he used. "He said that I started all this. He said that I have to pay up."

"Started what?"

"I wish I knew." I folded my arms on the table and dropped my head on them, overwhelmed with exhaustion.

"Let's have a break," Mareno said.

"Yeah." I closed my eyes.

Mareno fiddled with papers for a while, and then I heard him putting things into the carton. And then his footsteps as he left the big room. Leon's snoring devolved into a soft sort of purring.

I don't know whether I actually fell asleep, or whether I was dreaming or remembering.

Mareno had walked me down the long, cold corridor at the county morgue earlier that night. We had to wait while the attendants at the receiving bay processed Scotty in. It was late, and all the day's cadavers had been put away in the big coolers, but I could still smell them. The walls, the air ducts, were permeated with their singular odor.

Under the cold fluorescent light in the green hallway, Mareno's face was white. He asked me several times, "You okay?"

I said I was, but it was a lie.

The big receiving bay doors opened and Scotty was wheeled in on a coroner's gurney, the bed a big fiberglass pan instead of a mattress. The coroner on duty was an old man named Lipski. He greeted Mareno: "Bring your own bucket this time, Detective?"

Mareno covered his mouth with his hand and looked sick.

"Don't stand too close to Mareno, ma'am," Lipski warned me. "He has a history."

Scotty was wrapped in a heavy plastic sheet. As Lipski folded the sheet away from Scotty's face, someone set the brake on the gurney, make it sway. Scotty's corpse rocked gently back and forth, moving the way a living man stirs in his sleep. Mareno gagged, turned green, reached for support, and touched Scotty's leg by mistake. He fainted before he could snatch his hand away, dropped to the cold floor like a rag, bam, right at my feet.

Having to take care of him gave me something better

to do than go to pieces. He was embarrassed when he came to, muttered apologies, made jokes about opening his eyes and seeing the coroner's meat wagon with its doors open, waiting.

"Maybe I should hang it up," he said, sitting on the floor still with his back against the wall. "Maybe I've seen all the shit I'm ever supposed to."

Lipski, giving him a drink of Coke, laughed at the suggestion. "Hang it up, Mareno? Not you. The job's like sex to you; it's messy, but you can't get enough of it."

Mareno laughed then. "What's sex? I don't remember." Then he glanced at me, standing there next to the remains of my former husband, and he blushed furiously.

"Sorry," he said, deeply chagrined. "No disrespect intended."

And none was taken.

Scotty had looked like a wax doll. Waiting for Mareno to come back into the assembly room, I turned my face into the crook of my elbow and tried not to see Scotty's face.

How strange it is, I thought, the way a long relationship evolves. In the beginning constant sex, nearly uncontainable passion. Then after a while a deeper, more thoughtful sort of love emerges. Less sex, maybe, but no less passion. Looking back, I tried to remember when Scotty began to grow restless. When had the passion disappeared? Certainly it was on the wane before we moved into the San Francisco house.

One weekend stood out. We were working on the house shortly after we bought it. I was stripping old, dark stain off the oak wainscoting in the dining room, and Scotty was doing something in the basement. I remembered thinking, as I worked alone upstairs and he worked alone downstairs, that something was very wrong between us.

Scotty didn't like working with his hands. He was such a perfectionist that he never felt satisfaction with much of anything he did. Don't come downstairs, he had told me. He didn't want me to see his outbursts of temper.

But I went down anyway, on the pretext that I needed a hand with something. What I really wanted was to talk to him before we got any farther in debt over the house. I had decided that I wanted a trial separation. What was the point of staying together? We rarely saw each other.

At first, when I went down to the basement that day, I couldn't find Scotty. I could hear him, hammering away somewhere. When I called out to him, he answered from inside the wall. Actually inside the wall.

His reaction was so strange when he saw me; he was way too happy. We hadn't had sex for over a month. Too tired he'd say. Too much on his mind, the job, the new house, too much light coming in the new bedroom windows.

That day, right there on the cold, newly poured concrete floor, we had enjoyed each other with passion I thought we had lost forever. We christened the new house. Later, he painted a red heart on the spot, a commemoration, he said, of something perfect.

Maybe I was dreaming as I sat there in the police station, waiting for Mareno to come back. Because when I imagined that day in the basement, it was Mike's face I saw in my mind's eye, and not Scotty's.

I hadn't thought about Scotty as a husband for a very long time. How rare that day had been. It seemed to me that the only time Scotty was ever really happy was when he had a deal nearly set. Working on the house only made him cranky. What had he been so happy about that afternoon?

One other time Scotty had come close to that level of sweetness—the day of the San Francisco earthquake. When the shaker came, he was out of town on business, as he generally was. We were already separated. Scotty was so worried about Casey and me that he chartered a plane to get home to us.

We were okay. A crack in the basement floor—right through the red heart—and a back wall had come down. The foundation needed to be rebolted, and some things fell off shelves, there were plumbing problems. The repairs were costly, but compared to our neighbors, like Lyle, the damage was relatively mild. But Scotty came jetting home to help make the house secure again. We slept together the night of the earthquake for the very last time.

Someone kissed the back of my neck. Was I asleep? Had I actually been touched? I opened my eyes and looked into the tired face of Mike Flint.

I sat up. "How's Oscar?"

"Settling in." He gave me a going-over, from my matted hair to the hole torn in the side of my boot. Then he gently touched a bruise on the point of my cheek with the tips of his cold fingers. "Miss me?"

I walked into his arms and held on. "Scotty's dead."

"I know." His voice was like gravel. "You okay? You been checked out by a doctor?"

"I don't need a doctor." I tried not to cry, but I was so relieved to see Mike that I let my guard down. "I have to tell Casey, but I don't want to tell her over the phone. I talked to my dad. He said she's asleep. I want to be in Berkeley before she wakes up."

"What are you going to say to her?"

"A soft variation on the truth. Any ideas?"

"It's okay to go soft, as long as you tell it to her straight." He kissed the side of my head. "Who's calling Linda?"

"Mareno says he will. I think it's better to hear the bad news from the police than from the ex-wife, don't you?"

"I don't think there is a good way to hear bad news. Did Scott have other family?"

"None," I said. "Just us. Goddamn Scotty. Whatever the hell he was involved in, why did he have to put us into the middle of it?"

"When you figure it out, let me know." Mike turned to Mareno. "Can I take Maggie home now?"

"If you're going to be with her, okay. We haven't brought the suspect in yet, and we don't know what he might be up to."

"We're going to book as soon as we get cleaned up," Mike said. "Maggie needs to get to Berkeley."

Mareno nodded approval. "Let me know how to reach you."

"Count on it."

Mareno gave me a hug, an odd farewell to get from a hardened old cop. He said, "Take care."

We left Leon sleeping in his chair, a better place for him at the moment than his empty studio apartment.

The Blazer's dashboard clock said midnight when we pulled into our driveway.

Mike yawned. "We can get a few hours' sleep."

"Pedro was a scam artist," I said, as walked toward the house, "who got in over his head."

"Where did that come from?"

"I've been thinking," I said. "Pedro had quite a lot of cash on him. Where did he get it?"

"Probably, he earned it." Mike unlocked the back door.

"Didn't use a bank? Usually took his pay in cash to keep it off the books? Stashed his mad money in his socks, had a little in every pocket where he could get his hands on it."

"He'd still have his money if he had kept his clothes on."

"He'd have his money if he used a bank, too." I turned on the kitchen light. "But he was a scam artist and his cash was his bait. He wanted to attract a little something, instead he landed a shark."

"Fish analogies, huh? Why are you thinking about Pedro?"

"I'm talking about Scotty." I reached for Mike's arm. "I need you to drive me somewhere, before we head out."

Chapter 24

The old farmhouse in Westminster was dark. Dogs barked in the distance. A light drizzle fell.

I lifted the wire latch off its nail and pushed open the backyard gate.

"It's not too late to change your mind about knocking on that door," Mike said. "Anything this Yuen guy knows tonight, he's going to know in the morning."

"Tomorrow morning might be too late."

Inside the garage, the baby, Eric, started to cry.

Mike looked at me, seemed resigned. Then, with a deep sigh, he walked ahead of me and knocked on the door.

Ralph Yuen peered out through the door, sleepy-eyed yet alarmed. When he recognized me he relaxed, though he still seemed puzzled.

"Miss MacGowen." With a glance into the dark room behind him, he flipped on the outside light and stepped out, pulling the door closed. We stood huddled under the narrow eaves, trying to stay dry.

"Sorry to bother you," I said. I introduced Ralph Yuen to Mike. "I wonder if you would help me?"

He put his hands together and bowed.

I handed him a snapshot of Scotty. "Do you know this man?"

He held the picture up to the light and studied it. He said, "I did, once."

"Tell me how you knew him."

Yuen studied me for a moment, suspicion growing. "Is it Miss or Mrs. MacGowen?"

"Scott MacGowen was my former husband. He was killed tonight."

"Killed?" Yuen took a step back, seemed to bristle all over. "That is why you are here? But I know nothing."

"You know more than I do," I said. "I need some help. What can you tell me about Scotty?"

"So long ago." Yuen took a deep breath. "He was our conduit. I don't remember exactly what his official role was in Vietnam. But we used him for many years to move museum pieces secretly between Vietnam and Europe."

"He was the legal advisor to the American cultural attaché," I said. " 'We' means you and Bao Ngo?"

"Yes. And our associates."

"Khanh Nguyen and Minh Tam?"

"And others. Except Minh Tam did not participate so much. I believe Minh Tam only wanted to make sure the collection was preserved. He is a very idealistic man. His participation was limited to sending the true treasures out for safe-keeping in Swiss vaults. The rest of us were not averse to selling an item here and there for profit. Scott MacGowen arranged the sales so that the movement of funds and artworks could not be traced back to us."

"Did he get fair prices for you?"

Yuen smiled. "We were thieves. What could we expect?"

I handed him one of the pictures I had taken on the freeway shortly after my other visit to his house: the white Ford and its three occupants. "Know anyone here?"

"I told you, it has been a long time." He pointed to Dowd. "But he is not much changed. His name is Steinmetz. He was very loyal to your husband, Mrs. MacGowen. And he was perhaps the main reason why we did not complain about the terms of sale your husband arranged."

"He was loyal to Scotty?"

"Like a brother."

Mike held my elbow. "Find out what you wanted to know?"

"One more thing, Mr. Yuen. May I borrow your catalogue from the Da Nang museum?"

"Certainly."

"Can you point out which items were sold and which were sent to Swiss vaults for safekeeping?"

"I'll do my best."

The first flight out of Los Angeles put us in San Francisco at seven. We had crossed the northern edge of the storm just past Santa Barbara, and descended through a perfectly clear, brilliant blue sky.

At seven-thirty, a taxi dropped us in front of my house.

The morning was typical San Francisco winter weather: crisp and clear. From the front porch, we had an unobstructed view over the rooftops of the Marina District, across the Bay at the bottom of our hill to Sausalito on the far side of the water; the Golden Gate Bridge looked like no more than quick, deft strokes of orange-red against the deep blue of the cloudless sky.

I stopped to record the familiar scene in my mind's eye in case I never saw it exactly that way again.

"Here's where it began," I said. "When someone wanted to buy the house."

Uncle Max came out the front door. "Your dad is bringing Casey over. They just left Berkeley."

I gave Max a hug and said, "Thank you."

"How is my Maggot holding up?"

"One more task, Uncle Max, and I think we're there."

Max embraced Mike, and Mike tolerated it.

I led the way into the house and down the stairs to the basement.

"What are we going to find down here?" Max asked.

"If I'm right, buried treasure."

"Interesting. Whose is it?"

"That's the big question, Uncle Max," I said. I flipped on the basement lights. "Let's see if it's here, then we'll worry about whom it belongs to."

In the cupboard where we kept camping gear, I found

the long-handled ax we used for chopping firewood. Remembering the day I had found Scotty inside the wall, I tapped along the paneling with the butt of the ax until I heard a hollow echo. Scotty had put up a false wall. Unless someone had a set of the original blueprints to work with, no one would notice.

"There has to be an entrance of some kind," I said. "Scotty wouldn't have time to take down the whole wall every time he wanted in."

"In where?" Max asked as he felt along the wood.

"But I don't have time to fuss with it." I offered the ax to Mike. "Do you want to do the honors, or shall I?"

"Go ahead," he said.

I said, "Stand back," and swung the ax into the wall. The paneling splintered. I swung again, and again, until there was a hole large enough to see four sets of floor-to-ceiling cupboards that Scotty the perfectionist had built against the original foundation wall.

Mike took the ax from me and used the pick end to pry loose a whole sheet of the paneling. Scotty's room was narrow, just enough space inside to open the cupboard doors.

"I told you, Scotty was just like Pedro," I said. "Scotty kept his mad money in his socks."

"Who is Pedro?" Max asked.

"A dead fool," I said.

Max gripped my arm. "Give me some background."

"As soon as word got out that someone wanted to buy the house, bad things started to happen. The strangest thing was that Scotty wanted to buy the house, himself. When I learned that Scotty was the repository for artifacts pilfered from a museum, the pieces started falling into place. Who would Scotty trust to take care of a museum full of booty?"

Max thought for a moment. "Scotty never trusted anyone."

"Exactly," I said. "He stashed it right here, in his own basement. And he left it here when we split up because, first, he couldn't safely move it. And, second, he thought

I would stay in this house forever. The only time he worried about his stuff being discovered was after the earthquake. Remember? He chartered a plane and flew in?"

Max waffled his hands. "Vaguely, I remember. Your mother was afraid of a reconciliation."

"It wasn't me Scotty was reconciling with," I said. "It was his stolen booty."

Mike said, "Are you going to take a look or just talk?"

"I'm afraid to look," I said. "You do it."

All of the doors had padlocks. On three of the cupboards the locks hung open. Only the fourth was fastened. Mike went to the doors on the far left and opened them.

On the shelves, no glittering treasure. Nothing except empty wooden boxes, tufts of packing straw, torn scraps of yellowed paper wrappings.

The second set of doors was more promising. The shelves here were tightly packed with child-size shoe boxes from a cheap Taiwan manufacturer. He wedged one out and tossed the lid aside.

The box was brimful of stiff paper folders each roughly the size of a stick of chewing gum. Mike scowled. "What the hell?"

Max took a folder out of the box and opened it, showing us a micro-thin leaf of gold. "This is *chi van,* Vietnamese gold piasters. Except for American dollars, gold was the only currency Vietnamese tradesmen trusted. Still is."

"How much is all of this worth?" Mike asked him.

"It's peanuts," Max said. "There isn't enough gold in each of those boxes to make a decent neck chain. It's garbage."

We hit paydirt in the third cupboard, though the yield was hardly what I expected. A collection of small temple artifacts, old silver coins, and carved amulets of translucent jade. There were also some bronze pots and a short sword with a gold-inlaid hilt, large pieces of very old-looking jewelry with enormous, rough-cut stones that could have been sapphires and rubies. Maybe they were old glass, I couldn't tell. The richest find was a dozen kilo wafers of gold stamped *Credit Suisse*. Hardly ancient artifacts. Hardly worth dying for.

I reached into a wooden casket, littering the floor with Styrofoam packing chips as I felt around. I nicked my index finger on something sharp, and came away holding a tarnished brass box about the size of a video cassette. The chased patterns on the lid were worn nearly smooth. Full of expectation, I raised the lid.

The box was lined with red silk so old that in places there was nothing left of it except frayed wisps, showing the dark wood insert in which eight hollows had been carved. Six of the hollows cradled little jade figures about the size of my thumb, each in a different dance pose. Temple dancers, apsaras. I knew where the missing two were: One had been in Khanh Nguyen's purse with my name written on it. The other was in an evidence locker at the South Pasadena police station, smelling of salmon étouffée.

I handed the box to Mike. "Would you die for this?"

"I wouldn't walk across the street for it."

Max pulled a wooden crate about sixteen inches long and twelve inches high off the bottom shelf. On the side was stenciled: *Bank of the Republic of Vietnam*. Using the end of the ax, Max pried the lid off. Mike and I peered over his shoulder.

"Bingo," Mike said.

I said, "Bao Ngo, I presume."

The box was full of clean white bones, with a naked, grinning human skull on top.

"Don't touch anything," Mike said. "I'll go call the local cops."

He turned toward the stairs, but stopped so suddenly that Max and I turned to see what had happened.

"If you please." Minh Tam stood on the bottom riser, a dirty 9mm automatic held loosely in his grip. "Stay where you are, please."

I felt more afraid of the careless way he waved the gun than I did about his intentions.

As a lover who needed comforting might, I put my arm around Mike's waist and slipped my hand inside the back of his jacket. He wrapped his arm around me. My hand found the Airweight holstered at the small of his back. I unclipped the holster tab and lifted out the small gun. Mike's free arm went to his side and I pressed the butt of the gun against his open palm for an instant. He kissed my cheek, and then dropped his hand to the side where Minh could see it, yet in position to take the gun from me in a big hurry.

I challenged Minh: "How did you get here?"

"Your very efficient assistant, Miss Ferguson. She has been so helpful to me for the last two days, helping me to know where you are." He smiled wickedly. "You see, ever since you put me in the hotel room, Miss Ferguson has assumed you and I were friends. It was she who told me where you were dining last night. And with whom."

The light dawned. I said, "You were at the restaurant last night."

"I stand upon my right against self-incrimination."

"Dowd was mad at me because he thought I killed Scotty," I said. "But it was you."

Minh's gun came up level with my eyes. Mike's hand twitched and Minh saw it.

Minh snapped, "You, the policeman, I need to see your hands."

Without so much as a glance my way, Mike slowly raised his hands. I did the retiring violet thing, slipped behind Mike as if I needed a shield, used him as cover to slide the gun into my belt, covered by the front of my wool blazer.

"Policeman, move away from Maggie and turn around."

Mike did as he was told. Minh patted him down. "Don't policemen carry arms?"

"Not on airplanes," Mike said.

"All right," Minh said.

Mike came back and stood close beside me again. His hand bumped the gun butt under my jacket, making sure it was there.

"If you please," Tam said, waving that 9mm again. "I would appreciate very much if you would help me to wrap the collection for shipment. I have a truck outside."

Max tightened his grip on the ax handle.

"Take everything, Minh, and good riddance," I said. "You don't need the gun."

Minh walked over to inspect our discoveries. Everything we had found was laid out along one single shelf. He smiled as he fondled the jade dancers, but he never forgot about us.

"Where is the rest?" Minh demanded.

"We don't have a key for that last cupboard," I said. "Everything else is just what you see."

"There has to be more." Minh measured the cupboard with a dubious eye. Then he looked straight at me, angry. "You have sent many things away from here before I arrived. Where have you put them?"

"Nowhere," I said. "I've never seen this stuff before."

"But where has it gone?"

"My guess?" I said. "Over a twenty-some-year period it bought a lot of houses and cars, started a few businesses, paid off some debts. This is all that's left."

"Houses and cars?" Distraught, he picked up an empty box and threw it to the floor. The gun in his left hand swept the room. "Houses and cars? The legacy of my people sold off for crap?"

In a calm voice, Mike said, "Be careful that gun doesn't go off accidently."

Minh stopped flailing around, held the gun out in front of him stiffly. His face was red, but he was simmering down.

I said, "Until late last night, I had no idea anything was hidden down here. If I had, I would have turned it over to the authorities."

"What authorities would you call? Your government? The Vietnamese government? I will take everything with me now. Where is the key to these last doors?"

"You're not going anywhere." Dowd, coming from the laundry room under the stairs, aimed a .38 Magnum at Minh's sternum. Dowd looked bad. His right arm was in a sling, the scrapes on his face had fresh red scabs. Like mine.

"Minh Tam," Dowd said in a slow, controlled voice. "Put the gun inside that first cupboard and shut the door."

Dowd kept his gun trained on Minh until he complied. I was relieved to have that loose cannon out of the equation, but Dowd, well, here was a loose cannon of another variety.

Max squeezed my hand. Under his breath he muttered, "Look at the time."

I glanced at my watch. Casey and my dad could arrive at any moment. Whatever was going to happen here, I desperately did not want my daughter to walk into the middle of it.

Mike spoke to Dowd. "I don't know who you are."

"I am the business partner of the late, and lamented, Scott MacGowen." Dowd dipped his head at me. "My apologies to you. I heard what this asshole Minh said just now. You're right. I did think it was you who hit Scotty. And I thought for a while that it was you who hit Khanh Nguyen. I didn't see how it could possibly be anyone else. Now I get it. Minh, I should have shot you when I had the chance in 1975. You've messed me up royal."

"You were following me and my daughter," I said.

"Scotty asked me to look after you and the girl," Dowd said. "He and Khanh were afraid of what Minh here might pull. Guess he had reason to be scared."

"Khanh sent me off to find Minh," I said.

"And you did a damn good job. We sent a private dick in, but he didn't get anywhere. People were easier about talking to you." Dowd smiled, proud of something. "We kept you busy down south for a while, didn't we? Scotty needed some time, and Khanh agreed to give him some. She even had you looking for a dead man."

"Time for what?" I asked.

"See those cupboards?" Dowd's thumb pointed across the room. "Arrangements had to be made."

"What arrangements? We can get this stuff packed up in ten minutes and walk it up the stairs for you. Way too much fuss over a few artifacts."

"That shit is fluff. Nothing. Crate filler." I had made him chuckle, the sadistic bastard. "Mrs. MacGowen, why don't you go on over and open those locked doors?"

When I started across the room to get the ax from Uncle Max, Mike began to come with me.

"She's a big girl," Dowd said, training the gun on Mike. "She can do it all by herself."

I wedged the pick end of the ax in the hasp of the padlock and put all my weight on it. It took three tries, but finally the lock snapped and I opened the last set of doors.

It didn't hit me right away what I was seeing. There were four wooden crates, each the size of the coffin that held the set of bones lying on the floor beside me. The crates weren't very big, but their contents were heavy enough to make the solid shelving sag. Like the coffin, all of them had *Bank of the Republic of Vietnam* stenciled on the side.

"No." Minh screamed. He charged for the shelves and managed to rip the top off one of the crates, didn't seem to notice when he gouged his finger on a nail. He left a smear of blood across his face when he tried to wipe tears from his eyes. Stunned, he dropped to his knees and appealed, almost prayerfully, to Dowd. "Not this. Please. Where are the ivories? Where are the treasures?"

"Most of it's at the bottom of the South China Sea," Dowd said. "Been there since 1975. You didn't really think we'd let you waste valuable barge space on a bunch of old broken pots, do you? This is gold, asshole. Pure, solid gold."

"But Bao Ngo brought a cargo." Minh refused to believe. "It was reported. He came through Customs."

"Sure he did. We put enough of Bao's pots in the crates to make the shipment look legit. The crates were the thing. Bao brought shit in crates lined with bullion." Dowd caressed one of the wooden boxes. "This is what Scotty and I sent out with Bao. Or what's left of it.

"You see my problem here, don't you?" Dowd sighed. "The trick is finding a way to move the shit, and a place to stow it, without leaving a paper trail or witnesses. Not like I can rent a U-Haul. The sad truth is, without Scotty, I'm stumped what to do next."

I pointed to the open box on the floor. "Is this Bao?"

Dowd nodded. "Poor bastard."

"Khanh knew he was dead?"

"Oh, yeah. She did the ceremony, put the bones in the box, burned the incense."

"Who killed him?" Mike asked.

Dowd shrugged. "Doesn't matter now, does it?"

I didn't like the sound of that. It had occurred to me that the possibility was very good that all of us weren't going to walk out of the basement. From the brightness in his eyes, I knew that Mike had similar thoughts.

The ax was still in my hand. Mike came up beside me on the pretext of getting a better look at the loaves of gold inside the box Minh opened. He slipped an arm around my waist, in a reversal of the earlier exchange, and palmed the gun butt.

"What's all this worth?" Mike asked, looking owlish.

Dowd shrugged. "Plenty."

"Then I guess you're set for a while." Mike grinned at him. "None of us really gives a damn what you do from here. How about the rest of us just walk on upstairs and right out the front door? All I've had to eat since dinner last night was a bag of airline peanuts. I'm thinking a big breakfast down on the Wharf is a damn good idea. After we eat, we'll have a long walk, maybe take in a movie. Will that give you enough time to finish your business here?"

"Not hardly." Dowd laughed. "Look, you people are

okay. Mrs. MacGowen and me got off to a bad start, and I'm sorry about that. I think that if we could start over, we could get along okay. Be real nice for all of us to go on out and have that breakfast. But I know, and you know, that isn't going to happen."

Max, ever the litigator, stepped forward. "As I see the situation, and from what I've heard, Minh Tam is the only one here who is in legal jeopardy. Maggie, am I wrong?"

"No," I said. "Not from where I sit."

"You wouldn't have any reason to file any charges against Mr. Dowd for, say, assault, would you?"

"Not as long as I can go get breakfast pretty soon. I'm starving."

Max turned to Mike. "Anything to add?"

"One thing. I'll hook up Minh and drive him over to the local cop house. I seem to recall hearing him confess to the murder of Ian Scott MacGowen, late of Denver, Colorado."

"You're all very funny," Dowd said. He wasn't going to let us go. The strange thing was, he looked sad about what he had to do.

"Mom?" From upstairs, I heard Casey's voice. "Where are you?"

We all froze; I felt hollowed, nearly crazed with panic.

In the lull, Minh made his move. Screaming, "You bastards," he dove for the cupboard where he'd put his dirty little 9mm.

In the instant it took Dowd to raise his Magnum and find Minh in its sights, I snapped Minh on the legs with the ax handle, tripping him, sending him in a headlong roll across the concrete floor. The barrel of Dowd's Magnum bobbed as he adjusted and readjusted his aim. As I leaned forward to trip Minh, I felt Mike's Airweight slide up and away from my belt. Max flew into me, dropped me, covered me, so I never saw Mike actually fire the bullet that cleaved Dowd's skull.

A perfect red dot, like an Indian caste mark on Dowd's forehead, was two degrees off dead center.

Chapter 25

Bowser pulled against the leash, as anxious to get home again as he had been eager to go out. I wondered: If he knew this would be the last time we walked up our hill and turned a key in the door of the house at the top, would he be so eager? I confess, I felt more than a little wistful.

The morning air was crisp, freshened by a stiff off-shore breeze that carried the scent of roasting garlic up from the crab vendors on Fisherman's Wharf; whole bulbs as big as a child's fist, grown down south in Gilroy.

The gulls were on their morning migration between the produce district trash bins—rich when the loading bays closed at nine o'clock—and the prenoon return of the deep-sea fishing charters at the Hyde Street Pier.

When Mike and I paused to look back at the view across the San Francisco Bay toward Sausalito, a lone gull came down to eye us, lying nearly motionless on the airstream. He started to beg, a squawk so insistent that he made the dog bark.

I cracked off a bit of the last of the dog biscuits we had brought for bribes and rewards, and tossed it high. The gull swooped down, caught the crumb in mid-air, circled us once, hoping probably for something better, and then, when there was nothing, sailed back into the current to join his fellows.

"What a clown." Mike laughed. "Good catch, though. The Giants could use him."

"He's spoiled," I said.

We turned and started walking up the hill again. The

sun was warm on my face. The scrapes were nearly healed, the bruises easily hidden by makeup. It was nice to be able to walk around with Mike again without people staring, wondering whether he beat me.

"We've finished the rough cut on the new film," I said, slipping my arm through his. "I like it very much. We juxtapose Minh Tam with Shannon, fade from Dowd to Tina, overlap the crime scene pictures. Everyone talks about how much they ended up with, which is just about nothing, unless you count life without possibility of parole. The two threads of the story wind along in parallel and then they merge at the morgue."

I looked up at Mike. "Did you know that Pedro and Scotty were on the same tier of the big cooler at the morgue for a while? Guido's footage is incredible."

"I'm amazed you can talk about it so easily." Mike shivered.

"After you see a sequence of film enough times, it takes on its own reality. Does that happen to you when you're working a case for a long time? The details become disembodied. The blood doesn't represent pain after a while. It's just the spatter pattern on the northwest wall?"

"That's how we survive the job." He followed a gull's flight overhead, distracted by its antics. "Casey seems better the last couple of days."

"The sadness comes and goes," I said. "In a strange way, Dowd dying the way he did. . . ."

" 'Dying the way he did?' It's okay to say I shot him."

"Dowd dying the way he did"—I nudged Mike—"makes it easier for Casey to accept Scotty's death. Her father got in way too deep with some very bad people, trying to get something he wasn't entitled to. We were all in danger until you took care of Dowd."

"Scotty was a victim?" Mike's voice held a challenge. He was adamant that I not sugarcoat the truth for Casey. "That's how she sees it?"

"No. She holds Scotty responsible. But it's tough," I said. "She also has Khanh to sort out, that beautiful life-style based on stolen property. Khanh was always so sweet to her."

"What about you?" Mike had a wicked grin on his face. "I did the math. The Porsche Scotty was driving around that sucked you right into his web, made you decide you wanted to marry him, how do you think he bought it?"

"The same way Khanh bought her house and her restaurant. I'm sure the down payment on my house and more than a few mortgage payments came out of the stash in the basement."

"What does that make you?"

"I don't know, Mike. Ask me again next month when a check drawn against the proceeds from the sale of that house, bought with ill-gotten gains, goes to Trona to pay for Oscar's rehab."

He laughed and wrapped his arms around me. "I'll do that."

"There may come a day when you'll wish you had tucked away just one of those gold bars before the Feds came and took them all."

"I might. But I doubt it."

"My only regret is that we weren't able to have all that cash Scotty tried to give me for the house turned over to Linda. He left her and their babies in a mess."

"She'll be okay."

The house came into view ahead.

My neighbor, Felix Mack, serenaded the neighborhood from his front porch, playing "Big Butter and Egg Man" on his tenor sax, borrowing his phrasing from Louis Armstrong, using the racket of the gulls filling the sky above us for counterpoint.

We stopped below the porch steps to listen.

Felix ended his tune with a showy flourish. "Morning, Maggie, morning, Mike."

"Nice day," Mike said.

"A little nippy," Felix replied. Cold or not, Felix had his shirt open all the way down the front like the street musicians who hang out on the beach steps below Ghirardelli Square. Theirs was a life he craved.

Felix, a neurosurgeon by profession, could never get far enough past his sweet and nerdy essence to become a true hipster, not even with his big horn between his knees and all of his chest hair showing.

After my divorce, some of the neighbors assumed that Felix and I would hook up. We tried, but nothing ever stirred between us. Maybe it had something to do with all that visible chest hair, or his need to show it. Or maybe it was simply that he wasn't Mike Flint.

"Sorry to hear about Scotty," Felix said. "I saw him a few days before he died, just gazing up at the house. He didn't look happy. Didn't even say hello."

"He probably had a lot on his mind," I said. "Hope your new neighbors will be more quiet for you than we've been lately."

"I can hope," Felix chuckled. "I heard you sold the house. What'd you get?"

"All cash." I filled him in on the details. Mother wouldn't approve—never speak of money outside the family—but I thought that the price I got was Felix's business. The sale of my house affected the value of every house in the neighborhood.

"Cash, hmm?" Felix gave the Corinthian porch column beside him a possessive pat. "Who bought it?"

"Don't know. The name on the documents is a corporation. There isn't a human name to be found."

Bowser's patience wore thin. He sat where instructed, but he fidgeted. I thought Mike was encouraging him to fidget.

"Gotta be foreign," Felix said. "Chinese or Japanese. They like to pay cash. Did a *feng-shui* master come through before they made the offer?"

Mike said, "A who?"

"You know, *feng-shui*." Felix fiddled with his spit valve. "This guy comes to make sure the house has the right spiritual orientation. Like, if the stairs face the front door all your good luck will just spill right out and the Chinese won't buy."

"No *feng-shui* master," I said.

Felix blew "Shave and a Haircut" before pronouncing, "It's Japanese, then."

Mike frowned. "Does it matter to you?"

"Only academically." Felix turned and scanned across the front of his restored Italianate house, this time with a more objective eye. "Wonder what I could get."

Bowser barked, once. I don't know how, but I know Mike made him do it.

"Bowser says he's thirsty." Mike hooked his arm through mine. "See ya', Felix."

"The neighborhood won't be the same without you. I'll miss you."

Felix picked up his horn and played us out with a sweet rendition of "Sukiyaki" as we walked into the house for the last time.

TELLING LIES

Exposing the truth is investigative filmmaker Maggie MacGowen's business. She's smart, skeptical, and stubborn, with a hard-edged, wisecracking approach to life that hides her vulnerable heart. When Maggie's sister, Emily, is mysteriously shot in a Los Angeles alleyway, evidence shows that it's no accidental street crime. The twisted tale that emerges stretches back more than two decades. Using her formidable skills to unravel tangled threads of lies, deceptions, and buried secrets, Maggie comes close enough to the truth to put her in the same deadly jeopardy as her sister. This sharp and gritty mystery marks the debut of Maggie MacGowen, a relentlessly intelligent sleuth—with an unabashedly roving eye and a razor-sharp wit.

"Maggie is a character we won't soon forget!"
—*Denver Post*

MIDNIGHT BABY

Maggie MacGowen often spots the dark, hidden reasons people get lost, hurt, or even murdered. So when she comes across "Pisces," a fourteen-year-old hooker with a dangerous secret, she wants to help this young girl—but it's too late. Pisces is found the following night with her throat slashed. And it's now up to Maggie to uncover Pisces's true identity. It won't be easy. All Maggie has going for her is a nanosecond of videotape of the killer's face . . . and the shocking reality that no one protected Pisces from the quick, brutal death that claimed her. Grippingly authentic, this no-holds-barred mystery crackles with suspense.

"Sharp, harrowing, real and raunchy. . . . Wendy Hornsby doesn't fool around."
—New York Times Book Review

BAD INTENT

Maggie MacGowen finds herself in the urban war zone of South Central L.A. when a ruthless politician decides to get the minority vote by resurrecting a fifteen-year-old cop-killing case. He claims the police, including MacGowen's boyfriend, Mike Flint, coerced three black children into pointing the finger at an innocent man. Setting out to clear Mike's name, Maggie takes her camera and her sleuthing skills into the heart of an embattled city. But the witnesses she interviews start turning up dead. Cops, politics, and murder make for a devastating mystery that Maggie must solve—or lose what is dearest to her heart.

"Fast-paced . . . bristles with energy . . . MacGowen is a heroine for the 1990s."
—*Kirkus Reviews* (starred)

77TH STREET REQUIEM

Maggie MacGowen is initially intrigued by the twenty-year-old, cop-killing case of Roy Frady because her boyfriend, LAPD cop Mike Flint, had been Frady's partner. Twenty years ago, Frady was shot in the head, and the murder went unsolved. Maggie realizes there's more than she thought at stake as the Frady case is literally jumping with sex, jealousy, and violence. And she's soon out in the neighborhood, turning over rocks, looking at what crawls out from underneath. She doesn't realize that what she finds is still deadly enough to spread its poison into her relationships and to set off a rash of new killings that shatter her theories—and her life.

"A tour de force . . . explosive. . . . One of the most thought-provoking, gripping, and compelling mysteries of the year."
—*Publishers Weekly* (starred)